Published by Romance Ink
An Imprint of
ABCD Graphics and Design, Inc.
A Virginia Corporation
977 Seminole Trail #233
Charlottesville, VA 22901

A Long Way to Find Love
By Mariella Starr

eBook ISBN: 978-1-63954-547-6
Print ISBN: 978-1-63954-548-3

A LONG WAY TO FIND LOVE

MARIELLA STARR

PROLOGUE

aitlin Angela Ridgeway was five years old when she met her aunts for the first time. By that young age, she already knew that none of the sisters she lived with were her mother. The women were all sisters because they called each other sisters and wore white robes. The sisters in white told Caitlin she was going to live with someone else and that she would like where she was going.

She hid behind Sister Luke's white robes when the two women visited. One lady was nice. She smiled and gave Caitlin a small bag of candy. The other woman was dressed in black. She snapped her fingers, frowned, and pointed to her feet.

"Get over here, child," the woman in black demanded.

"Don't frighten her!" the nice lady in blue scolded, and she bent down to talk to Caitlin. "My name is Florence, and this is my older sister, Beaula. We are your aunts, and we are going to take you home with us."

"I'm not scaring the brat," Beaula snapped. "I want a better look at her. Look at that God-awful red hair!"

Five-year-old Caitlin twirled her fingers in her curls and decided she didn't like the woman in black. Most grown-ups liked her hair. She'd been told it was fox-red and beautiful, although she didn't know what a fox looked like.

The woman in black scared her, and she tried to hide behind Sister Luke's robes, but she was pulled out and told to go with the women who called themselves aunts.

Caitlin cried when she was taken to a large house and taken to a room with a bed, toys, and baby dolls. She was told a woman she'd never met before was her nanny, and she was to obey her.

She was also warned by the woman in black to never leave the room without permission. And, no, she would never return to the orphanage or see the orphans or the sisters again.

By the age of seven, Caitlin could distinguish the footsteps of her aunts in the hallway outside of her room. Florence was light-footed, always smiling, and friendly when visiting the nursery. Beaula didn't walk; she stalked, and Caitlin knew to hide from her.

Beaula always had something to complain about, and she pinched and hit Caitlin when no one was around to see or stop her.

When Aunt Florence became sick and bedridden, Caitlin was told it was her duty to attend to her Aunt. She was ten years old, and Aunt Florence wanted her to read to her. Reading newspapers and books wasn't hard, and it quickly became a favorite getaway. Caitlin had grown to love her Aunt Florence.

Had anyone asked, Caitlin would have described the aunts as different as night and day or sweet and sour. Not that anyone ever asked because when she was dressed up and brought out for display, Aunt Beaula's female friends told her she was a lucky orphan to have been taken in as a stray.

Caitlin didn't like Aunt Beaula but had to obey her. Under Beaula's instructions, Caitlin was given more chores as she grew older. Cleaning was at the top of Aunt Beaula's long list of tasks. She was expected to clean every day and care for Aunt Florence. The house staff was dismissed one after another until only Caitlin and Jilly, the cook, were left to maintain the house. Aunt Beaula never had a good word to say about anyone or anything unless she was putting on what Jilly called *'the act.'*

In addition to learning how to dust and scrub, the chauffeur taught her how to drive the buggy and take care of the horse. Through hard work and constant criticism, Caitlin became self-sufficient. Under Jilly's guidance, she learned how to steal a few nickels and dimes at a young age. Aunt Beaula saw no reason to pay her niece for the work she performed. Caitlin was fed and dressed. Why should she be paid when she was living a life of luxury? When she was scrubbing floors on her knees, it didn't feel like a luxury.

Every night in her prayers, Caitlin prayed to whatever deity was listening to cure Florence Ridgeway of her ailments. She also asked to be freed from Beaula Ridgeway's clutches.

Then, suddenly, one day, she was freed, although not in any manner Caitlin would have guessed.

CHAPTER 1

1883, Philadelphia

CAITLIN DROVE the buggy into the stable and cared for the only horse left, ironically named Spirit. The old horse didn't have much spirit left as he was nearing the end of his life and should have been put out to pasture. Beaula Ridgeway would force the old guy to work until he dropped dead. Caitlin carried a box of groceries through the backdoor and set them on the kitchen table.

"Where have you been?" Jilly Mason demanded, pointing a chubby finger. "The Miss has been having a fit because you weren't here!"

"I went for the groceries you told me you needed, and I interviewed for a job," Caitlin answered with a smile. "I think I got the job, but I won't know until Friday. If Beaula thinks I'm staying here now that Florence has passed, she is out of her mind."

With hands on her well-padded hips, Jilly nodded and

hugged Caitlin. "There's a lawyer in the study with her. He's been here for hours waiting for you to come back. He told the Miss he wasn't leaving until he talked to you."

"What about?"

Jilly gave Caitlin a look of frustration and smacked her bottom lightly. "How would I know? Get on in there and find out for yourself!"

Caitlin checked her appearance in the hallway mirror and smoothed a few strands of her bright cherry/orange hair into place. Then, she squared her shoulders and entered the study.

"Where have you been?" Beaula demanded.

"That is none of your business," Caitlin said bluntly, shocking her aunt. She turned to the attorney and offered her hand. "Mr. Deveraux, we meet again. What can I do for you?"

"I have the will of Miss Florence Gwendolyn Ridgeway, ma'am, and my instructions are that you were to read and officiate it first."

"My niece is not capable of understanding a legal document," Beaula interrupted.

"I find that difficult to believe," the attorney said, and he handed Caitlin a folder.

Caitlin walked over to the window, pulled the heavy velvet curtains aside, and opened the folder. After reading several paragraphs, she sank onto the arm of a chair, looking pale and stunned.

"Florence was my mother," Caitlin whispered, looking at her aunt in disbelief. "Aunt Florence was my mother, and you wouldn't let her keep or claim me!"

"My sister was a weak woman, and she was pregnant without a husband," Beaula spat. "I wasn't going to allow her to besmirch the Ridgeway name! I did what was best for both of you."

Caitlin closed the folder but held it tightly against her chest. "Mr. Deveraux, may I have this evening to read these documents? Could you come back tomorrow, or should I come to your office to discuss these matters?"

"Would ten o'clock tomorrow morning suit your schedule, madam?" the attorney asked.

"Ten would be fine," Caitlin agreed, walking him to the front door.

"What has she written in that will?" Beaula demanded, following her niece.

"You'll find out tomorrow," Caitlin said, continuing to walk up the stairs and away from her aunt, although Beaula followed on her heels.

"I did what was best for my sister!" Beaula spewed. "I did what was best for her and you. Having an illegitimate child would have ruined her reputation! I did what was right, and we took you in as a bastard child!"

Caitlin stopped on the staircase's first landing and turned to look down at the bitter woman who had terrorized her younger sister and cared for no one other than herself.

"You've been wearing black since your father died, and you've always told people it was out of respect for him. I don't think that's true. I think it's because you have a black heart, and wearing black was the only way you could disguise how sick and depraved you truly are."

Caitlin was awake most of the night. She blocked the door in her room by pushing a chair against the doorknob, although she knew she was the only one with the key to the old nursery.

Beaula had pounded on the door several times, demanding entrance. Long after midnight, Caitlin tiptoed from the room she'd occupied since she was a small child and crept downstairs and into the study. She removed a small palm pistol from a desk drawer, checking it to see if it was still loaded. As far as she knew, the little pistol had never been out of the drawer or fired. Carrying it to her room, she locked the door behind her. If what she'd read was true,

Beaula was capable of anything. Caitlin opened her door to Jilly the following morning, and her friend brought her breakfast on a tray. They waited for the front doorbell to ring.

Descending the stairs, Caitlin wore her best dress, a gift from Jilly when her daughter-in-law had outgrown it. Mr. Deveraux was invited in and followed her to the front parlor.

Caitlin followed him, and Jilly, the cook, hovered protectively near Caitlin.

"Get back to the kitchen!" Aunt Beaula ordered.

"Stay where you are," Caitlin countered, turning to her friend. "Please. Take a seat, Jilly."

Beaula flounced into her chair in front of the fireplace. Caitlin had always considered the oversized, red velvet-covered chair Aunt Beaula's throne.

"Mr. Deveraux, please read the will out loud," Caitlin said.

Beaula turned on her niece. "Don't think you'll get away with this insolence!"

"Sit down and shut up!" Caitlin snapped.

"How dare you!"

"Oh, I dare," Caitlin said, distancing herself from her aunt and closer to the attorney. "You are going to discover how much I dare! Have a seat, Mr. Deveraux, and please read the will aloud."

The devil himself couldn't have shrunk more than Beaula Maud Ridgeway did as Mr. Deveraux read Florence Gwendolyn Ridgeway's will aloud.

"This can't be true," Beaula exclaimed.

"I can assure you the will is legal," Mr. Deveraux said. "Miss Florence Gwendolyn Ridgeway has left her daughter, Caitlin Angela Ridgeway, the entire Ridgeway trust and inheritance. As you know, your sister inherited the estate from your father twenty-four years ago. You were excluded from his will then. You have been excluded from your sister's will as well."

"The house?" Beaula demanded. Her voice broke, and she sounded panicked.

The attorney looked uncomfortable. "Yes, ma'am. Everything belongs to your niece." He turned to Caitlin. "Miss Ridgeway, I will be available to explain in detail what the inheritance covers. You are a wealthy young woman and may need guidance."

* * *

SIX MONTHS LATER, Caitlin stood in a nearly empty house. The Ridgeway Mansion had been sold, and most of the interior furnishings had been sent to auction houses.

"I checked the kitchen cupboards again," Jilly said. "They're clean as a whistle."

"I spent most of my life here, yet I never belonged," Caitlin said, looking around.

"They weren't all bad years," Jilly said. "Are you sure you want to do this?"

"It's too late to change my mind. I've already signed all the papers. Are you second-guessing your decision to come with me?"

"Did I say that?" Jilly demanded. "I will not let you take off to God knows where by yourself!"

Caitlin smiled. "Texas is not a foreign country. With the letters I found among Florence's personal items, I might be able to locate my father. I have his name now and where he lives."

"You may be going on a wild goose chase," Jilly huffed.

"True, but I only have one tie here, and I'm taking you with me!"

"Are you going to tell Beaula where you're going?"

"No," Caitlin said, shaking her head. "Beaula is settled in a small brownstone and will receive a stipend once a month. It might not be up to the standard of living she's hosted for years, but that's her problem. She doesn't deserve better, and I will not feel guilty. I wouldn't have been that generous had I found Florence's diary and the stack of letters she wrote before I made those arrangements. Florence was terrified of her bitch of a sister."

"Ouch," she complained when Jilly smacked her across the bottom for swearing.

Looking around the spacious foyer for one last time, Caitlin wished she did feel a sense of loss, but she didn't. "Let's go. We have a room at the Independence Hotel tonight, and our train leaves at eleven in the morning."

Waking hours before the train was due, Caitlin and Jilly went to the cemetery to lay flowers on Florence Ridgeway's grave. Caitlin had made arrangements for her mother's burial site to be changed. It had cost a ridiculous amount of money, but she did not want Florence to spend eternity beside the woman who had made her life miserable. Anyone as evil as Beaula had to die eventually, and no one would mourn her passing.

Caitlin laid roses on the granite tombstone at the new plot site. She could only hope that her mother had finally found peace.

The trip to Tyler, Texas, wasn't the comfortable adventure the railways advertised. The passenger cars were crowded, and the meals were far from delicious. There were several layovers, where they spent several hours waiting for the next connection. She and Jilly found mercantiles to purchase food that was better than what was offered in the dining cars.

Six days later, the train pulled into Tyler, Texas. Caitlin flagged a wagon and asked the driver to take them and their luggage to the Tyler Hotel. The three-story building was the tallest building on the main street of businesses. The town had a typical layout for most western towns they'd passed. The wagon driver delivered their luggage to the lobby, accepted a fee, and left.

"Hello?" Caitlin called out at the front counter.

"Hold on to your britches," a man shouted from somewhere behind the counter.

Caitlin and Jilly exchanged looks of amusement.

"Sorry, ma'am," a tall man exclaimed as he wiped his hands with a towel. "Do you want a room?"

"We have a reservation," Jilly said.

"Which one of you is Ridgeway?" the man asked.

"That would be me," Caitlin said.

"I got your telegram. Most people don't bother," the man said. "I'm Daniel Foster, and I own this place. I go by Daniel, not Dan. You're going to have to share because I'm almost full."

"That's okay," Caitlin said. "Is there someone who can bring our luggage upstairs?"

"Yep, that would be me," Daniel said with a grin. "How long are you ladies going to be here?"

"I don't know yet," Caitlin said.

"Well, usually I'm not that busy, but Hudson McFarlane has brought in a bunch of outsiders to teach Magnolia farm how to plant peach trees. Did you ever hear of such? This is ranch and farming country. Has been since the town was settled, but now Hudson is taking the word of some citified men from back east who claim Texas soil will grow peach trees. They call themselves hor-ti-culturists. I think I said that right, but that's just another fancy name for farmers, and what would they know about what will grow in Texas? They hail from Virginia!

"Ya'll make yourselves comfortable. The Rusty Pot is three doors down next to the mercantile if you get hungry. The eatery is my younger sister's business. Eleanor will give you a ten percent discount if you tell her you're staying here."

"That's convenient," Jilly said with a smile.

"Yes, ma'am. My sister makes the best food in town, not

counting our Ma. Don't let her talk your ear off," Daniel said as he set down their bags and closed the door.

"He does a good job of bending the ear himself," Jilly said with a smile.

"That could work in my favor to find out about my father," Caitlin said.

It didn't take long to discover Tyler's history and who the most prominent men in town were. Caitlin was trying to be discreet while asking questions. Daniel was right. His sister Eleanor was a good source of information, as were others in town.

After talking to Frank, the man who owned the livery, Caitlin and Jilly hired a buggy and drove to the entrance gate of Magnolia Ranch.

"I've heard that it's still five miles to Mr. Angus Ballard's house and outbuildings," Caitlin said. "The Magnolia Ranch combines ranching and farming, and he owns over four hundred thousand acres. Can you imagine that?"

"Have you got the nerve to face him?" Jilly asked.

"Not yet, and it wouldn't do me any good if I did. Angus Ballard is visiting his daughters in California. I can wait him out."

"For how long?" Jilly asked.

"As long as it takes," Caitlin answered, turning the horse around and giving a hitch to the reins. "I like the town of Tyler and the people here. They're friendly."

"That could turn on you. It might not be so friendly if Ballard denies that he fathered you," Jilly warned.

"I believe the letters Florence wrote to him, and I believe they never reached their destination. I think Beaula hid them before they were mailed. Angus Ballard was the love of Florence's life. I'll take my chances," Caitlin said.

A knock on the hotel door, well after dark, surprised

Caitlin. It was Daniel, and he motioned for Caitlin to come outside into the hallway. He handed her a telegram.

"It's for Miss Mason, ma'am," Daniel whispered. "It's bad news."

"Thank you," Caitlin said, but what she was thinking was that telegrams should be private. She nodded at Daniel, closed the door, and handed the envelope to her dearest friend. "Sit down, Jilly, it's for you."

Jilly sat. She looked scared and handed it back. "Read it!"

Tearing the envelope open and reading the bad news, Caitlin joined her friend on the lounging sofa. "It's from your daughter-in-law, Della. Lincoln is in the hospital. The doctors are saying he may not survive. She's asking you to come home."

"Oh, my God," Jilly cried. "What do I do?"

"You go back to Philadelphia," Caitlin said firmly.

"You have to come with me. I can't leave you here by yourself!" Jilly wept.

"Yes, you can," Caitlin said, consoling her friend. "I'm a grown woman, and as much as I love you, I can't come between you and your son. You need to go home to Lincoln. I will be fine here. I'll ask Daniel if he can find out when the next train going east comes through town. Have a good cry, and start packing. I'll be back in a few minutes."

In the early morning hours, just past daybreak, Caitlin and Jilly walked to the rail station. They each carried a suitcase, and Daniel followed with another.

"Are you sure you're going to be all right?" Jilly cried.

"Yes, and I want you to take this," Caitlin said, tucking a roll of money into Jilly's hand.

"I can't take..."

"Hush," Caitlin scolded in a whisper. "You might need it and more. I'll send a telegram to Mr. Deveraux authorizing him to help you financially. Don't hesitate to ask, and keep me posted about what is happening. Telegrams are expensive, but send them anyway!"

"I will, and you need to come home after meeting that man," Jilly whispered as she hugged Caitlin.

"I am home; I just didn't realize it," Caitlin said to herself as the train pulled out and she waved goodbye. She went inside the station and sent a telegram to Mr. Deveraux.

Giving the telegraph agent a lookover, Caitlin glanced at the nametag on his uniform. "Mr. Thomas, I will be sending and receiving private telegrams while I am in town. Should anyone speak to me about these matters, I will not hesitate to inform your employer about a breach of confidentiality. Do you understand?"

"Yes, ma'am," the agent nodded.

Caitlin returned to the hotel and waited for the Tyler Peoples Bank to open. She went inside and asked to speak to Mr. John Bones, the Bank President.

Escorted into the office by a male secretary, Mr. Bones stood and offered Caitlin his hand. She shook it, introduced herself, and sat in a leather chair across from the large desk.

"How may I help you, Miss Ridgeway?" Mr. Bones asked.

"I would like to open an account," Caitlin said, handing over a bank draft.

Mr. Bones looked at the amount, blinked, and nodded. "Tyler Peoples Bank would be pleased to accept you as a new client."

"Any bank would," Caitlin said. "But, the reality is that I don't want anyone to know how much I'm depositing into this bank. Privacy is important to me. For now, I have decided to make Tyler my home, and I don't want to spend my time in a boarding house. I would also like to know what properties are for sale and who handles them?"

"Unless it's a private transaction between two parties, I usually arrange the sales," Mr. Bones agreed. "I must warn you that there aren't very many properties available, but I'll be more than happy to show them to you."

"I would appreciate it, and please remember this transaction is private."

Secrecy was almost impossible in a small town, but generally, bank employees could be relied on. After the bank draft cleared, Mr. Bones took his second wealthiest client out on a Sunday morning while most people were attending church.

Caitlin was shown several properties, but they required a lot of work to make them livable. After looking at several similar homes, she turned to the banker. "Is this all you have to offer?"

"That's it, except for the Henasee property," Mr. Bones said.

"Why haven't you shown that property to me?" Caitlin asked.

Mr. Bones looked disconcerted. "The property has been up for sale for quite some time. It's far too much for a woman to take on. The house is large, and there are almost a thousand acres. Negotiations between Mr. Henasee and another client have been ongoing for quite some time."

"Show me the property," Caitlin said bluntly.

"Ma'am," Mr. Bones said, "I have a client who is determined to purchase the property."

"Do you, or do you not want me to be a client of your bank and sell me a house?" Caitlin asked.

"I'll show you the property, but I must warn you that the owner hasn't vacated yet, and he is... well... cantankerous."

As Mr. Bones drove, Caitlin was told the property was five miles from town. The brick house looked to be in good condition, although neglected. The lawn was overrun with weeds and bushes, and the wooden fence surrounding the house and large yard was broken in places. The wooden parts needed repair and painting. In some ways, the large house reminded her of the Ridgeway Estate she'd sold before leaving Philadelphia. The house was considerably larger than the other homes she'd been shown so far but not as large or pretentious as the mansion she'd grown up in and maintained for years.

Upon entering the house, they were met by an elderly man. "What the hell do you want?" Hubert Henasee demanded.

"Please be civil, Bert. This is Miss Ridgeway, a newcomer to town," Mr. Bones said. "She wanted to see the property."

"Have you got a husband that can afford it?" the old man demanded.

"No, but I have a bank account that can afford it if the price is right," Caitlin answered.

"I've been wrangling with Angus for the last year, and he ain't come up with the right price yet," Henasee said, aiming his words at Mr. Bones. "He wants to tear down my Pansy's house!"

"You know his reasons for wanting the property," the bank manager said.

"I don't care what he wants. Ballard thinks he will outlive me, but that ain't happening. I'm too ornery to die and give him what he wants! Go sit on the porch, Bones. Let me talk to this little gal," Henasee ordered.

"Miss Ridgeway," Mr. Bones began to say something, but he was interrupted.

"It's all right," Caitlin said, and the banker mumbled something she couldn't hear, but he went outside to the porch.

"How old are you, little lady?" the old man demanded.

"Mr. Henasee, I turned twenty-one last month."

"Why ain't you hitched yet?"

"Well, to tell the truth, I haven't been asked. I've spent most of my life caring for my two spinster aunts. One was a wonderful woman, and I loved her very much. The other was a cold-blooded bitch, and I couldn't wait to get away from her!"

Hubert Henasee threw back his head and laughed. "You remind me of my Pansy. She was the best wife a man could have, but boy ol' boy, she had a temper and a mouth. She didn't pussyfoot around with words, either. What will you do with this house if I sell it to you?"

"I'm going to learn how to live on my own. I'm going to draw, paint, and grow beautiful flowers, mostly roses. I like this house because it feels familiar. You've let it get somewhat run down, but that is fixable."

"But why does a city girl want to live in the country?"

"Pure pleasure," Caitlin answered with a smile. "I haven't had much pleasure in my life, and quite frankly, I'm overdue. For the first time since I was five years old, I can do as I please."

"This house holds dear memories to me," Hubert Henasee said, squinting his eyes and looking around. "Will you tear down my memories of my Pansy?"

"I haven't seen enough of the house to know," Caitlin said, looking around the foyer. "Will you be taking your furniture with you?"

"No, ma'am. I live in a cabin past those damn peach trees in the back lot. I took what I wanted and paced off ten acres I won't sell. That's why Ballard hasn't agreed to my terms. He wants all or nothing, and I won't let him tear down my Pansy's house. He's used to getting his way, but I'll be plum tickled if he got nothing!"

"I don't need that much property. I'm more concerned with the house and the yards," Caitlin admitted. She offered her arm. "Why don't you give me a tour, Mr. Henasee?"

"I like a little lady with grit," the old man said with a snaggletoothed grin. "Mr. Henasee was my pappy. I've been going by Bert for seventy-six years."

"I'm not sure what grit is," Caitlin admitted. "But, I'm open to learning."

Bert Henasee opened his front door an hour later and confronted Banker Bones. He slapped a piece of paper against the banker's chest. "I'm selling the property to Miss Caitlin

Ridgeway. All of it. Get off your duff and bring the papers around tomorrow for signing."

"What about the offer from Angus?" Mr. Bones demanded. "He's not going to like this!"

"Why the hell should I care?" Bert cackled. He gave Caitlin a nod and a wink. "I'll see you tomorrow, little lady. Mr. Bones, see that you get here early!"

Banker Bones wasn't happy about the transaction, but Caitlin didn't care.

"Why so glum?" Caitlin asked. "You sold the property, and I'm sure you didn't do it for free."

"I wish you'd change your mind," Bones said. "Angus Ballard and Hudson McFarlane are not going to like this."

"I've heard about them already," Caitlin admitted. "Owner and Manager of the Magnolia Ranch and the Magnolia Farm. Mr. Ballard owns half the county. Doesn't he have enough property?"

"Angus Ballard will never have enough land. Miss Ridgeway, you have put me between a rock and a hard place," the banker complained, helping Caitlin into the buggy.

As the banker walked around the buggy, Caitlin snorted and whispered to herself, "I was forced to live in that hard place because Angus Ballard did not accept his responsibilities. He doesn't get any sympathy from me!"

CHAPTER 2

"*A*re you sure about this?" John Bones, the President of the Tyler Peoples Bank, asked, holding onto the last piece of paper that would close the deal.

"You've been asking me that same question for two weeks," Caitlin said. "For the last time, yes!"

"Get on with it, Bones," Bert Henasee growled.

The banker slid the deed across the table. Caitlin signed it, and then Henasee signed it. "Welcome to Tyler, Miss Ridgeway."

Caitlin smiled. "It's about time! I've been living here for over a week as Bert's guest!"

When the door closed behind the banker, Bert Henasee was all smiles, and he hugged Caitlin. "Every day that goes by, you remind me more of my Pansy. Angus will be fit to be tied when he finds out I've sold the place. Hot damn, I'm looking forward to him finding out!"

"He's going to have a bigger fit when I tell him I'm his daughter," Caitlin said in a low voice. She knew Bert couldn't hear because he was hard of hearing in his left ear. The old man had offered her the house to live in so she could leave the hotel, while Mr. Bones, the Bank President, had tried to delay the paperwork to finalize the property deed transfer. He was hoping Angus Ballard would return from his trip.

"What are we doing today?" Bert asked.

"Frank at the livery has offered to sell me two horses and a used buggy," Caitlin said. "One horse is for riding, and the other is harness trained for the buggy. I could use your advice on the horses and the buggy. I've already sent some telegrams, and I should have a rail delivery at the station soon."

"You've got it, darling," Bert grinned.

Caitlin knew Bert was pleased that she wanted most of the house furniture. She hadn't kept much when she'd sold the Ridgeway Estate. Most of the furniture had gone to an auction house. Beaula had been given most of what she demanded, although she no longer had the right to demand anything. Caitlin had burned the red velvet chair and several of Beaula's favorite pieces in the backyard as an exorcism of the forced labor, slaps, pinches, and hair-pulling she'd received before the age of twelve when she learned how to fight back. She'd had to shove her aunt back on her ass several times before Beaula realized her abuse wouldn't be tolerated any longer, and then there had been the biting episode, something she didn't like to think about.

Caitlin had boxed a few things belonging to her and Florence and stored them until she decided where to settle. She had also boxed her memories of the nursery. There was a huge dollhouse where make-believe loving parents and brothers and sisters had existed in her imagination. A rocking horse she'd ridden far, far away, but neither she nor the wooden horse had left the room until she was old enough to serve and work.

Her easels, painting supplies, and paintings had always been hidden in attic rooms that had initially housed servants. They had been carefully crated and stored to be shipped wherever Caitlin decided to live. For now, it was going to be Tyler, Texas.

* * *

It took ten days before the news of Bert Henasee selling his property reached Hudson McFarlane. He'd been offsite dealing with cut fences and wandering cattle. When he was told, he was pissed. That property should have always belonged to Augus Ballard. It was only a thousand acres, but that strip of land split Magnolia Ranch from Magnolia Farm. That land now belonged to an outsider, a silly city woman to boot.

Caitlin Ridgeway was the woman's name, and he'd gotten a look at her when he was in town picking up supplies. At least, he thought the woman he'd seen and the woman described as the new owner of Henasee's land were the same. The description was the same, and how many women had hair that looked like blazing fire in the sunshine? He'd admired her from a distance for a few seconds before he'd moved on to finish his errand.

That was before all hell had broken loose at Magnolia Ranch. He'd thought she was a train passenger passing through. It wasn't uncommon for travelers to wander from the station to the mercantile if there was a delay. There weren't many pretty and single women in town. If they did show up, they didn't remain unattached for long.

Hudson was going to Bert's house to talk to the new owner when he saw her leave in a buggy. He continued to the house and saw the changes already made. Since his wife died, Old Bert hadn't done much with the oversized house. He hadn't lived there for years, and the house had stood as a memorial to his wife.

It was a house like no other in the county, built of brick and three stories high.

There was a sign newly painted, naming the property Rose Hill. The fences that had been falling down were now fixed and freshly whitewashed. The bushes had been trimmed, and the grass scythed. Someone was working on the neglected property.

Turning his horse, Hudson rode over the hill to the log cabin Old Bert had moved into after his wife of nearly fifty years had died.

"Howdy, Hudson," Bert Henasee said when he was approached.

"Why did you do it?" Hudson demanded.

"Cause I could," the old man said with a cackle. "Those Ballard bastards can't have everything they want."

"Whatever your problems were, they were with Andrew, not Angus. They had nothing to do with Angus. It was fifty years ago," Hudson said.

"Wrong is wrong, and that bastard branded me a thief," Bert growled. "I should have put a bullet in him before my eyesight went bad!"

Hudson shook his head. "Andrew claimed on his deathbed to Angus that you stole the land in a crooked faro game. Both of you are acting like fools."

"If Andrew was still alive, he'd give you a hiding for saying that," Bert snarled.

Hudson shook his head and laughed. "I never met Andrew, and I'm not a kid anymore."

Riding into town, Hudson saw Miss Ridgeway's buggy in front of the Ellison mercantile. He tied his horse to the hitching post and went inside, looking around.

"Looking for somebody?" Rob Ellison asked.

"Miss Ridgeway," Hudson said.

Alma Ellison smiled. "I'm filling her order now. She went down to the Rusty Pot. Said she was in the mood for some of Eleanor's apple pie."

"Thanks," Hudson said, and he walked out.

"I'd like to be a fly on that wall," Alma told her husband.

Rob laughed. "So would I."

Caitlin was sitting at a table facing the sidewalk. She saw a tall, good-looking man dressed as a rancher stride to the door and enter the eatery. He had the deep tan of a man who spent many hours in the hot sun. He removed his hat, and his hair was a dark mahogany color with streaks of blond.

He looked around and made a beeline for her table.

"Miss Ridgeway?"

"Yes," Caitlin answered.

"I'm Hudson McFarlane, foreman of the Magnolia Ranch."

"Have a seat," Caitlin offered.

Hudson pulled out a chair with his back to the rest of the nearly empty eatery. "We need to talk, ma'am."

"In here or outside?" Caitlin asked. "Not that it will make any difference. I am the owner of Rose Hill now."

"Ma'am, I don't think you realize..."

"I do realize," Caitlin interrupted him. "I own the property, and I'm not selling it to Angus Ballard. Mr. Henasee and I have an agreement, and I will honor it."

"Ma'am, Bert Henasee is senile."

Caitlin smiled. "I don't believe Mr. Henasee is infirm for a second. Cantankerous and stubborn, maybe, it was his property to sell. He's a shrewd negotiator. He got exactly what he wanted. So did I."

Hudson looked into the soft lilac eyes of the woman across the table and shook his head to clear it. She was the same woman he'd seen before. Her hair was flaming orange, what he could see of it that had escaped from a flower-covered hat. "Miss Ridgeway, Bert Henasee was negotiating with Angus Ballard and me for that property."

"Not very successfully, from what I understand," Caitlin said, smiling. "From what I understand, Mr. Ballard and Mr.

Henasee have argued over that property for quite some time. Mr. Henasee believes I am a better fit for his previous home."

"My boss, Angus Ballard, will be coming home soon. He's expecting the deal on that land to be completed," Hudson complained.

"I am sorry, Mr. McFarlane, but I bought Rose Hill, and I am pleased with my purchase. Is there anything else I can do to help you?"

Hudson knew instantly what he wanted, but he couldn't and wouldn't voice it. He wanted Caitlin Ridgeway in his bed and under him. His body was reacting to her physically, and Hudson hadn't responded to a woman that way in a long time. He stood, wondering if he was being vamped. He'd heard about women having that ability but had never believed it.

Shoving his chair back under the table, Hudson shook his head, gave her a nod, and walked out.

"That didn't go well," Caitlin said to herself, aiming her words at Hudson McFarlane's back. "I'm looking forward to discussing a few matters with Angus Ballard myself."

"Is something wrong?" Eleanor asked, bringing a slice of pie to the newcomer's table. "I wish Hudson would seek me out."

"He is a handsome man," Caitlin admitted. "But, I think we're destined to be adversaries. Is he married?"

"Not now, but he was," Eleanor said. "His wife Malinda was killed in a wagon accident a few years ago. Something spooked a team of horses, and she was trampled. His little girl, Charlotte, was only four years old and saw it happen. She hasn't spoken a word since."

"The poor child," Caitlin said with sympathy.

Hudson rode home to the Magnolia Ranch, reviewing his short conversation with the Ridgeway woman. He'd been told she was of legal age to sign a contract, but she didn't look it. She looked about sixteen. The other descriptions he'd heard were correct. She was a small, good-looking young woman who didn't waver under pressure.

Miss Ridgeway was probably right about the verbal agreement because Banker John Bones had allowed her to purchase the property. From the look of it, she was either a hard worker or could afford to hire help. From an inside perspective, Hudson would be the one who had to face the wrath of his boss, Angus Ballard, for not stopping the sale, even though he'd been a hundred miles away dealing with cattle thieves.

Caitlin didn't give much thought to her encounter with Hudson McFarlane. Other than being impressed with his good looks, the conversation had been lacking. Later that evening, she stood in front of a full-length mirror and looked at herself. Before the inheritance, she'd never had a single young man approach her. Even if she had, she wouldn't have had a proper dress for an outing. After the news of her inheritance spread through gossip, men sought her company and left their fancy printed cards for a formal introduction.

That wasn't going to happen. If those eligible young men hadn't been interested in her poorer self, she had no use for them after she had become an heiress. Caitlin had been kept close to the Ridgeway Estate, and most of Beaula's so-called friends thought she was a hired servant, a distinction her aunt never bothered to correct.

Caitlin had always had Jilly, but now Jilly was gone, and she and her daughter-in-law were caring for Jilly's son Lincoln.

After the will had been read and with money suddenly available, Caitlin had splurged on pretty dresses, shoes, and hats for the first time in her life. Not only for herself but for Jilly, too. She'd made up for all the years of doing without and neglect. The boxed and crated clothing was on a train between Philadelphia and Tyler. The problem was that what she had bought was too fancy to wear in a small Texas town, and she would have to correct that problem. Her art supplies and other personal items would make her new house feel like a home.

For the first time in her life, Caitlin wasn't at the beck and call of someone, and she wasn't being berated if she didn't fulfill the expectations of others. The truth was she didn't quite know what to do with herself. She and Bert, along with three older boys he'd hired, had cleaned the yards of debris, trimmed the bushes, fixed the fence, and whitewashed it. Caitlin had cleaned, polished, and rearranged the furniture to her liking with the help of Bert's strength.

Realizing she was bored and lonely, Caitlin decided to ride her new horse, Bucky, into town to see if she could purchase a sketching pad. The one she'd brought with her was full of her drawings.

She stopped at Bert's cabin to see if he was well. He hadn't shown up at her house for a day or two. Sometimes, she tried to cook for him, but her attempts weren't very good. Burt was gentle with his truthful comments, and she was learning. She had never worked in the kitchen except to help with baking. There was a reason for that, but she didn't like resurrecting those awful memories.

Bert wasn't home, so she continued into Tyler.

Caitlin stopped in front of the Ellison mercantile and tied her horse to the railing.

"Good morning, Miss Ridgeway. What can I do for you?" Rob Ellison asked.

"First, you can call me Caitlin," she said with a smile.

"Yes, ma'am," Rob agreed with a smile. "I'm Rob, and my wife is Alma. How can I help you?"

"I'm looking for a sketch pad."

"A what?" Rob asked with a frown.

"A sketch pad," Caitlin said, pulling her pad from a leather case. "It looks like this. The paper is a bit rough."

The mercantile owner shook his head. "I don't think I've got anything that looks like that. But you sure can draw good." He turned to his wife. "Alma, see if you can find what Caitlin is looking for in one of our catalogs."

"I think we have some of this paper," Alma said, looking at the pad. "Remember that surveyor who came through town a few years back. He ordered this same kind of paper tablets out of a catalog, but then he left town, and we haven't seen him since."

"I do remember him," Rob said. "And, now I remember where I put his order. On second thought, I'll get it. I put his order on a top shelf, under that heavy box of duck decoys that didn't sell. I figured the weight would keep the paper from curling in the summer heat. Those boxes are too heavy for you to lift."

Rob disappeared behind a curtained doorway, and a few minutes later, he appeared with a good-sized box. He opened it and handed Caitlin a tablet. "Will these do?"

"They're perfect," Caitlin exclaimed. "I'll take all of them. How much?"

"Nothing, they were already paid for in advance, and we have no use for them," Rob said with a smile.

"Thank you! I'll take one today because I rode in, so I'll have to return for the others. I don't think I can balance a box and a sack on horseback."

"We'll hold them for you," Alma said. "How are you doing out there at Bert's place?"

"I love living there," Caitlin answered truthfully. "I grew up in Philadelphia, so it's taking me a bit to get used to living in the country," She hugged the large sketch pad to her chest and then put it back on the counter. "Thank you, and I'll be back in a few minutes for my order."

Caitlin quickly walked to the Rusty Pot and waved at Eleanor.

"I'm not full if you want a table," Eleanor said.

"I'm not hungry, but could I buy a whole pie as a gift?"

"Sure," Eleanor said, surprised. "Today's pie is apple, and it would be forty cents. Is that too high?"

"No, it's fine. Thank you!" Caitlin exclaimed.

Caitlin was carrying the pie very carefully. With Eleanor's permission, she would give the pie to the Ellisons for being so helpful and frankly honest.

Anyone who didn't draw or paint couldn't understand what it meant to create. Caitlin had found it profoundly satisfying after a horrible day of Beaula complaining that she was worthless. Her drawing had always been a secret between Florence and Caitlin. Since she'd left that environment, Caitlin had found an even deeper satisfaction in her drawings.

Carefully watching her step on the uneven sidewalk boards, she didn't notice the woman at first, but she did recognize the words and the harsh, nasty tone of voice.

"Worthless! Stupid! Simple-minded Dummy!"

Caitlin raised her head, and pure fury raced through her. "Stop it!" she screamed.

The heavy-set woman barely looked up. She was striking the little girl with every demonized word with a wooden ruler.

"Stop it!" Caitlin screamed again.

"Mind your own business!" the woman snarled.

Caitlin threw the pie at the woman at the same time that the little girl bit into her arm. Caitlin grabbed and pulled the little girl behind her. The little girl was crying, but there were no sounds of terror.

"Awww!" the woman yelled, raising the ruler to attack.

Caitlin took the blows and turned her body to block them. She raised her arm and slammed her elbow into the woman's face, knocking her into the side of the building, where she slid to the ground.

"What the hell is going on?" Rob Ellison demanded as a crowd of people was gathering.

"Call the sheriff," the woman on the ground demanded. "She attacked me!"

"Call the sheriff and have her arrested!" Caitlin countered. "She was beating this child!" She picked up the little girl in her arms and sat on the sidewalk, rocking the sobbing but silent little girl in her arms.

"Y'all break it up and go about your business," a man with a sheriff's badge said to a growing crowd. "Jimmy, see if you can round up Hudson. He must be around if his kid and her nurse are here."

"She broke my nose!" the woman on the ground bellowed.

"You deserved it and more!" Caitlin spat.

"Ma'am, who are you?" the sheriff asked of the woman holding and rocking Hudson McFarlane's daughter.

"My name is Caitlin Ridgeway."

"Well, that don't tell me much," the sheriff said. "Who do you belong to?"

"I don't *belong* to anyone," Caitlin snapped. "Even if I was married, I wouldn't *belong* to a man or his family!"

"All right. You two, just sit tight for now and stay away from each other."

Caitlin hugged and rocked the little girl in her lap, whispering into the child's ear. "It's going to be all right, sweetie. I think I know your father. Well, I've met him once, and…"

"Leeroy, what's going on?" Hudson demanded, weaving his way through a crowd of people, but his attention was caught by his daughter sitting in Caitlin Ridgeway's lap, and she wasn't fighting to get away from her. There was a short list of people Charlotte would allow to touch or hold her. In long strides, he reached the sidewalk and squatted down. Charlotte went into his arms, still sobbing silently.

"What happened?"

"That woman assaulted me, and she broke my nose," the woman on the ground wailed.

Hudson looked at Caitlin. "What's your version?"

"She's wearing the apple pie I bought for the Ellison's as a thank-you gift," Caitlin said, slightly rattled. "I didn't think. I just threw it at her, and when she turned on me, I elbowed her in the face. She was beating this child, who I assume is your daughter."

"She even admits it," the woman on the ground wailed. "She tried to kill me!"

"I admit to hitting you, and I'm glad I did. You should be ashamed!" Caitlin exclaimed, facing Hudson, not the sheriff. "Look at your daughter's back and her legs. That disgusting excuse of a woman was beating her with a wooden ruler."

"What!" Hudson demanded.

"Worse yet," Caitlin said, covering Charlotte's ears with her hands gently. "She was calling this child horrible names. Worthless! Stupid! Simple-minded and Dummy! And those are the ones I heard. Who knows what she spewed before I stopped her!"

The sheriff was looking at the woman on the ground now with no sympathy, but he was more concerned with the look of pure disgust in his friend's eyes. There was pure murder in Hudson McFarlane's eyes.

Hudson shifted his daughter and pulled the top of her dress down, and then he gently looked down the back of her dress and rolled down her stockings. He looked over at the sheriff. "She has welts on her back and legs, and that's all I can see without undressing her."

"I was disciplining her," the woman wailed.

"Take her over to Doctor Martin," Hudson ordered, nodding toward the woman on the ground, and the sheriff nodded. "Tell him I'll bring Charlotte to him, but only after he's done with that piece of trash!"

Hudson turned his attention back to the woman. "Deloris Campbell, you are fired! Have your things packed and be gone by the time I get to the ranch." He looked around and nodded to a young man. "Sidney, drive her back to the ranch and have Mrs. Brimmer pay her what is owed. Then bring her back to town. I don't want her to spend one minute more at Magnolia that isn't necessary. Then I want her out of Tyler!"

"Yes, sir," the young man nodded.

Caitlin leaned closer to Charlotte and opened her arms. To Hudson's surprise, his daughter crawled into her lap and snuggled against her.

"I want you to know something very important, Charlotte," Caitlin said gently while wiping the little girl's tears with her skirt. "Some people say hurtful words, but that doesn't mean they are true words. You don't have to listen or let those bad words hurt you. You are a smart little girl whose father loves you very much. I'm sure there are lots of people who love you!"

Charlotte turned her wet eyes to her father, and Hudson nodded. "More than anything," he said softly.

"And, most important," Caitlin continued. "Words can't hurt you if you know they aren't true. Now, you should go with your father to the doctor. I'm sure you're okay, but when a father gets scared for his little girl, he needs someone like a doctor to tell him she's okay."

Charlotte nodded, stood up, and hugged Caitlin. Then she took Hudson's hand.

"Thank you," Hudson said as he picked up his daughter and walked away.

Caitlin went to stand up, but found she was a little wobbly. She was helped to her feet by Rob and Alma Ellison.

"I was going to treat you to an apple pie for being so nice to me earlier," Caitlin said. "But that horrible woman is wearing it."

Eleanor laughed. "I have another that I'll give them."

"You're quite a woman, Miss Ridgeway," Rob said.

Caitlin smiled. "It's just Caitlin, please. I'm not big on

formalities, and I hope we can be friends. I don't usually go around knocking people down."

"She deserved it, and I'm sure we will be friends," Alma said with a smile.

"Why don't you come into my place, sit for a spell, and I'll make you a cup of tea," Eleanor offered.

"Thank you. I think I could use one," Caitlin agreed.

CHAPTER 3

$\mathcal{R}$iding home from Tyler was a bit uncomfortable for Caitlin. The closer she got to her house, the more pain she was feeling. The woman she'd tackled was taller and at least fifty or sixty pounds heavier. The woman had hit her a few times with the ruler before she elbow-hit the woman in the face, and she had dropped the ruler.

Caitlin had learned how to hit with her elbow from the gardener before he had been fired. She had used that defense several times against Beaula, teaching her aunt that hair-pulling would no longer be tolerated.

Arriving at Rose Hill, she took care of her horse, Bucky, and stored her precious sketch tablet. Then she went to the kitchen, dragged a tub into the pantry, and prepared a bath.

The bath helped, although it uncovered more darkening bruises, sore spots, and scratches, especially on her elbow and arm. It wasn't the worst she'd experienced, but it had been a while since Beaula dared to strike her.

Wandering through the big, empty house, wearing only a wrapper, Caitlin picked up her new tablet and a pencil and went outside to the back veranda. She climbed into a hammock Bert had strung up in the backyard and began to sketch.

By the time Hudson finished in town, half the day was gone. Charlotte wasn't hurt badly, but the red welts left by the ruler still had him grinding his teeth in anger.

Deloris Campbell had a broken nose and two eyes that were blackening and was now missing two front teeth. Her injuries were well-earned as far as Hudson was concerned. Gossip spread fast in Tyler; he'd already heard that no one wanted to house Deloris for the night. Gossip claimed that she would sleep on the train station outdoor bench. The town of Tyler depended on Magnolia Ranch and Farm for their livelihoods, and Hudson represented the ranch.

He had fired her, which should have been enough humiliation, but the townspeople were taking Deloris' downfall further. Even Hudson couldn't be hard-hearted enough to make a woman sleep on a wooden bench on the train station platform.

Hudson talked to Harriet Wilder, who ran a woman's boarding house in town. He promised Harriet that Deloris would be leaving Tyler on the morning train. His next stop was the train station to ensure Deloris had purchased a ticket.

While there, Hudson was informed that Miss Ridgeway's expected freight from Pennsylvania had arrived. There were three large freight boxes, and two smaller ones stacked on the freight platform. As expected, the large boxes were heavy, but surprisingly, the smaller ones were heavier.

Hudson's original plans for being in Tyler were brought to a grinding halt. He took Charlotte to his sister Nell's house, explained what had happened earlier, and left his daughter in her capable hands. She had been a nurse before marrying, and Dr. Martin had examined Charlotte and declared she would be fine in a day or two.

Charlotte had looked upset at his leaving, but when Hudson

explained that he had to do something nice for the lady who helped her, his daughter smiled and nodded.

The rest of his day was spent hiring drivers for rented wagons to deliver Miss Ridgeway's freight boxes to Rose Hill. Hudson gave Rob Ellison his list of supplies and told him he would return later. He drove his wagon to the train station and loaded the two smaller crates into the wagon bed.

When he arrived at Rose Hill, Hudson jumped down from the wagon. He knocked on the front door, but there was no answer. He walked around the house, but his eyes were on the paddock, and horses were there. Now, he was intrigued. He opened the back gate, but stopped in his tracks.

Caitlin was asleep in a hammock, stretched out, and only wearing a wrapper. The wrapper material had provocatively twisted around her, showing more of her feminine charms than any woman would display except to a husband.

Hudson had to admire the female curves, but he frowned when he saw deep purple bruising on her arm and a long scratch on her thigh. He cleared his throat and turned his back to her.

"Miss Ridgeway!" he said louder.

"Hmmm," was the only reply he received.

"Caitlin!" Hudson said sharply.

Caitlin was disturbed from her sleep and almost turned over. She grabbed the sides of the hammock and closed the wrapper to cover herself. "What are you doing here?" she demanded.

"I came to thank you again," Hudson said. "I also came to help you unload two of your freight boxes.

"Oh," Caitlin exclaimed, climbing out of the hammock carefully. "I need a few minutes to get dressed."

"Stop," Hudson ordered before she went through the door."

"What?" she demanded.

"I couldn't help but notice," Hudson said. "I saw the long

scratches on your... ah, limbs. "Are they deep? Do you need the doctor to look at them?"

Caitlin smiled at his embarrassment. "Mr. McFarlane, I'm not a tree. I have arms and legs, the same as men. I didn't notice the scratches at first, but I treated them with alcohol after I got home. It hurt like the devil, but I don't think they are anything to worry about. How is your daughter?"

"She's with my sister, Nell, who lives in town. She was a nurse before she married," Hudson said, his hands tightening into fists. "I didn't know Miss Campbell was mistreating Charlotte. She didn't have permission to discipline my daughter. Not at all. Why didn't I know?"

"Because your daughter can't speak, and she was probably threatened and scared," Caitlin answered. "The shame is on Miss Campbell. She took what she thinks is discipline too far. There's a difference between smacking a child's bottom and beating them."

"I agree," Hudson said. "It's true in marriage, too."

Caitlin raised an eyebrow at that remark. "I'll only be a few minutes. I need to get dressed."

"Is there anything in those crates that I shouldn't see?" Hudson asked. "If not, I'll pry off the tops before carrying them inside."

Caitlin smiled. "The two smaller crates are filled with painting supplies and good memories."

On his way out of town, Hudson had borrowed a crowbar and a hammer from Sammy King at the livery. He quickly pried off the tops of the wooden crates.

Caitlin rushed out of the house, wearing loose men's trousers, a man's shirt, and men's boots. She climbed into the wagon, looked through the shredded cardboard, and tossed it aside. "Oh, good! Everything looks intact."

Hudson joined her and pulled out smaller boxes from the crate, clearly labeled as brushes, paints, canvas, and other supplies. What he assumed were paintings were covered with heavy wool cloth. Before carrying them inside, Caitlin scrutinized at least a dozen large paintings for damage. She didn't uncover them, and he helped her carry the packages into the house. Hudson nailed the lid back on the empty freight box. Then he opened the second crate and looked down at something that looked like a roof. It was a roof, and he uncovered a huge dollhouse.

"You paid the freight on a doll house from Philadelphia?" he asked incredulously.

"Yes, I did," Caitlin said with a smile. "And it was worth every penny."

Hudson scratched his head, but didn't make any comments. It wasn't his bill to pay. "It looks like there are a lot of wrapped pieces inside. It would probably be better to carry it inside while still in the crate.

Caitlin reached to pick up one side of the crate.

"Are you sure you can lift it?" Hudson asked, stopping her.

"There's no harm in trying as long as we don't drop it."

"With Hudson on one side and Caitlin on the other, they lifted the doll house crate and moved it cautiously off the wagon bed. The weight was distributed evenly, and they were moving together. Suddenly, there was a strangled sound from Caitlin, and her side of the box jolted downward.

"Don't break it!" Caitlin screamed.

"I'm trying not to!" Hudson said, lowering his side. "Let it go!"

There was a jolt as the crate hit the ground.

Caitlin was on her knees, sitting on the ground. "Is it broken?"

"Not that I can see," Hudson said. He stood and pulled her to her feet, but his eyes lowered to her trousers, where one pant leg was darkening with blood. "You've busted your leg."

"There was a nail that I didn't see," Caitlin said.

With a sweep of his arms, Hudson picked her up, carried her to the kitchen, and sat her at the table. Looking around the kitchen, he pumped a pan of water and banged cabinets open and shut before finding a towel. He went to one knee and began rolling up the trouser leg.

"Stop!" Caitlin cried. "You can't do that!"

"It's a little hard to stop the bleeding if I can't see what I'm doing," Hudson growled.

"I can fix it," Caitlin protested.

"Be quiet, and let me tend to this!" Hudson ordered.

"Don't yell at me!" she snapped back.

"I'm not yelling! Yet," Hudson growled. His whole attention was on the cut below her kneecap. He pressed down on the wound, but every time he released the pressure, blood gushed from the laceration.

"What the Sam Hell is going on?" Bert Henasee cursed as he stomped into the kitchen through the back door.

"Not now, Bert," Hudson said. "I can't stop the bleeding!"

The old man got down on one knee and squinted at the cut. "It needs sewing! Put her back in that wagon and take her to the Doctor."

"I'll be okay if you would just stop," Caitlin pleaded. "I bleed a lot if I'm cut. I always have. It will stop."

"Are you going to listen to that dripple while she bleeds out?" Bert demanded of Hudson.

"No, I'm not," Hudson said. "Hold that!" he ordered Caitlin, removing his hand from the wet towel and placing hers over the bloodied cloth.

"Good man," Bert said with a grin. "Old Angus ain't ruined you yet."

"Bert!" Caitlin complained.

"Hush up, Little Darling," the old man said. "I saw my share of gushers during the war. You'd best do as you're told!"

"I'm not budging until my dollhouse crate is brought into

the house safely. The skies look like rain is coming, and I won't have it ruined!" Caitlin said stubbornly.

"Damn it!" Hudson growled. "Save me from a stubborn woman! Come on, Bert. If we don't do it, she'll blame us if the damn thing gets wet!"

The men stomped out of the kitchen, and Caitlin hopped over to the water pump, twisted the towel under the water, and when it was clean of blood, applied it to the cut under her knee.

A few minutes later, the men stomped back into the kitchen.

"What the..." Hudson growled, seeing that Caitlin was sitting on the pump sink.

"It's stopped bleeding," Caitlin said, removing the towel. "And the cut isn't that deep."

Hudson walked over to inspect the cut with Bert at his side. "What do you think, Bert?"

"Well, she's right, it ain't bleeding. But that don't mean it can't start up again," the old guy said.

"What about the other scratches and bruises?" Hudson asked Caitlin.

"What other scratches and bruises?" Bert demanded.

Hudson crossed his arms and gave Caitlin a look that made her swallow and flinch, but she raised her chin defiantly. "Bert, our pretty Miss Ridgeway is a scrapper. She was in a catfight this morning. Now, I'm not faulting her for it because she was protecting my daughter. But, it seems she was hurt more than she admitted to this morning." Hudson nodded to the bruises on her leg. "Those didn't come from dropping the crate."

Twenty minutes later, Caitlin was still trying to stand her ground but was losing the argument. Hudson and Bert insisted that she return to town and see the doctor.

"I can't," she told Hudson. "You said you hired men to

deliver the other crates. I have to be here to make sure they aren't careless and leave them out in the rain."

"I'll stay here," Bert volunteered.

Hudson was so frustrated he felt the palm of his hand twitch. It crossed his mind that the feisty little woman wouldn't be so stubborn if he gave her bottom a lesson in behaving. As it was, she wasn't giving an inch.

"Don't look now, but you're bleeding through the bandage you put on your leg," Hudson said.

Caitlin bent over to pull her trousers away from the bandage, and the next thing she knew, she was hanging over Hudson's shoulder.

"Let me down," she shouted. "Bert! Make him stop!"

"I can't do that, Little Darling," old Bert said, following them outside to the wagon. "I may not agree with Hudson or his boss most of the time, but this is different. He asked you nicely, and you ain't listening! I'll be here when the wagons get here, and I'll have those fellows be real careful with the freight boxes and put them inside."

Hudson set Caitlin down on her feet and loomed over her diminutive figure. She only came up to the third button on his shirt. He leaned down to her level and whispered, "I'm going to lift you into the wagon seat and take you to town. If you try to make a run for it, I'll catch you and turn you over my knee for a well-deserved spanking. Then, I'll still take you to Tyler. Your choice! Behave or keep fighting me."

Caitlin looked up and silently cursed her small stature for the millionth time. "I'll go, but it's a waste of time!"

Caitlin didn't speak until she saw wagons coming in their direction. "Are they bringing my freight boxes to Rose Hill?"

"Yes," Hudson said. "They'll unload the crates under Bert's watch."

"Who do I pay? Caitlin asked.

"It's already been taken care of," Hudson said.

"By you?" Caitlin asked. "I'll repay you."

"You can repay me by not behaving like a spoiled brat," Hudson said gruffly.

"Me? Spoiled?" Caitlin snorted. "Until a few months ago, I was Cinderella."

"Who?" Hudson demanded.

Caitlin shook her head. "Shame on you. You have a daughter. Every little girl knows about Cinderella. She's a character from a children's book. A little girl who was used and abused by her stepmother and stepsisters. At least her story ended well because Cinderella married a prince in the happy ever after ending."

She shrugged and looked up to an overcast sky. "Maybe I didn't have it that bad. Only one of my aunts was wicked and horrible. My other aunt treated me well. It was unfortunate that she was sickly. She didn't have the stamina to fight her older sister."

"What happened to your parents?" Hudson asked.

"They never married. I discovered my mother only after she died and left me with a sizeable inheritance."

"What about your father?" Hudson asked.

"I know his name, but I've never met him," Caitlin said. "I was raised in an orphanage until I was five. Then, I was taken to live with two women who claimed to be my aunts. When I was ten, I became my bedridden aunt's nurse and caretaker. My other aunt used me as an unpaid servant, and I was supposed to be grateful and indebted to her. I wasn't."

Hudson turned to look at her with a half-grin. "How long did it take you to tell the wicked aunt to kiss your... well, you know what I won't say in front of a lady. What was your revenge?"

Caitlin took a deep breath. "I wanted to be vengeful. I really did. The bad part of me wanted to make her homeless and destitute. I would gladly have given her an old hat and a tin cup and let her beg on street corners for pennies. She would have done the same to me.

"Instead, I sold the house I'd scrubbed and cleaned for years. My despicable aunt receives a monthly stipend. It's enough to survive on but not enough to get fat on or allow for extras. The real revenge she brought on herself. When her so-called society equals discovered her financial downfall, they pretended she didn't exist."

"Why did an heiress from the northeast decide to live in Tyler?"

"Why not?" Caitlin said, returning his question. "I've found that most people here are friendly and nice. Do you know the town doctor?"

Hudson recognized the question was a dodge from further information. "Our town doctor is Harold Martin, but I'm not taking you to him. I'm taking you to my sister Nell. She was a nurse before she married our local lawyer, Ben Rogers. I thought you might be more comfortable seeing a woman. I'll take you there if she thinks you need to see the doctor."

"I guess that's fair," Caitlin said. "I've never been to a doctor before, and the one who came to see my aunt was a horrible little man."

Hudson pulled the wagon to a halt beside a picket fence and lifted Caitlin to the ground. He knocked on the door, and it was answered by his sister, who was obviously with child. She was tall like her brother and had the same coloring and features.

"Nell, this is Caitlin Ridgeway. She's the young woman..."

"Who saved our Charlotte," Nell exclaimed, drawing Caitlin into a hug. "Thank you! I never liked that woman, and I was right!"

"She came highly recommended," Hudson said. "Sis, would you take a look at Caitlin. She has a gash under her knee and other scratches and bruises. Don't look at me like that! I was there when she got caught on a nail. Seeing the scratches and bruises was an accident. Anyway, I thought someone should look her over."

"I told him it wasn't necessary," Caitlin protested. "But he won't listen to me."

"Welcome to the story of my life," Nell exclaimed. "Come in, please come in!"

"How is..." Hudson questioned but was cut off.

"Charlotte is taking a nap, and she's fine. Are you going to spend the night here?"

"Yeah, I have to take Caitlin home and return the wagon. Then I have some business with John Bones. It will be too late to head up to the ranch by then."

"Get along with your business, brother. I'll take care of your lady friend," Nell said, closing the door after a kiss on his cheek and a wave. She turned to Caitlin. "Now, let's see how much damage was done when you rescued my niece."

A few minutes later, Nell turned a nearly naked Caitlin this way and that, inspecting the scratches, bruises, and the cut below her knee. "These are all surface wounds, although we'll keep a tight bandage on the cut. It could have taken a stitch or two, but it's not deep enough to do any damage."

"I tried to tell Hudson that, but he wouldn't listen," Caitlin complained.

Nell laughed. "No one can tell my brother anything once he sets his mind on something. I'm surprised that he's restrained himself from going after that horrible woman he hired. My brother is very protective of the women in his life. That's Charlotte and me. He's been that way since our folks died. He was only sixteen, to my ten, but he raised and supported us. Sometimes, I think he had to become a grown man far too soon."

"How long has he worked at Magnolia Ranch?" Caitlin asked.

Nell thought for a moment. "It's been sixteen years now. He's been the top foreman for the last seven years. He keeps a tight rein on everyone who works for Magnolia, both on the ranch and the farm. My brother has earned his reputation of being a good man."

"He's a stubborn man," Caitlin said. "I apologize for taking up your time."

"Oh, I wanted to meet you," Nell exclaimed. "You've been the talk of the town for buying the Henasee property, and now today. Everyone was talking about how you protected Charlotte. Oh, how I wish it could have been me who gave that woman a broken nose, black eyes and knocked out her front teeth!"

"I did?" Caitlin exclaimed.

Nell giggled and hugged Caitlin. "Yes, you did, and you're my hero!"

"I wanted to make a good impression on the townspeople," Caitlin moaned.

"You have!" Nell exclaimed. "Believe me. You have!"

Hudson was sitting in John Bones' office talking to the banker. The bank President had already told him that there was no way to reverse the sale of Bert Henasee's property to Caitlin Ridgeway.

"You knew Angus Ballard wanted that land," Hudson said. "Why didn't you hold off on the sale?"

"I tried, and you should have expected something like this when trying to deal with him," the banker said. "Bert has had a fifty-year feud with Andrew and now Angus. As determined as Angus was to get that land, Bert was just as determined that he wouldn't. I think Bert was just stringing Angus along and had no intention of selling that land to him.

"Bert took a shine to Miss Ridgeway right away. I tried to postpone the transfer, but Bert said he would take it to Nell's husband if I didn't do the paperwork. The old coot marked off ten acres around the original cabin he built when he and Pansy came here fifty-some years ago. He's been living there off and on for a couple of years, and there is a stipulation in the deed that when he dies, that land will revert to the property owner of the house. It's a done deal, Hudson. There is nothing I can do about it."

"How much did she pay for the property?" Hudson asked.

John Bones shook his head. "That's private information."

"Angus is due back in a couple of weeks, and there will be hell to pay."

"Maybe he can bargain with Miss Ridgeway," John suggested.

"I've only spoken to her a few times," Hudson said, shaking his head. "She is a stubborn young woman, and she's got Bert tucked in her pocket."

"There's nothing I can do," the banker said. "Has that Campbell woman left Tyler?"

"Not yet. She has a ticket for the 8:20 train heading west in the morning, and it will be good riddance," Hudson said.

"Was Miss Ridgeway hurt in the scuffle?" Thomas asked.

"I dropped her off at Nell's place because she was injured more in that scuffle than she originally admitted to."

"Give her my best wishes," John said.

"I will. I've got some more errands to run today," Hudson said, shaking the banker's hand.

Going about his business, Hudson got a dose of small-town gossip. Every person he encountered had an opinion about the fight. Most of the hearsay favored Miss Ridgeway's reaction to stop Charlotte from being hurt. He was lectured several times about being more careful about whom he hired to look after his daughter.

With his errands completed, Hudson returned to his sister's house. Nell was all smiles, and she assured him that the scratches and bruises would fade with time. The cut he'd worried about was bandaged, and Caitlin had been instructed how to dress it.

"I told her to take it easy for a day or two," Nell said.

"How is Charlotte reacting to what happened?" Hudson asked.

"Surprisingly well, but unfortunately, I'm interpreting that this was not the first time that woman has mistreated her. Children are resilient. Charlotte has a few welt marks on the back of her legs, but they will fade. Her response to Caitlin is amazing," Nell said.

"I saw that this morning," Hudson admitted. "She went to Caitlin, a total stranger, sat in her lap, and hugged her."

"I know. I saw the same thing when Charlotte woke up from her nap. Caitlin has been reading to her. I haven't seen that many smiles since... well, it's been a while," Nell said.

"Yeah, I know," Hudson agreed, thinking of his deceased wife, Malinda.

"I like Caitlin," Nell said. "The scuttlebutt around town is that she's a wealthy runaway."

Hudson frowned. "That may be true. She told me she'd cut all contact with her past. And now she has bought that land old man Henasee refused to sell. Angus already considers that land his."

"Is there trouble coming?" Nell asked.

"I think trouble arrived when Miss Ridgeway got off the train," Hudson said.

CHAPTER 4

*C*aitlin looked around her foyer, and she was pleased with her efforts. The paintings on the walls were her labors of love and had traveled a long way to be hung and displayed for the first time.

She had spent many hours watching and learning from Aunt Florence while Beaula was visiting with her snooty friends.

No, Caitlin corrected herself mentally. Florence wasn't her aunt. Florence was her mother. Restricted to her bed, her *mother* had spent hours teaching her how to sketch and draw. Beaula hadn't known about the room in the attic, where Caitlin painted in the early hours before the household was awakened.

Jilly knew. There wasn't much that happened in the Ridgeway Estate that Jilly hadn't known about. She had been Caitlin's only support and protection from Beaula's cruelty. She had taught Caitlin to stand up for herself and to ignore the cutting remarks and the mocking sneers.

Finished with uncrating the large boxes, she and Bert had carried the empty crates to his wagon, and he'd returned them to the rail station for her. While unloading the containers, Hudson's words echoed in her mind.

He'd called her a spoiled brat, and she knew that wasn't true. After exhaustive trips carrying as much as she could lift upstairs to the bedrooms, she would admit to being impulsive. She had spoiled herself by spending a lot of money on clothing, shoes, boots, and frilly undergarments that no one would see except herself. The fancy hats she'd purchased in Philadelphia probably wouldn't be worn again. She hadn't noticed the women of Tyler wearing anything fancier than bonnets, if they wore a head covering at all. The fancy dresses she'd bought weren't suitable for working around the house or painting. Shopping had been a giddy experience after realizing she would never have to wear the gray uniform of a servant again. Her extravagance resulted in her having dresses that were too fancy to wear in Tyler. She could, over time, remake them plainer so they could be worn.

Caitlin had prayed for freedom as she'd grown older. But she hadn't wanted it at the expense of losing Florence. She still woke in the middle of the night, wondering why. Why hadn't Florence told her the truth? Why had she been abandoned in an orphanage for five years? Why hadn't she been told she had a living mother and father?

Even after Florence's death and the reading of the will, Beaula had sneered and refused to answer her questions. The hatred Beaula displayed had been so frightening that Jilly had moved from her room off the kitchen to Caitlin's nursery bedroom to protect her.

There was a knock on the door, and Caitlin opened it to Bert. "I'm going into town for supplies. Do you need anything or want to come along?"

"I'd love to come along," Caitlin exclaimed with a smile. "Can you give me a few minutes to change?"

"Have you got any of those little sweet cakes left over?" Bert asked.

"I do, and you can help yourself," Caitlin agreed with a smile.

"Well, howdy, you can take as long as you need. I'm getting a pretty lady for company and 1 2 3 4 cakes as good as my Pansy used to make them!"

A few minutes later, Caitlin entered the kitchen in a different dress. "When we return, you can have the rest of that batch."

"Why are they called 1 2 3 4 cakes?" Bert asked, biting into the small cake as he followed her outside.

"Because the recipe is so easy," Caitlin said, climbing into the wagon. "1 cup of butter, 2 cups of sugar, 3 cups of flour, 4 eggs, 1 cup of milk, and 1 spoonful of baking soda. They are easy to make, but I have to half the recipe because they have to be baked in cups, and I only have six."

"So, Little Darling, what have you been doing for the past few days?" Bert asked.

"Sketching and finding a place for everything I had shipped from Philadelphia. I've also been writing letters to Jilly and a few friends. I have to go to the Post Office at the rail station."

"You also need to pick up some oats at the livery," Bert said. "We can drop off our lists at the mercantile and the mill and run our other errands."

"I'll treat you at the Rusty Pot when the dinner rush is over," Caitlin said.

"You've got a deal," Bert said with a grin.

The trip into town was companionable. Bert had a lot of stories about his younger days. He'd been a rancher and a wrangler in his earlier days.

"Never was much of a farmer," Bert said. "Except for a garden my Pansy planted every year.

"Can't you be both?" Caitlin asked.

Bert threw his head back with laughter. "Little Darling, your citified ways are showing. Don't ask that of a Texan. Farmers grow crops. Ranchers raise beef and horses. Most don't cross over. Men are cowpokes or farmhands. And, if Angus Ballard gets his way, there will be orchard workers here, and I don't know what they call themselves."

"What's wrong with being both or all three?" Caitlin asked. "Isn't Hudson McFarlane the foreman or overseer for both of Mr. Ballard's properties?"

"Well, you got me there," Bert said. "He's been Angus' right-hand man for a long time, and I can't fault Hudson. He's a man's man and deserves respect, regardless of who he works for."

"What does that mean?" Caitlin asked.

"What does what mean?" Bert asked.

"A man's man," Caitlin repeated.

Bert was quiet for a few moments. "Well, I reckon a *man's man* is a man who has a reputation for being courageous, trustworthy, and respectful. He has to be a leader, sure of himself, and sometimes be as tough as nails. I reckon Hudson has those traits. Both men and women look up to him."

"So, he's perfect," Caitlin said.

Bert laughed. "Sweet child, there ain't been a perfect man put on this earth yet. Some come closer than others, but most have good and bad habits. The same goes for women!"

"I don't know much about men," Caitlin said. "I've only lived with women."

"If some yahoo comes knocking on your door, and you ain't asked for his company, you fire off that rifle I put behind the coat tree in the foyer, and I'll come running," Bert said seriously, and then he looked over to her again. "You ain't never been taught how to shoot, have you?"

Caitlin shook her head. I have a Derringer, two-shot. The

man I bought it from showed me how to put the bullets in, but I've never had to fire it."

Bert shook his head. "A Derringer ain't a gun. It's a toy. You've got some learning to do. You can't live in Texas and not know how to handle a weapon."

"I'm not sure I want to know how to shoot."

"You will tomorrow!" Bert said firmly. "I ain't putting up with your citified ways!"

Bert pulled up in front of the mercantile, but there was no room for the wagon. He handed a list to Caitlin and said he'd run his errands and meet with her later at the Rusty Pot.

Saturday was a big day for merchants. The Ellisons were busy, so Caitlin gave both lists to Rob and told him she'd be back later. She stopped at the Rusty Pot to speak to Eleanor, but she was busy with every table taken.

Seeing a large group of people at the train station, Caitlin stepped into the hotel and asked Daniel what was happening there.

"It's an Orphan train," Daniel said. "It's the second one arranged by Reverend Cormack. This group of orphans came from Baltimore. He's been posting advertisements all over town.

"I read stories about the orphans in the newspapers. The cities don't want the burden of building orphanages, and they are sending them to western farming communities," Caitlin said.

"It's probably better than them sleeping in empty buildings and stealing to eat," Daniel said. "They should be about done by now. If no one here wants them, they'll move on to the next town."

Caitlin wandered over to the depot and made her way through a group of people until she could see and hear a man in a black suit shouting at potential parents. A heavy-set man holding a Bible stood behind him. Only four children were left on the platform: two boys and two girls.

"Come on, folks," the man shouted. "Here are two boys, Sam and Mike. They will grow to be strong young men. Think of your fields and the work it takes to harvest. You can train them to work on your farms."

"I'll take them," a man said.

"Thank you, Mr.?"

"Hammersmith," the man said. "I've got a homestead south of here."

"Good, good!" the man said. "Step over here with the Reverend and sign the papers. Now, all we have left are these two sisters. We don't want them separated, but these little girls need a home. Come on folks, they can help in the fields, and if you've got sons, they'll grow up to be wives."

"Hey," a man standing to the side of Caitlin shouted, and he elbowed a man beside him and pointed to a young man. "I, I, I, needs a wife to teach him how to talk!"

Several men laughed, and a young man standing a few feet from Caitlin turned away, looking embarrassed.

"How old is the bigger girl?" the uncouth man behind Caitlin demanded.

The promoter looked down at the list in his hand. "The older girl is ten!"

"That's two years before marrying age," the man behind Caitlin shouted. "Will you learn to talk by then, I, I?" he roared, laughing, and there was more male laughter.

Caitlin looked to her side at the loud-mouthed man in filthy overalls and his cohorts. "Ask her if she can cook, I, I!" the man demanded, and the young man shook his head and made his way through the crowd.

Caitlin looked at the girls, clinging to each other and shaking in fear. She stepped forward and raised her voice. "I'll take them. Both of them!"

The promoter looked at Caitlin and then looked around. "Ma'am, you don't look old enough to take on children. Are you married?"

"No, I'm not, nor do I need to be married. I can afford to raise these children. If you doubt me, please speak to Mr. Bones at the bank."

The promoter turned to the Reverend, and they put their heads together. There was some talking and nodding, and then the man faced her with a put-on smile. "Step up here, ma'am, and sign these papers. These little gals are yours for the raising."

"Hey, lady," the mouthy farmer behind her complained. "I was going to take the older one."

"Children should not be separated from their siblings. Nor should they be used for free labor or to fulfill your mean-spirited jokes," Caitlin said coldly, and she moved forward. She walked over to the Reverend.

Meanwhile, the promoter was waving off the crowd, and it was dispersing.

"Are you sure you want to do this, Miss Ridgeway?" the Reverend asked. "I've been meaning to come out to your place and invite you to join our church."

"Where do I sign?" Caitlin said, ignoring his invitation.

"Here, here, and here," Reverend Cormac said, pointing to three blank spaces. "Both copies, please. One copy is for you, and the other will be sent to the organization that sent them here. This makes you their legal guardian. Now about..."

Caitlin signed the papers, folded her copy carefully, and put it into her reticule. "Thank you, but I'm not interested in joining a church that would condone humiliating children as you've done here today." She turned and approached the two girls huddled together against the station wall.

Holding her hands out, one to each girl, Caitlin waited patiently until the older girl took her hand. The younger one waited until she got a nod from her sister and did the same. "I'm not here to hurt you. My name is Caitlin Ridgeway, and I will take care of you. I want us to become friends, and you have my word that I will treat you decently," Caitlin said gently. "What are your names?"

The older girl was biting her lip. Finally, she said, "My name is Maisey Jean Frost, and my sister's name is Naomi May Frost."

"Those are very pretty names," Caitlin said with a smile. "Did you come with any luggage?"

The smaller girl tugged on Caitlin's dress.

"Yes?" Caitlin asked, bending over.

"What is luggage?" Naomi whispered.

"Oh, that's a suitcase or a box that holds clothing for you," Caitlin explained.

The older girl, Maisey, shook her head. "We had a sack, but someone stole it."

"Well, we're not going to worry about that," Caitlin promised. "Shall we go? Our first stop will be the mercantile, and our second will be the Rusty Pot for something to eat."

As Caitlin walked away with the girls, she saw the crowd was dispersing. Wagons and buggies were disappearing down the road, leading them away from town. The uncouth man stared at her with his hands on his hips and a sneer on his face.

When Caitlin entered the mercantile, Alma's eyes widened. "You didn't!" she exclaimed.

"Yes, I did," Caitlin answered. "Do you have any already made dresses that would fit these two young ladies? This is Maisey and Naomi."

"In the back room," Alma said. "Did you tell Hudson you were going to adopt orphans?"

Caitlin shook her head. "Why should I? I didn't know I would adopt them until I saw them. Why is it any of his business?"

Glancing at her husband, Alma stammered, "Uh, I guess it isn't. Come with me into the back room. I'm sure we can find something that will fit them."

The mercantile had a selection of already-made dresses that would fit the girls, with a few modifications to make them fit better but with room for growth. The dresses had wide hems that could be taken down as they grew. Several calico dresses were picked out for each girl, along with an assortment of undergarments, shoes, bonnets, and hair ribbons. With every selection, the girls were looking both amazed and scared.

Very discretely, the worn-out rags they had been wearing were hidden from sight, and their faces and hands were washed before being dressed in the new clothing. Caitlin noted that full baths and hair washing were warranted before they would be given beds to sleep in.

The girls were almost unrecognizable when they left the mercantile. The new clothing was boxed and added to the merchandise stacked on the sidewalk, waiting for Bert to return with the wagon. In addition to the clothing, each girl was holding a baby doll of her choice. Caitlin couldn't resist when she saw the girls staring at them.

As they left the mercantile, Naomi pulled on Caitlin's skirt.

"What?" Caitlin asked.

"Can we keep the clothes?" Naomi asked shyly. "Do we have to share?"

Caitlin smiled. "Yes, you can keep everything. It's yours now, and no one can take it away. The only person you have to share with now is your sister."

Holding a hand with each girl, Caitlin left the mercantile, walking the few steps to the Rusty Pot. They entered and took a table.

"You did it!" Eleanor said, coming over.

"I did," Caitlin said with a smile. "News travels fast in Tyler.

This is Maisey and Naomi. They'll be living with me now. Girls, this is my friend Eleanor. What's on the menu today?"

Eleanor smiled at the girls. "Caitlin is a city-bred woman. I don't have a menu. I have a chalkboard. Can you read it?"

"Beef and potatoes, roasted duck, and chicken pie," Maisey read aloud.

"Oh, good," Caitlin exclaimed. "I love a chicken pie that I don't have to cook. Girls, what would you like?"

"Do we have to share?" Naomi asked.

"No, but I'll give you smaller portions," Eleanor said. "If you want more, you only have to ask for it. Our grown-up portions are big enough to fill a man-size stomach."

"Can we sit here for a few minutes? I'm expecting Bert to join us," Caitlin said.

"He's already stuck his head in looking for you. He'll be back in a few minutes. It was nice meeting you girls," Eleanor said with a smile. "Dessert is on me today. This should be a proper celebration."

When Bert came in, he was shaking his head. "Gal, now you've stirred up the Preacher. Are these your girls now?"

"Yes, they are, and I couldn't care less about what Reverend Cormac thinks," Caitlin agreed. She laid her hand on one of the girls' heads. "This is Maisey Jean, and she is ten years old." She moved her hand to the other child. "And this is Naomi May, and she is seven years old. Girls, this is my neighbor and good friend, Mr. Henasee."

"Hello, sir," Maisey said, looking frightened and chewing her lower lip again.

"Well, I reckon I've got three pretty ladies to watch over now," Bert said with his toothless grin. "I've already been to the mercantile to pick up our supplies. Now I could eat a bear!"

"Bear isn't on the chalkboard," Naomi said, shaking her head and pointing.

Bert turned his head, and he chuckled. "No, it's not, and

thank you for noticing, Miss Naomi. I reckon I'll have the beef and spuds."

"What's a spud?" Naomi asked.

"Spud is another name for potatoes," Caitlin said as Eleanor approached to get their orders.

Later, when Bert stopped the wagon in front of Rose Hill, Maisey and Naomi stared at the large house with wide eyes.

"Is this another orphanage?" Maisey asked, looking worried.

"No, this is my house," Caitlin said.

"Are we going to live here?" Naomi whispered.

"Yes, we are," Caitlin said with a smile, nudging the girls forward. She'd had the same reaction at the age of five when she'd been taken from the orphanage to live with her aunts at the Ridgeway Estate. Silently, she swore an oath to never mistreat these precious little girls. These two little girls would never be used, abused, or feel unwanted again!

* * *

HUDSON DREW his horse to a stop in front of his sister's house, dismounted, and swung his daughter to the ground.

His brother-in-law, Ben, opened the door.

"It's about time you got here," Ben exclaimed.

"Is Nell okay?" Hudson demanded.

"She's fine, and so is our son, Benjamin Hudson Rogers, " Ben said. "Rita Rodriguez, the midwife, was with her during the delivery."

"Congratulations," Hudson said with a smile. "Can I see her?"

"The midwife is in charge, not me," Ben grumbled.

Hudson knocked on the bedroom door and was allowed in. "Hey, squirt," Hudson teased his sister. "Are you okay?"

"Fit as a fiddle," Nell said smiling. "It's okay, Rita. I want my brother to see the baby."

Hudson played with the baby's tiny fingers. Looking into his sister's eyes, he asked again, "Are you okay?"

"Where have you been?" Nell asked.

"Working, as usual," Hudson said. "There was a problem on the farm. A revolt that had to be squashed."

"While you were gone, Caitlin Ridgeway has stirred up the town gossip again!"

Hudson frowned. "What has she done now?"

"She adopted two girls from the orphan train that came through, and apparently, she had words with Reverend Cormac about mistreating children. Half the town agrees with her, and the other half, mostly the farmers, think she should mind her business. You need to go talk to her."

"Miss Ridgeway is entitled to her opinions," Hudson said. "Why should I get involved?"

Nell gave him a long look. "You're not fooling me, brother, or anyone else. Most men in town know not to go near her because you've claimed her already."

"I have not!" Hudson denied. "I was helping her because she was hurt defending Charlotte. If anything, she's caused me a lot of trouble for buying Henasee's property. We need that land to plant the peach orchard Angus wants to experiment with."

"If you don't court Caitlin, you are a fool," Nell exclaimed. "Didn't you see how Charlotte responded to her? She hasn't done that since Malinda died.

Hudson drew back from her words.

"I'm sorry, brother," Nell said earnestly. "I know how much you loved Malinda, but she's gone. You like Caitlin whether you want to admit it or not. I've seen you with her and how protective you are of her. Charlotte needs a mother, and she clung to Caitlin. She hasn't done that with any of the nurses or nannies you hired. If you're really not interested, why did you go out of your way to make sure she wasn't hurt? Why did you help her move her things from the depot to her house? Brother, it's okay to love another woman. It's been four years, and Malinda wouldn't want you to be alone. She wouldn't want Charlotte to be raised without the love of a mother."

Hudson left his sister's house with Charlotte riding in front of him in the saddle. It wouldn't be long before she would be too big to share a saddle.

It was early in the day, and it was officially his day off, but that had never stopped him from performing his duties as the foreman of Magnolia. Pulling the reins, Hudson stopped in the middle of the road, where it split in two directions. Without much thought, he turned east, although the road to Magnolia Ranch was west.

CHAPTER 5

*A*pproaching the Ridgeway house, Charlotte hammered her hands against Hudson. She was pointing and smiling as she recognized Caitlin in her front yard. Hudson almost lost his grip as Charlotte struggled to get down. When her feet hit the ground, she ran to the woman who knelt down and hugged his daughter.

Caitlin had set up two makeshift easels in the yard, and it looked like she was teaching the girls she'd adopted, to draw.

As Hudson dismounted, Caitlin turned to introduce the girls. "Mr. McFarlane, Charlotte, these are my daughters, Maisey and Naomi. She leaned over and whispered something in Maisey's ear, and the older girl nodded. She took Charlotte's hand and walked her to the easel.

"Hello," Caitlin said, approaching Hudson.

"Hello," he responded. "Charlotte wanted to see you, and we were out for a ride."

"I'm delighted to see her. I heard Nell had her baby, but I haven't had time to visit."

"We stopped in this morning," Hudson said. "Would you

mind watching Charlotte for a few minutes? I need to speak to Bert."

"May I show her how to draw?"

"Of course," he mumbled, then he turned to his daughter, expecting her to throw a fit, but she was smiling and waving goodbye. Hudson mounted, and Caitlin returned to whatever she was showing the girls.

Hudson rode down the road a piece, but he didn't have a destination in mind. He didn't need to talk with Bert. The old man had pissed him off the last time they'd spoken about the sale of the property. The old coot had intentionally sold the property to foul Angus Ballard's plans. He rode down to a freshwater pond, dismounted, and considered his sister's words.

He knew he was fighting his attraction to Caitlin. Every time he'd seen her, even if he was scolding or they were arguing, he was aware of her as a woman. Yes, he was attracted, and he wanted her. He was a man, and the physical attraction was natural.

What he didn't know was how she felt about him. She had reasons for disliking him. Almost every time they'd spoken, he'd tried to convince her she'd done wrong by buying Bert's property. She was also nine years younger if she'd told the truth about her age. She might think he was too old for her. He had to admit he found her confusing. Sometimes, she behaved immaturely, but at other times, she acted much older. He wasn't sure where he stood.

When Hudson returned to the house, he was surprised to see Caitlin and the girls lying on their backs in the grass, pointing to the sky. They were shouting and giggling. Dropping the reins of his horse, he approached them.

"There," Caitlin exclaimed, pointing to a cloud formation. "Do you see the puppy?"

Naomi giggled. "I see it! I see the eyes and the tail!"

"There!" Maisey pointed. "It's a man with a big belly!"

"Sketch it!" Caitlin exclaimed, and the girls jumped to their feet and ran to the easels. "Keep looking at the clouds because the angels change them very quickly."

"Look there, Charlotte," Caitlin exclaimed, pointing. "It's a rabbit. Look at the ears! Draw it!"

Hudson watched as his daughter jumped to her feet and smeared a brown color across a tablet with a brush. He looked to the sky, but all he saw was white clouds, moving quickly before a darkening sky that threatened an incoming storm.

Caitlin sat up, saw him, and blushed. "Girls! It's time to clean up. Go to the water basin and wash your hands. Use the towels to dry your hands, not your skirts." She followed the children and helped Charlotte wash and dry her hands. She ran to her easel, took her drawing, and ran to her father.

"I painted an angel, Papa," Charlotte said, pointing to the sky.

Hudson went to his knees in shock. He hugged his daughter, and he didn't let go until she giggled. When he raised his face, he was crying. "You're talking, baby girl!"

Charlotte looked at the sky and pointed to the rolling clouds. "I'm not a baby, Papa. Momma's angel is gone, but I'll see her again. I didn't know where to find her."

"It's going to start raining any minute," Caitlin said when thunder rolled overhead. "We should go inside."

Hudson wiped his eyes on his sleeve and stood up. "I'll need to put my horse in your barn?"

Charlotte tugged on the leg of her father's trousers. "Why are you crying, Papa?"

"Because I love you," Hudson said.

Charlotte smiled. "I love you too, Papa!"

Thunder rolled over their heads again. "Run to the house," Caitlin instructed Charlotte, but she ran to the yard and grabbed the easels to take them inside.

Hudson led his horse around the house to the barn and put his mount in an empty stall. He would have to run for it as the rain was pouring down. But before he moved, he buried his face in his horse's mane and closed his eyes. "Thank you, God. You've sent me a message and a miracle. I'm listening now."

When Hudson entered the kitchen, he couldn't help feeling overwhelmed. Tears were in his eyes as he listened to his daughter laughing and talking.

There was a loud crack of lighting, and all the females screamed, including Caitlin.

"All right, that's enough," Caitlin said. "If we can't play outside, maybe it's time for reading. Maisey, would you pull the drapes in the parlor and pick a book to read.

"Yes, ma'am," Maisey said. "But I'm not supposed to light the lanterns."

"I'll do that," Hudson volunteered, following the girls. He'd not seen the inside of Caitlin's home when it wasn't full of wooden packing crates.

He lit the fancy oil lamps and admired the room's wood-work and paintings. When Maisey began to read, he returned to the kitchen to find Caitlin peeling potatoes.

"The house looks better than when Bert lived here," he said.

"No saddles on the dining room table?" Caitlin teased.

"That's true, although the house is in good shape. The barn is something else. It needs a new roof."

"I'll get to it," Caitlin said. "Bert has mentioned it several times, but I told him he is not climbing a ladder at his age. It made him angry, but he gave me his word. I'll get around to it."

"Not personally. It's not a job for a woman. I can give you the names of several men who would take on the job," Hudson said sternly. He looked around the clean kitchen, removed his hat respectfully, and hung it on a hat rack by the back door. Then he sat at the table across from Caitlin. "How did you do it?"

"I didn't," she said.

He took the knife from her hand, pushed the bowl aside, and took her hand. "I've taken Charlotte to every doctor within three hundred miles, some further. I've written to doctors back east and California. She's been examined countless times, but she remained silent."

"I don't know," Caitlin said gently, looking into his deep brown eyes. "Maybe it was just the right time. I really don't know. We were playing a game I play with my girls. On days like this, when the clouds are moving fast, we look at them and see what our imaginations can make of the clouds. We see puppies and turtles and whatever. It was a game my Aunt Florence played with me as a child. She was bedridden, but we could see the clouds through the windows.

"Charlotte saw an angel in the clouds and pointed it out to us, and she spoke. Her first words were, *That's my mommy in heaven.'* I didn't do anything except allow her imagination to see what she wanted to see.

Hudson blinked away tears. "You may not think so, but I consider this a miracle."

Caitlin smiled but shook her head. "If I could perform miracles, I would have performed one on myself long ago." She disengaged her hand from his, surprised that she hadn't noticed when he'd taken her hand in his. She returned to peeling potatoes.

Maisey appeared in the doorway. "Ma'am, can I help fix supper?"

Caitlin smiled and then slid a sneaky glance toward Hudson. "No, sweetie. Mr. McFarlane has volunteered to cut up the smoked ham Mr. Bert dropped off a little while ago."

"I did?" Hudson questioned.

"Yes, you did," Caitlin said, returning her attention to Maisey. "Thank you for asking, and you can set the dining room table and keep an eye on the girls."

"Yes, ma'am," Maisey said.

"It's only been a few weeks, but I don't think Maisey trusts me yet. Naomi is younger, and she's been easier to convince that I will not abandon them or send them back to the orphanage."

"When our parents died, the do-gooders tried to split Nell and me apart. She was ten to my sixteen. They didn't care about me and said I was old enough to support myself. But I wasn't going to let them take my sister away and give her to strangers."

"What did you do?"

"I broke into the orphanage office, emptied the cash box, and stole my sister in the middle of the night. We hopped on a train and got as far as Tyler before getting caught and kicked off. I got a job on Magnolia Ranch and kept Nell hidden for a while."

"How did you do that? Where did you put her when you were working?"

"In a shed that wasn't being used," Hudson said. "The foreman found her and hauled me in front of Angus."

"What did he do?" Caitlin asked, forgetting what she was doing and looking at him with wide eyes.

Hudson leaned back in the chair. "Angus made me tell the truth and then gave me one hell of a licking for lying to him! He told me he'd help me, but I would never lie to him again, and I haven't. Then he had that old shed fixed up with two bunks and a stove and moved it behind the foreman's cabin. My job was to shadow Brett Abbot, the foreman, and to learn from him, and I did. I didn't know it for a long time, but Abbot was ill. He died when I was twenty, and I became the foreman working directly with Angus."

"Who took care of Nell?"

"Nell was schooled by Mrs. Brimmer. She's the housekeeper at Magnolia. By then, Angus' two daughters, Emma and

Abigail, were married and living in California. They married into influential and wealthy families. I've only met them once."

"Angus Ballard must be a decent man," Caitlin said. "He's not the bastard that Bert claims him to be."

Hudson frowned. "I know you think you're grown up, Caitlin, but being vulgar will get you spanked!"

Caitlin's mouth dropped open in surprise. "Excuse me, but you have a double standard!"

"In what way?" Hudson demanded.

"I've heard you swearing. You seem to think it's acceptable for you to swear as a man, but I'm not allowed to swear as a woman!"

"Well, I reckon that's how it's supposed to be," Hudson agreed. "Women are supposed to be genteel and behave like ladies, and men have to take care of their womenfolk."

"Papa?" Charlotte said from the doorway.

Those damnable tears flooded into Hudson's eyes as his daughter ran into his arms.

"I'm hungry!" Charlotte said.

"Well, we're going to fix that," Hudson said. "Why don't you go play with your new friends. Miss Ridgeway and I will get busy fixing supper."

Charlotte shook her head. "Not Miss Ridgeway, Papa. Caitlin," she corrected.

"If that's all right with her, we can call her Caitlin," he agreed and looked over to the woman in charge.

"It is," Caitlin said, and she smiled at the child but frowned at Hudson when Charlotte ran out of the kitchen.

Hudson stood up. "Where's the ham?"

"It over there on the sink," Caitlin pointed, then jumped and squealed at a crack of lightning nearby. "If the weather wasn't so bad, I'd ask you to leave for threatening me!"

"It wasn't a threat," Hudson said, honestly. "It was a fair warning."

The storm outside didn't let up for hours. There was a lot of flashing lightning, and they could hear strikes nearby.

When it was time to send the girls to bed, Caitlin had no choice. She couldn't send her guests out in a lightning storm.

"You're going to have to stay the night," Caitlin told Hudson.

"Charlotte can stay with you and the girls," Hudson said. "I'll sleep in the barn."

"That's silly," Caitlin said. "The roof leaks. You said so yourself, and I haven't had time to get to the outbuildings yet. We are adults, and there are four empty bedrooms upstairs and a small room off the kitchen not being used."

Charlotte wanted to sleep in the bed that Maisey and Naomi shared, and Hudson was shown to the bedroom the furthest down the hall.

Hudson couldn't sleep. The room he'd been shown was better than his own in his cabin, but the bed wasn't long enough to accommodate his height. Even so, it wasn't the discomfort that was keeping him awake. He feared that Charlotte would go silent again.

Would his daughter be able to talk when she woke up? He still couldn't get over the miracle of her voice returning. He turned over several times, but sleep was elusive. Finally, he pulled on his trousers and crept down the hall barefoot. He opened the door to the bedroom where his daughter was sleeping and smiled at the tangle of little girls in the center of the large bed.

He silently went down the stairs and into the kitchen.

Caitlin was backing out of the pantry and almost dropped the bowl of 1234 cakes when she realized she wasn't alone. Her eyes widened at Hudson's appearance. He was wearing trousers, but his chest was bare. He was a muscled man with a patch of dark hair on a broad chest. He was slim-waisted.

"Sorry," Hudson said. "I didn't know you were still up."

"I didn't know you were either," Caitlin said, setting the bowl on the kitchen table and then looking down at her sleep gown. She was covered from her neck to her toes. "Would you like some cakes? I make them for Bert once a week, but I have to put them in a basket or a box. He forgets to bring my bowls back.

Hudson turned toward the stove. "Is there any coffee left?"

"If there is, it's probably strong and bitter," Caitlin warned.

"I'm a rancher. We learn to drink it that way," Hudson said, walking over and pouring himself a cup. "Do you want any?"

Caitlin shook her head as she filled a basket with the small cakes. "Couldn't you sleep?"

"No," Hudson said. "Today was a miracle, and I keep thinking that Charlotte will be silent again tomorrow."

"I was shocked by her first words," Caitlin said. "Her voice was weak, but the more she laughed and played with Maisey and Naomi, the stronger her voice became. I don't believe she'll be silenced again."

"I still can't thank you enough," Hudson said.

"I didn't do anything," Caitlin protested. "But please be careful when hiring a replacement for her caretaker."

"I haven't found anyone yet," Hudson admitted. "Mrs. Brimmer has been watching over her, but that's not her job. She keeps reminding me to hire someone. The Magnolia Ranch and Farm covers over four hundred thousand acres. That's six hundred and twenty-five miles of land. I oversee the property and have fifty men working under me. It's a lot to keep track of, and sometimes, I can be away for a week or more. I try not to be longer, but it is what it is.

"Deloris Campbell isn't the first caretaker I've fired, although she was the first to be fired for being abusive. I don't want that to happen again!"

Caitlin covered the basket of small cakes with a piece of muslin and turned to leave the kitchen. "If you're going to ask if I will watch over Charlotte in your absence, the answer is yes. My girls get along with her wonderfully."

"I was getting to that, and thank you," Hudson said, finishing his coffee.

"Good night then," Caitlin said, turning to leave.

"There is one more thing bothering me," Hudson said, moving closer. He circled his arm around her and pulled her against his bare chest. He lowered his head, capturing her lips with his. Her hands pushed against his naked skin, but then her fingers gently explored his flesh as Caitlin leant herself to the kiss. She felt a shiver run up her spine, and then Hudson's hand stroked her breast through her nightshirt, and she felt a hardness against her stomach. She stepped back.

"That's how I feel about you," Hudson said, breathing hard and letting her go. "Think about it," he said. "That comes within the bonds of marriage." He walked out of the room.

Caitlin remained in the kitchen for a while. She touched her lips gently, her breast, and stomach. She knew what happened between men and women, or at least she thought she knew. She'd been approached by men after the news of her inheritance was leaked to the newspapers and high society, but she hadn't been interested. She wasn't living in Philadelphia now, and she'd already discovered Western men were more direct. Several men had already brashly introduced themselves to her. One young man had ridden out to her house with an offer of matrimony, but Bert had chased him off.

Making her way through the dark house, Caitlin wondered what Jilly would have thought of Hudson's offer, and she smiled. Jilly might have hit him over the head with a rolling pin! Maybe it was good that Jilly wasn't here because Caitlin was intrigued by the idea of having a beau.

Hudson left with Charlotte at the break of dawn. The girls were upset because their new friend had to go home. Hudson said he needed to leave early to tell Nell about Charlotte's miraculous recovery.

Over the next few weeks, Caitlin settled into a routine with the girls without any problems. Maisey and Naomi were happy and enjoying their new lives. Bert was an adopted grandpa addition to their unusual family. When Caitlin decided to make a trip into town, the girls were dressed in their best, and she drove the buggy. The first stop was at the mercantile to drop off a list of supplies needed. The second stop was to Nell's house, where they were introduced to the new baby boy.

"Where have you been?" Nell asked.

"We've been busy," Caitlin said. "Is Charlotte okay? Is she still talking?"

"She's become a chatterbox," Nell said with a smile. "Not that we are complaining."

"Is she staying with you?" Caitlin asked.

"Yes, she's been staying here and with Mrs. Brimmer out at the ranch," Nell said. "That storm that came through did a lot of damage at the ranch. A tornado hit two of the barns, and the lightning started a fire. Three men were seriously hurt. They'll be laid up for a while, and my brother broke several fingers rescuing one of his men."

"Hudson was hurt?" Caitlin asked, suddenly feeling scared.

"Not seriously," Nell said. "His fingers were splinted, but it hasn't stopped him. He's still the head honcho, supervising his crews. He'll whip that place back into shape in no time."

"If you need help, send Charlotte to my place," Caitlin offered. She nodded toward the three girls playing together. "They get along well. Flag Bert down. He comes into town several times a week to play cards with his buddies."

"I might do that," Nell said with a smile and a glint in her eyes. "What has brought you into town?"

"I need to talk to Sally Rogers, the school teacher. I want to continue the girls' education, but Rose Hill is too far for them to come alone. The only good thing about them being in an orphanage was that they were taught well. I want her advice on what books to order."

"From what I've heard, she is a good teacher."

Caitlin walked around town, holding hands with her girls. They stopped at the hotel to talk to Daniel and ate at the Rusty Pot. When the bell rang, meaning school was over for the day, Caitlin introduced herself and the girls to the teacher and asked what books she would need to teach the girls.

Sally Rogers was helpful, and Caitlin returned to the mercantile to look through catalogs with Alma to order what she needed from the Sears Catalog.

"No!" A scream from Maisey had Caitlin running out of the store. The large man who had been obnoxious at the orphan train station had Maisey by the arm.

Caitlin reached into the leather bag Bert had given her and pulled out a revolver. "Let her go!

Still, in filthy overalls, the man raised his hands and looked surprised. Maisey ran to Caitlin.

"I wasn't going to hurt her," the man claimed, looking around at the people on the sidewalk. "I wasn't."

"Go away!" Caitlin ordered. "And, never come near us again!"

The man stepped forward, and Caitlin cocked the revolver as she'd been taught. "I wasn't going to hurt her!" he bellowed. He ran across the street and disappeared down an alley.

Caitlin hugged Maisey and Naomi to her. "Are you all right? Did he hurt you?"

Maisey shook her head. "He said he wanted to talk to me. He said something about pulling a prank on a man who can't talk. I said no, he took my arm, and I screamed."

"Good girl," Caitlin said, putting the pistol back into her bag. "From now on, I want you girls to stay close to me when we're in town."

"Yes, ma'am," the girls said together, and they followed her into the mercantile.

"I'll get this order in the mail tomorrow," Alma said. "It might take a while to get here."

"That's all right. I'll take a package of writing paper and two slates, for now. Oh, and I'd like a pair of boy's overalls for each of the girls and an extra set in Naomi's size. A little big so they can grow into them. They're learning to fish with Bert, and I don't want them ruining their dresses."

"Maybe they should have little boy shirts, too?" Rob suggested with a smile.

"Good idea," Caitlin agreed, digging into her reticule again for another list. "I'm also supposed to purchase shotgun shells for Mr. Henasee. Do you sell them?"

Rob Ellison raised his eyebrows at the request, but he nodded. "Yes, ma'am." And then he looked over as the Sheriff came through the door.

"Ma'am," Sheriff Bensen said with a curt nod toward Caitlin.

"Hello, Mr. Bensen. Or should I call you Sheriff?"

"Sheriff will do. I just had a complaint about you pulling a gun on someone outside."

"I did," Caitlin agreed. "A man had his hands on my daughter, and I told him to leave her alone."

"Well, ma'am, I'm sure you thought Chester Brigham was dangerous, but he's not. He's a little on the dim side, but he's usually harmless. My problem, ma'am, is that Tyler has a no-gun-carrying law. If you're carrying a gun, it must be turned into my office for the duration of your stay in town. We don't want any trouble."

"Then I suggest that you tell Mr. Brigham, who is, as you say, usually harmless, not to scare little girls or their mother. He should keep his distance and keep his hands off of little girls. He's the same man I heard harassing a young man in the crowd when the Orphan train came through. He thought he was funny. He wasn't. He was hurtful, and while tormenting and making fun of someone may not be against the law, maybe it should be!

"I was advised to carry a gun and to protect myself and my children, and I fully intend to do so. Not all men are harmless, and I am being taught how to defend myself!

"The next time I come to town, if I bring a gun, I'll be sure to stop by your office, Sheriff. Although, I am not convinced that this town is safe, especially for children. Good day, sir!"

CHAPTER 6

*N*ell was sitting in a rocking chair feeding her newborn when her husband came looking for her.

"Is everything all right?" Ben asked.

"Of course," she said with a smile.

"Then why has your 'worry' line appeared?" Ben asked, tracing his finger across her forehead gently.

"The worry isn't about me," Nell whispered. "It's my brother."

"It takes time to repair the damage Magnolia Ranch sustained during those storms," Ben said.

"That's why they have a full roster of men, and Hudson has already hired replacements for the men who were hurt," Nell said. "He's taken two days off that I know of since the big storm, and we've had multiple storms since."

"Without Angus there, everything falls on him. Is taking care of Charlotte too much for you right now with the baby?"

"No. I love Charlotte as my own. It's my brother's problem I'm worried about."

Ben frowned. "Would you like to narrow that down for me?"

"Hudson needs a wife," Nell said. "The perfect woman is right under his nose, and he's not doing anything about it!"

Ben shook his head. "That's your brother's business, not yours!"

"Of course, it's my business," Nell exclaimed. "I love Hudson, and I want him to be happy. He just needs a little push in the right direction!"

Ben shook his head. "Stay out of it! Come back to bed and try to get some sleep."

Nell nodded, but she was already thinking and planning. Most men didn't have a clue when it came to women, and her husband was no different.

When Ben got up the following day, Nell was still asleep. Their little boy had an appetite and was waking his mother several times every night. He found a sealed envelope on the briefcase he carried to work and a note asking him to drop the envelope off at the saloon for Bert Henasee. He tapped the letter in his palm several times and considered opening it. Then, he looked over his shoulder and smiled. If his wife was interfering with her brother's love life, Hudson was more than capable of setting her straight. Everyone knew Bert came into town several times a week to play cards.

Caitlin was climbing a rickety ladder propped against the barn when she heard the excited voices of the girls. She jumped the two rungs to the ground and ran to the front of the house. Bert was unloading two valises along with Charlotte McFarlane.

"I've got a present for you," Bert said, grinning. "Mrs. Rogers said she was a little under the weather, and you'd offered to care for Charlotte."

"I did," Caitlin said as Charlotte ran to give her a big hug.

"Aunt Nell said I can stay here until my Papa comes for me."

"We're glad to have you," Caitlin said with a wide smile.

"She also sent this letter," Bert said, handing over an envelope. "Magnolia Ranch and the farm have taken some hard hits from these storms."

"I heard," Caitlin said, but she didn't mention the additional damage to her barn roof. She didn't want a man in his mid-seventies on the roof of her barn. "Is this normal weather for this area?"

"Our weather depends on what's going on in the Gulf of Mexico," Bert said. "Some years are good, and some are bad. This year is gonna be a wet one for sure."

Bert's prediction was correct; it started raining and didn't stop for days, and the overcast skies threatened more. The house roof was sound. Caitlin checked the whole house, including the attic, for leaks, but she hadn't found any, although she did find a lamp she liked up there. The barn was another matter. She moved the horses out of the stalls to a dryer area, dragged the feed sacks out of the range of the dripping rain, and raked the dry straw into a large pile.

* * *

SINCE ALL BUT inside construction was impossible, Hudson gave orders to his top men and headed to Tyler. He hadn't seen Charlotte in nearly two weeks, and while he felt guilty about it, he knew she was safe with his sister.

Only Charlotte wasn't with Nell when Hudson reached his destination. She had used a slight break in the weather a few days earlier to send his daughter to Rose Hill. Hudson wasn't an idiot. He knew what his sister was up to, although she denied the interference. He stayed to visit a little while and gave his sister a condensed version of what he'd been doing at Magnolia. When he said he had to go and spend some time with Charlotte, he caught the sneaky gleam of satisfaction in his sister's eyes. She walked him to the door, kissing him on the cheek. She turned at the cry of her newborn in the bedroom, and Hudson smacked her a good one across her bottom.

"Oh!" Nell squealed.

"That's for meddling!" Hudson said firmly.

Nell rubbed her stinging bottom but looked out the window with a smile. Her brother was heading in the right direction.

Looking upward at the sky, Hudson knew he would be drenched long before he reached Rose Hill, and he wasn't wrong. The downpour of rain was relentless, occasionally adding sleet to its wrath. When he finally arrived at his destination, he rode his horse around the house to the barn to find the door open. Entering the barn, he dismounted and looked upward at the roof that wasn't keeping much of the rain out. Then he heard hammering and thought, 'Hell no! Bert must be on the roof.'

He went outside and saw an old ladder propped against the roof. The ladder looked too unstable to hold his weight.

"Bert!" Hudson shouted, backing away from the barn so he could see him, and his heart stopped when Caitlin stood up with a hammer in her hand.

"Get..."

Hudson didn't get to finish his shout. There was a loud crack and a scream as Caitlin disappeared. He ran around and into the barn and found Caitlin lying in the pile of straw. She was trying to catch her breath.

"Are you hurt?" Hudson demanded.

"I don't think so," Caitlin gasped. She took a few deep breaths, wiped the rain from her face, and looked up at the hole in the roof. "Damn it to hell!"

"Are you hurt?" Hudson demanded again, giving her a shake.

"No, but now there is an even bigger hole in the roof!" she complained.

Hudson looked to the roof roughly fifteen feet above his standing height. The hole was leaking a constant stream of water. "What the hell were you doing on the roof?" he demanded furiously.

"Planting tulips," Caitlin said sarcastically, getting to her feet and shaking her arms and legs.

"Anything broken?" Hudson demanded.

"I don't think so," she exclaimed.

"Good," Hudson said, gripping her arm with his good right hand. He dragged her to an old trunk filled with odds and ends and slammed the lid down.

"What are you..." Caitlin didn't finish her sentence because Hudson sat down, tossed her over his knees and landed a hard, stinging wallop to her bottom.

"No!" she screamed, but Hudson had just started. He delivered a spanking that would not be forgotten for some time. When he finished, his work-calloused right hand was stinging as much as his injured left hand. He sat Caitlin upright on his lap, ignoring her tears and sobbing.

"Don't you ever, EVER, put your life in danger again!" he growled. "I've lost one wife, and I won't lose another. Am I making myself clear?"

"Yes," Caitlin sobbed. "But I'm not your wife!"

"The way I feel about you, it's close enough!" Hudson growled. "Now get in the house and get dry. I'll figure out a way to temporarily cover the hole in the roof!"

Caitlin ran from the barn sobbing but huddled against the wall of the house on the back porch. She was crying, her bottom was aching, and she was soaking wet. In all the years of Aunt Beaula's mistreatment, she'd never been spanked.

In the early days before Jilly, Aunt Beaula's arsenal had been slapping, pinching, and grabbing her by the hair or the ear and insults. Always insults.

Most of that mistreatment had stopped when Jilly had

started working at Ridgeway. Jilly was a big woman and scary when she was angry. When she interfered with Beaula's mistreatment, Beaula tried to fire her. But Jilly had stood up for Caitlin. She threatened Beaula with a butcher knife, with calling the police, and telling everyone in the community what a horrible, nasty person she was. Jilly was the only person living at Ridgeway who wasn't afraid of Beaula. Beaula had backed down with the threats to her standing in a community of wealth.

Jilly had stepped up as a fierce protector. Jilly occasionally gave Caitlin a swat on her bottom over the years, but those were only warnings.

Caitlin had never had a full-out spanking before, and it hurt! She was confused by Hudson's actions and words. When she could control her tears, she entered the house through the kitchen door and used the back staircase to run upstairs to her room. She didn't want the girls to see her this upset.

Washing her face and holding a cold cloth to her eyes, Caitlin took a few minutes to gain control of her emotions. She had to regain control of the feelings and confusion she felt. She was still too upset to let the girls see her.

Belatedly, she realized how foolish she'd been. She'd fallen from the roof. If she hadn't landed in the pile of straw, she could have been seriously injured. In hindsight, she realized how stupid she'd been to go on the roof. Hudson's words were right, but he had acted as a parent or a husband, and he was neither.

Caitlin never realized how many times she sat down while getting dressed. She was very aware this time because her still stinging bottom kept reminding her of Hudson's hard hand. Buttoning her shoes was the worst. Fully dressed and hoping that she was not showing any signs of a sore bottom, she returned downstairs using the front staircase.

With Bert's help, they moved the large dollhouse into the

empty space under the stairs. The girls loved playing with it as much as she had as a child.

"Did you fix the roof?" Maisey asked.

"No, Mr. McFarlane is fixing it," Caitlin answered.

"My Papa is here?" Charlotte squealed.

"Yes, but he's working in the barn," Caitlin agreed. "Girls, it's time for lessons."

"Can we play until my Papa comes in?" Charlotte asked.

"No, we've had these discussions before. Maisey and Naomi have school lessons, and you have yours too. When your father comes in, you will be excused to visit with him unless he wants to take you back to your Aunt Nell," Caitlin explained.

"I don't," Hudson said, entering the foyer. "If you're happy here, you can stay here until the weather improves. We'll have time later, sweet pea." He motioned with a leather bag in his hand. "I've got some dry clothes in this pouch. Where can I put them while I work in the barn?"

Caitlin didn't look in his direction. "Leave them on the table. I'll take them upstairs to the room you used before."

Hudson gave her a nod and went back outside.

"It's lesson time, girls," Caitlin announced, and the girls ran into what used to be an office. They were to study quietly for the first hour, and then she would review what they learned the previous day and add to it.

Caitlin went to the kitchen and took a mop from the butler's pantry. She mopped the water Hudson had left behind. Then, gathered the ingredients to make bread. She was forming the loaves when Hudson entered the room and stood dripping on a rag rug.

"The roof is only temporarily fixed. When this weather finally clears, I'll send a crew over to replace the entire roof and, from what I've seen, some of the support beams," Hudson said.

"I can hire men to do that," Caitlin said.

"No, you can't," Hudson said. "I've got every carpenter, builder, and every man with building experience within a hundred miles on the Magnolia Ranch payroll. If you try to hire someone, the job won't get done for months."

"I'll wait," Caitlin snapped. She slammed the bread loaves behind the stove to rise and tried to leave the room.

Hudson blocked the door. "Why are you so angry?"

"How can you ask that after what you did to me?" Caitlin demanded in a whisper. "You beat me!"

"I did not," Hudson denied. "I spanked you, and it was well-deserved! When you fell through that roof, I lost about ten years of my life. I know you've been told by Bert and myself to stay out of the barn until it can be fixed!"

"I don't have any other shelter for the horses. This is my property, not yours or Bert's. What I do or don't do here is my business!" Caitlin exclaimed.

Hudson shook his head. "You're a stubborn little cuss, Caitlin. You should be ashamed of yourself. Bert is looking out for you, and so am I."

"You... you... How could you?" Caitlin wailed. She ran across the room and turned her back to him, looking out at the constant, miserable rain.

She stiffened when she felt Hudson's hands on her shoulders. "You are not alone anymore, Caitlin. When people care about someone, they become involved with their lives and the troubles that come with them.

"You're a lone woman in a man's world in Texas. Texan men care about their women, and we show it. Not only in supporting her, but also in protecting and caring for her. With that protection comes an understanding that we're not trying to hurt you but to guide you. When a woman pushes too far, she has to be reined in, and that was what I was doing. The next time you take on a job you know you can't handle, you'll remember that spanking and not want another like it. Those memories might keep you from doing something you know damn well that you shouldn't be doing."

"You hurt me," Caitlin whispered.

"I gave you a sore bottom," Hudson said, turning her to face him. "It might have been your first, but I have a feeling it won't be your last."

"I will not be mistreated again!"

"There's a big difference between being mistreated and being spanked," Hudson said. "I would never beat you, but I do believe in spanking when I think someone that I love is misbehaving and deserves it."

"You can't love me," Caitlin whispered.

"It's too late to claim that now," Hudson said, kissing her. "I'm already there."

"You don't know me," Caitlin said.

"Sometimes, love can be at first sight," Hudson said. "I know because it's happened to me twice."

"Charlotte's mother?" Caitlin questioned.

"Yes," he nodded. "And, when she died, I thought I'd never find another woman to love, but I have."

"I won't be a substitute for your deceased wife!"

"You're not," Hudson said with a chuckle. "You are nothing like Malinda, and I wouldn't expect you to be. I want you for who you are."

"You don't know," Caitlin whispered. "You don't know."

"What don't I know?" Hudson said.

"Excuse me?" Maisey said, standing in the kitchen door. "It's time for our lessons."

"I'll be there in a minute," Caitlin said, glad Hudson blocked Maisey from seeing her tears.

"We'll continue this discussion later," Hudson said firmly. "I know this is sudden, but I have no choice but to believe in fate."

Caitlin followed Maisey to the office, now used as a school room, but she was keeping an eye on the time, and in the middle of an arithmetic lesson, she moved the girls to the kitchen. While Maisey read ahead for the history lesson, Naomi and Charlotte practiced cursive letters.

Caitlin checked the rise of her bread, put more wood in the stove, and slid the bread pans into the oven a few minutes later.

"What's for supper?" Charlotte asked.

"Leftover vegetable stew from yesterday and fresh bread," Caitlin said with a smile. "Strawberry jam on bread for dessert."

"Where's Papa?"

"I believe he's still working in the barn," Caitlin answered, although she knew he was there because she'd seen him through the open doors. He was still wearing his soaked clothing. While she'd been in the office teaching, Hudson had carried a lot of chopped wood to the back porch so the wood would dry out. She didn't know what he was doing in the barn.

* * *

Hudson was rearranging the barn. He'd found a small tack room behind a pile of discarded wagon wheels and junk that needed to be carted off and buried. He opened the door and found old saddles, bridles, and horse-related equipment that looked usable. Bert had probably blocked the tack room to prevent passersby from looting the barn when he'd moved over to his cabin.

Hudson had found a stack of old tarpaulins and carefully climbed the old ladder, fearing it would give way under his weight. He spread and tacked them over the roof's worst parts. Measuring the distance between the support beams, Hudson walked over the roof, stepping carefully, not trusting any of the structure with his weight. When he finished, at least part of the barn was dry, and he dragged the sacks of grain into the tack room. It was the driest area in the entire barn. Then he took the ax and chopped the old ladder into four parts to ensure Caitlin wouldn't be tempted to use it again.

When Hudson decided he'd done as much as he could, he returned to the main house.

Charlotte jumped out of her chair to greet him, but he stopped her.

"I'm soaking wet and filthy, sweet pea. Let me wash up, and then we'll spend time together."

"There's plenty of hot water in the stove reservoir," Caitlin offered.

"Thanks. If I didn't know it was June, I'd swear we were in the middle of February."

"Swearing is bad, Papa," Charlotte scolded her father.

"I agree, and it's not appropriate for little girls or young ladies," Hudson agreed, shifting his eyes to Caitlin. "But the word swear is not a bad word by itself."

Hudson dipped a bucket of hot water from the stove reservoir and carried it upstairs to the room he'd slept in once before. He'd known the clothes in the leather sack were damp, but now they were spread out on the bed, dry and ironed. It was a simple kindness that made him smile.

Caitlin was still angry with him, but that couldn't be helped. As a newcomer to Texas, she had to learn that some jobs weren't suitable for women, especially a city-raised one.

Supper was tasty even though it was leftovers, and when it was over, Caitlin suggested that it was time for Hudson to spend some time with his daughter while she and her girls did the dishes. She washed, Maisey dried, and Naomi carried the dishes to the pantry.

Hudson enjoyed supper and the company, although most of the talking was done by the children. He'd lived off of chuck wagon fare for the last few weeks. Magnolia Ranch and Magnolia Farm were huge operations. His job was to keep track of everything and ensure that everything was running smoothly during Angus' absence.

Charlotte took him into the school room, where there was a stack of cards and board games. The games weren't new, so they must have been in those massive crates Caitlin had brought from back east. Hudson listened to his happy little chatterbox as they played checkers and a game that depended on a teetotum to jump around the board.

After an evening together, Charlotte asked if her Papa was staying, and Hudson had to admit that he couldn't.

"I'm sorry, honey. I can only stay until morning," Hudson said honestly. "I have to return to the ranch. There were a lot of buildings damaged in the bad storms, and I'm responsible for getting them fixed or rebuilt."

"Do I have to go too?" Charlotte asked, shaking her head. "I don't want to go back home. I don't have anyone to play with!"

"I have to discuss that with Caitlin," Hudson said.

"She's nice to me, and Maisey and Naomi are my friends," Charlotte said, looking like she was about to burst into tears.

There was a knock on the door. "It's bedtime," Caitlin said, turning to Hudson. "I'm assuming that you are staying the night?"

Charlotte clung to her father. "Will you be here when I wake up?"

"Maybe," Hudson said. "But I need to leave early."

Hudson felt like someone had stabbed him in the heart when his precious daughter left to go to bed with the other girls. When Angus Ballard returned, they would talk long and hard about his responsibilities and how his job was interfering with raising his daughter. He went to the kitchen and poured the pitch-black leftover coffee into a cup.

"You're going to have stomach problems if you keep drinking coffee like that," Caitlin said, entering the kitchen. "I'm thinking of buying a cow. Would one cow make enough milk for five people? Children need milk, and Bert could teach me how to milk it."

"More than enough," Hudson said. "Cows have to be milked twice a day."

"Really? I didn't know that," Caitlin said. Crossing the kitchen, she sat down gingerly. "You owe me an apology."

"No, I don't because you earned that spanking," Hudson said. "Tell me what you wouldn't tell me before. You've thrown enough hints that I know you were brought up rough, yet you're wealthy according to the rumors in town."

"Tyler has a privacy and gossip problem," Caitlin said. "I was left at The Sisters of St. Joseph Orphan's Asylum after I was born, and I lived at the orphanage until I was five years old. One day, I was introduced to two women who called themselves my aunts, and I was told I had to live with them. I was then taken to the Ridgeway Estate in Fairmont Park. That's a very wealthy and exclusive district of Philadelphia. I was put in a nursery with a nurse and rarely left that room for the next five years. My Aunt Florence would visit me there, play with me, and buy me toys. My other Aunt Beaula never darkened the door unless it was to insult me.

"Then, at ten years old, I suddenly wasn't considered a child anymore. The nurse was fired, and I was given the job of caring for my Aunt Florence, who was bedridden. Florence was a kind person, and I genuinely grew to love her.

"My problems stemmed from Aunt Beaula. She was, and still is, a miserable human being. I won't go into the details because it's over, and I don't want to think about it. My Aunt Florence died eight months ago. At that time, I discovered she was the beneficiary of their father's estate. Beaula must have been a nasty daughter because her father left her nothing. Nothing, not a penny.

"In her will, Aunt Florence left the family inheritance to me. I was the illegitimate daughter of Florence Ridgeway, and she made me the beneficiary of the estate. I inherited an obscene fortune and nearly doubled it when I sold the mansion and the properties. The Ridgeway fortune is highly invested in companies. Twice a year, I will receive an amazing amount of money that my lawyer called dividends."

"None of that matters to me," Hudson said. "I've fallen in love with a beautiful young woman who is courageous and has the amazing ability to take in and help the young and old. Your wealth is yours. I'm not the kind of man who would marry for money."

"Hudson, I came to Tyler to find my father," Caitlin said in a rush of words. "He abandoned my mother when she was pregnant with me. I am the illegitimate daughter of Florence Ridgeway. Angus Ballard is my father."

CHAPTER 7

"What!" Hudson exclaimed, sitting back in his chair. "Angus, is your father?"

Caitlin nodded. "And you are his right-hand man."

Hudson stared at Caitlin. "You've got his red hair. It's more gray now than red, and he's gone somewhat bald, but when I first met him, he had your red hair."

Caitlin closed her eyes and winced when she moved to leave the chair to stare out the window. "I have a diary and copies of Aunt Florence's letters to Angus. She had a habit of writing draft letters before rewriting the letters she sent. She kept the first drafts. I also have letters sent to her from Angus Ballard. She begged him to come back to Philadelphia. He countered that she should come to Texas.

"Florence was a gentlewoman, afraid of her shadow. She was too browbeaten by Beaula to believe she could survive on her own. She was the person who should have been controlling the purse strings, not Beaula. The day after Florence died and before I learned of the will, Beaula was vile.

"I discovered her in Florence's bedroom, and she was trying to destroy everything. Jilly and I threw her out of the room and

88

wouldn't allow her to return. I believe she was trying to find and destroy what Florence had left behind for me to learn the truth.

"In Florence's diary, she wrote that when Angus refused to return to Philadelphia, she was heartbroken. Then she discovered that she was with child. His child. Beaula hid Florence behind the walls of Ridgeway Estate to hide her shame. I was that shame, a bastard child, and Beaula paid the nuns at an orphanage to care for me from birth until I was five years old. The Ridgeway sisters supposedly adopted me, although I found no records of an adoption. What they told me was a pack of lies. I wasn't adopted because Florence was my birth mother."

Hudson went to Caitlin, pulled her into his arms, and rocked her gently. "Caitlin, none of that was your doing, and you shouldn't shoulder any guilt for the mistakes made by others. If the railroad tracks aren't washed out between here and California, Angus will return. The man I know will welcome you into his life."

"You can't know that."

"I do," Hudson said firmly. "Angus has been a father to Nell and me for sixteen years. He took a raw kid in and has greatly influenced my life and Nell's.

"What if he doesn't want me?" Caitlin asked.

"Then he's the fool," Hudson said, rocking her. "And the man I know is far from being a fool."

"But..."

"Hush," Hudson whispered. "Marry me, Caitlin."

"What?" Caitlin squeaked.

"Marry me," he repeated. "You exasperate the hell out of me with your boldness, and yet you make me so proud I could bust. Your foolishness makes me want to spank you, which I have already done, but that's because I won't allow you to put yourself in danger. I want to love, protect, and care for you and the girls, yours and mine. Marry me!"

Caitlin looked up at Hudson and saw love in his eyes. It was a strange feeling that made goosebumps rise on her arms and other places that didn't show.

"Promise me no more spankings," she whispered.

"Not in a million years," Hudson said, chuckling. "I won't be a husband you can run over to get your way."

"Where will we live?"

"We'll figure out the details later," Hudson said. "Just tell me you love me."

"I believe I do, hard hand and all," Caitlin whispered. "I've missed you while you've been gone. It's strange because we haven't spent that much time together, but I missed you, and it's been driving me crazy. We don't know each other."

"I know enough," Hudson said. "I've heard of mail-order brides marrying within a few hours of meeting their husbands-to-be, and those marriages last. We haven't spent much time together, but what I feel inside is important. I want to love you, care for you, and be there when you need me."

Hudson tucked her head under his chin, rocking back and forth. "Guess what?"

"What?"

"It's stopped raining, and there's a quarter moon showing its face again," Hudson said.

"That means you'll be leaving in the morning," Caitlin said.

Hudson nodded. "I won't ask you to share my bed tonight, but will you rest beside me on the sofa? I need to feel you in my arms, where I know you're safe."

Caitlin nodded in agreement.

"If it's not raining in the morning, I'm going to take it as a good omen," Hudson said. "But I have a lot to do, and I have to delegate a lot of responsibilities. When I return, we're going to the preacher!"

Caitlin shook her head. "I'd rather go to a Justice of the Peace. I don't like Reverend Cormac. He's the kind of preacher who believes he knows best for everyone and sticks his nose in other people's business."

"Whatever it takes," Hudson agreed. "And be aware, Caitlin, that I'm not after your inheritance, but as your husband, I won't let you fritter it away carelessly either."

Hudson left the following morning after breaking the news of their impending marriage to the girls. Privately, he gave Caitlin several stern warnings and a light smack on her bottom. "Keep the girls out of the barn, and that goes for you, too!"

"I can't," she protested. "I have to feed the horses."

"I've already fed them this morning, and I'm dropping them off at Bert's place on the way out. He can fit two more horses in his stable."

"What if I need to go out?" she protested.

"Bert lives a quarter-mile over that hill," Hudson pointed. "Close enough to walk or run in an emergency, and he'll check on you as he has done since you arrived. I'll be back as soon as possible." Bending over, he kissed her, long and slow. When he stood straight again, he smiled and heaved a deep breath. "I'll be back as soon as possible."

Bert wasn't happy about the impending marriage. "Are you sure you want to do that? Angus has Hudson in his back pocket!"

"You were the one who told me that Hudson was an honorable man."

"Gal, as soon as you say 'I do,' by Texas law, your property becomes his. Angus wants this land for his peach tree folly!" Bert grumbled.

"Hudson has made promises to me," Caitlin assured the old man. "Your feud with Mr. Ballard needs to stop! I promised not to sell the land to Angus, and I'm a woman of my word. Hudson will not make me break my word to you."

Caitlin had promised not to enter the barn, but she couldn't contain her curiosity. She tried to open the door, but Hudson had nailed it shut. That didn't stop her. She found a loose board at the back of the barn, squeezed through it, looked around, and found the tack room. Now that the sun was shining again, the barn didn't look that bad.

Hudson appeared in a buggy nearly two weeks later, leading four wagons filled with lumber and an army of men.

"Pack a bag for the girls," Hudson said with a broad smile. "We have an appointment with Ed Marcal, the Justice of the Peace, and we're getting married."

"You are impetuous," Caitlin teased.

"I have a good reason to be," he whispered in her ear. "God, help them, but I asked Bert to check on the crews. It should take them about a week to finish the roof and make the improvements listed on their worksheets."

"How much is it going to cost?" Caitlin asked.

"That's not for you to worry about," Hudson said. "You need to pack for a week. I've already sent a telegraph to the hotel in Thedford to hold a room for us. It's the next stop on the railroad, going west and not too far away if something goes wrong and we are needed. The girls will stay with Nell while we have a few days of privacy and get used to being married."

Caitlin dressed the girls in their best dresses and packed extra clothing for everyday wear. She went through four wardrobes full of clothes from her extravagant Philadelphia spending spree. Finally, she decided on a pale lilac gown for her wedding. Changing clothes, Caitlin covered herself with a long cloak. She didn't want to take a chance of ruining her dress and wanted to look her best. She wrapped the girls in sheets to prevent mud splattering on their dresses.

The trip to Tyler seemed to take forever. Hudson knocked on his sister's door, and Ben answered.

"Long time no see, brother-in-law," Ben said.

Nell entered the room carrying the baby. "What's going

on?" she asked, although her eyes were wide with expectation when she saw Caitlin's dress cover and the three girls dressed in their finest, with flowers pinned in their hair.

"Well, we are going to a wedding," Hudson said with a smile. "We have an appointment with Ed Marcal at three o'clock. I thought you might want to be there."

Nell handed the baby to her husband and hugged her brother. "It's about time you came to your senses," she said in his ear. "I told you she was perfect for you."

"I already knew it," Hudson said. "I was just having a hard time accepting it. I've got a surprise for you, too."

"What?" Nell asked.

"Payback for your interference," Hudson said with a devious smile. "The girls are staying with you for the next week. We'll pick them up next Monday on our way home."

"I don't know where we'll put them, but we'll manage," Nell exclaimed, smiling. She hugged Caitlin and each of the girls.

Then, with a broad smile turned to Ben. "Let's get dressed, husband. My brother is getting married!"

Caitlin had never been to a wedding before. In Philadelphia, she hadn't been in the society circle where weddings were celebrated as a social event. She'd read articles in the newspaper announcing the unions and then describing the marriage ceremony in full detail. Those events hadn't meant much to her, and she didn't need all the pomp and grandeur.

Standing before the Justice of the Peace, she listened to words while never losing eye contact with Hudson. They were making a commitment to share each other's lives and to support and comfort each other in difficult times. When the part came to exchange wedding rings, Hudson produced two gold rings, and they pledged their lives to each other. They didn't kiss. Kissing was a private matter, not a public display.

Then, signing the papers in front of him with a flair, Ed Marcal handed the certificate to Hudson.

Nell was crying, and the Justice of the Peace offered a glass of wine to the recipients, although he, Ben, and Hudson were the only ones who accepted it.

Leaving the office and going into the sunshine, it felt good to feel the heat from the sun. Hudson checked his watch and turned to his sister. "We barely have time to return to your place to change and beat the train if it's on time."

"The trains are never on time," Nell said.

When all the hugs and goodbyes had been said, Hudson carried their bags onto the train. It was only a half-hour trip to Thedford. By the time the locomotive reached its top speed, it had slowed down to stop at the Thedford station. Hudson had picked the town because it had a decent hotel and wasn't too far away in case of an emergency or something going awry at Magnolia or something happened to the children. Mrs. Brimmer was the only one beyond Nell and Ben who knew where they were going. She could send a telegram if he was needed.

"This is our stop," Hudson said, reaching for their bags.

They walked across the station platform and looked at the small town similar to Tyler. And, like Tyler, the road through town was a mud pit. Hudson flagged a wagon down and asked the driver to take them to the hotel.

"Sure," the driver said. "You don't want the pretty Miss sloshing through the mud!"

Hotel Thedford was about the same size as Tyler's hotel, except a restaurant and bar were on the first floor.

Checking in, the clerk ran through a series of do's and don'ts for the hotel. "Breakfast starts at six-thirty and ends at eight. Dinner starts at eleven-thirty, and supper meal is available from five to seven-thirty. After that, no food is available, and we don't allow food in the rooms. After seven-thirty, alcohol is available at the bar. If you want a bath, we need a three-hour notice. Washstands are in every room. Water is available from a pump at the end of the hallway. Don't throw your used water out of the windows. If you don't carry your luggage upstairs, tip the bellboy!"

At the top of the stairs, Caitlin could hear the hotel clerk repeating the same information to the next guest. She covered her mouth to stifle her laughter when the clerk put a red bellboy hat on his head, picked up the set of luggage from the other guest, and started climbing the stairs.

Opening the door to their room, Caitlin felt a hint of panic. She moved to the window and looked out to see the rest of town.

Hudson set their carpet bags on the floor and closed the door. He walked up behind her and put his hands on her shoulder. "Scared?"

"A little bit," Caitlin admitted. "I overheard some men talking among themselves, once about being with women."

"Men do spend time bragging about things that should remain private," Hudson admitted. "Especially the single men."

"Women don't, and I didn't have a mother to tell me," Caitlin said. "The only men on staff were the gardener and the driver. The driver was the first to go, and last was the gardener. I think I was about fourteen at the time. They weren't fired. They quit, as a lot of the servants did. They couldn't stand being constantly berated by Aunt Beaula when they knew they'd done their jobs correctly. Only Jilly stayed, and I think she stayed to protect me."

"I didn't get to meet Jilly. I'm expecting you to be a virgin, but if you aren't, it's not world-shattering."

"I'm more than a virgin. I'm stupid," Caitlin exclaimed. "I don't know what I'm supposed to do or what is expected of me."

Hudson lifted her face up. "You may be untried, but you are not stupid. Being your first is a gift to me. I don't want to scare or hurt you, and I will teach you. Let's take a walk and see what Thedford has to offer."

The town didn't provide much more than Tyler. There was a mercantile, where they bought apples and sweet shortbreads, fully intending to ignore the rule of no food in the rooms. Wandering further, they discovered a bookstore. Tyler didn't have a bookstore, and they spent some time and money on books.

"I'll have to go back there before we leave," Caitlin said. "Maisey is a big reader, and ordering books through the Ellison mercantile takes weeks." They wandered through the town until it was time for supper, and they returned to the hotel. The food wasn't as good as Jilly's or Eleanor's, but edible.

It was difficult for Caitlin not to think about what would happen when they returned to their room. Hudson had been married, and he would already know. When the meal was finally over, they walked upstairs.

Looking into his eyes, Caitlin was more curious than scared. He wasn't pushing her, and tired of waiting, she drew his head down to her level and kissed him.

Hudson took full advantage of the kiss, smiling when he finally raised his head.

"Are you ready?"

"I think so," she said, chewing her lower lip.

"This isn't a fight, Caitlin, and I won't hurt you. It's two people doing what they were made to do naturally." He began to unbutton her blouse. "We'll take this slow and easy."

Caitlin wasn't a coward. For every button he unbuttoned, she did the same to his shirt.

When their tops were open, Hudson shucked his shirt, and with a tug, his undershirt was pulled over his head and tossed onto a chair.

Caitlin tossed her blouse in the same chair and removed her

chemise. She didn't wear a corset as she was small-waisted and thin.

Hudson's eyes lit up with interest as her breasts were exposed. Then she reached to unbutton her skirt and stepped out of it and her bloomers.

Hudson followed her lead, unbuttoning his trousers. He wasn't a man who bothered with hot and uncomfortable longjohns in the summer months. Except for his socks, he was naked.

A shiver ran through her, but Caitlin was determined not to show fear. She faced her naked husband, a little surprised at what a grown man looked like without clothing.

"You're beautiful," Hudson said.

Caitlin knew she was blushing, but she took a deep breath and looked at him again. "You look bigger without your clothing. How is that possible?"

Hudson threw back his head and laughed. "Maybe it's because a particular part of me has grown just looking at you. He stepped closer and kissed her long and sweet before leading her to the bed.

"Don't be frightened. Sex is sort of like riding a horse. You might be scared the first time you climb on, but that first ride makes you want to do it again and again." He kissed her while running his hands over her breasts. She was small, and he moved downward to kiss and suckle the dark rose-colored nipples.

Hudson heard a gasp, and he could almost feel her fears float away as she was enjoying his attention. "Let it come," he whispered, stroking his hand over and down her ribs and hips. Caitlin's body relaxed under his touch but stiffened as his hand moved further downward. "Easy, easy," Hudson crooned as he would with an unbroken colt.

With one hand, he began stroking between her legs, and he shifted his weight. This was Caitlin's first time, and he knew instinctively to be gentle. He didn't want to hurt or frighten her. Although it was killing him, he moved slowly, gently, so she wouldn't be frightened. When he broke her, it would hurt, and if he wasn't gentle, he could ruin this first time for her. He started pumping his fingers inside her, stretching her while he was keeping her preoccupied with his kisses.

His cock was aching to be inside her. Covering her with his body, he spread her knees apart and settled between her legs. Sliding his dripping cock against the wet lips of her sex gently, he continued to feast on her lips while breaking through her virginity with a deeper stroke. She gasped, and he continued to stroke deeper.

Feeling a sharp pain made Caitlin gasp, but the pain only lasted for a few seconds.

"It only hurts the first time," he soothed.

Caitlin nodded. He moved slowly, pushing gently and allowing her body the time to stretch around his sex. He continued to thrust deeper into her, and she was surprised when the stroking began to feel good.

Hudson was watching Caitlin carefully and felt her acceptance as she relaxed. Their bodies had now joined as one.

"Are you good?" he asked.

"Is that it?" Caitlin asked.

Hudson smiled. "No, that was your introduction to being a woman. Let's see if I can show you why sex is a gift both men and women enjoy."

He was being careful this first time. If a man misused a woman, chances were that sex would become a drudgery she had to tolerate instead of enjoying. He didn't want that to happen to Caitlin. He was aroused and needed his release, but he wouldn't enjoy himself at her expense. Tempering his body, he removed himself.

"Do you know what a woman's orgasm is?" he asked, aligning his tall body against her much shorter one.

Caitlin shook her head.

"I'll teach you. It may not happen right away, but you'll know it when it happens," Hudson said. He kissed her as his fingers began to stroke her sex.

"Oh!" Caitlin whispered as sensations she hadn't felt before rippled through her. "What was that?" she stammered.

"Relax and enjoy. This is what being a grown woman and wife is all about. I can make you feel this good with my fingers, my tongue, and especially with my penis."

Although his words were shocking, Caitlin thoroughly enjoyed what his fingers were doing to her. Then suddenly, ripples of pleasure seized and left her gasping for breath.

"What was that?" she stammered.

"That, my innocent, is called an orgasm. Sometimes it's called a climax," Hudson said. "It's my job as your husband to ensure you have one every time we make love."

Hudson was patient. His job was to teach his innocent wife so she wouldn't be frightened. As the night progressed, neither of them got much sleep. She was awakened every few hours and taught how to please her husband. There was a strangeness about waking up beside a man... now her husband, but Caitlin knew she would get used to it. When he was inside her, it made her feel good. If this was marriage and sex, she saw no reason not to enjoy it.

Daylight came, but there wasn't the usual scramble to do chores. A pattern of sleeping a couple of hours and then making love continued until hunger drove them from their marital bed.

Breakfast had come and gone in the hotel dining room. It was mid-day, and a few heads looked in their direction but returned to their meals.

"Do you think they know?" Caitlin whispered when they were seated at a table.

Hudson shook his head, laughed, and whispered, "No, and

even if they guessed, it has nothing to do with us. We are a couple now, and that's what married couples do. There are no rules except the ones we make. We can do it whenever we feel like it and have privacy. Making love and having sex is an important part of being married."

Caitlin blushed. "What are we going to do today?"

"Eat and walk around town a bit to stretch our legs and enjoy that we don't have chores or work to do," Hudson said. "Then we will return upstairs and enjoy each other."

True to his words, they walked around the small town and went into a few shops, mostly purchasing things for their daughters.

Finally returning to the hotel, there was a surprise for Caitlin. A large tub was in their room. She turned around to ask Hudson if he'd ordered it, but he went to answer a knock on the door. Wearing the busboy hat, the hotel clerk stood outside with two buckets of hot water. He poured the water into the tub, and Hudson tipped him two bits, shut the door, and closed the window drapes.

Hudson smiled, came to her, and began to undress her.

Caitlin wasn't scared like she'd been the day before. The bathtub was large enough for both of them, and they enjoyed being so close together until the water turned cool. What was left of the daylight hours was a repeat of their previous night. There was no need to be nervous or embarrassed. This was marriage.

CHAPTER 8

*T*he days of their honeymoon went by quickly, and there wasn't much to do in Thedford. They visited the bookstore several times, and there was a growing stack of books in the hotel room. The sun's heat was drying out the land, and the mud was hardening. They rented horses and rode them until they came upon a posted sign that warned that they were on Magnolia Ranch property and trespassing.

"I guess this doesn't apply to you," Caitlin teased.

"No, it doesn't," he agreed. "But I have no intention of getting any closer. When we return, I want to take you and the girls to the ranch and introduce you to everyone."

"I don't want to go there until I can confront Angus Ballard, the man himself," Caitlin said.

"He's not the ogre Bert has made him out to be," Hudson laughed. "Angus' great-grandfather John Ballard laid the original claims to Ballard land sixty years before Texas was a state. John Ballard's son, Edwin, took that claim, bought out homesteaders or ran them off their land, and doubled the ranch's size. He was the one who named it Magnolia. No one knows why.

"How can one man own hundreds of miles of land?" Caitlin asked.

"When Texas became a state, the men making the laws questioned that too. They took Edwin to court and tried to break it up, but Edwin Ballard was smart enough to make good friends with politicians before the case went to trial. Three other ranches are as big as Magnolia in Texas, and the owners organized themselves and declared war against the interlopers and the government. It was a bad time for homesteaders, who had been told the land was free. The trial lasted four months, and nine men were dead before the courts made their decision. The result was the established landowners kept their ranches intact.

Angus' father, Andrew, lost the thousand acres you now own to Bert Henasee in a faro game."

Caitlin gave him a confused look. "If Andrew lost the land in a card game, why does Bert have a feud with Angus?"

Hudson shook his head. "If it's not one thing, it's another. Bert raised and trained some of the finest horses and beef on the market in his time. He built that fancy house for his wife and had a profitable ranch for a long time. I've heard that Bert pampered Pansy. Anything she wanted, he made sure she got it.

"When she died, he took it hard and quit everything. He sold off his stock, went into the bottle for a while, and moved out of the big house and back to the original cabin he'd built.

"Bert's feud with Andrew is legendary, and Angus wanted to buy back the land from Bert. He wanted Bert's land, and they were talking, but then Angus did something stupid. He was so sure he was going get the land that he had peach trees planted on Bert's land as a test to see if they would grow. That land didn't belong to Angus yet, and those trees set off the feud again.

"I've lived and worked under Angus' supervision for over sixteen years, and he's been square with me from the beginning. "Bert bottled all his resentment against Andrew and poured it on Angus when he inherited the property. Angus will not be happy about you swooping in and buying the place while he was gone."

"Too bad," Caitlin said. "I've got a private bone to pick with him myself."

"I know you made promises to Bert, but you have to give Angus a fair chance," Hudson scolded. "One thing I know for sure. If Angus had known about you, he would have claimed you. You can't blame him for decisions made by your mother and aunt."

After returning the horses, Caitlin wanted to revisit the bookshop again. This time, though, they were greeted with For Sale placards in the windows. Going inside, there were books in stacks everywhere.

"Why are you going out of business?" Caitlin asked the proprietor bluntly.

"Because I'm not making enough to pay the rent," the young man behind the counter said. "I've sold more books to you and your husband in the last couple of days than in the last four weeks. It was a mistake opening here. I was promised by the mayor that business would be good, but I've seen no trace of it. I've been open for five months, and it's been a downward spiral since I opened the doors."

"You should move to Tyler," Caitlin said, looking around at the shelves of books. "Tyler can use a bookstore."

"Excuse me?" the young man said.

"Caitlin," Hudson said disapprovingly.

"Why not?" Caitlin asked, turning to Hudson. "If Mr..." she looked at the young man expectantly, and he spoke up. "James Bennett, ma'am."

"Do you want to close your shop, Mr. Bennett?"

"No, ma'am," the young man said, shaking his head. "But I don't have the funds to relocate either."

"There's an empty shop next door to Ben's office," Caitlin said, turning to Hudson. Who owns it?"

"I don't know," Hudson said.

"Have you had any offers to buy you out, Mr. Bennett?" Caitlin asked.

"No, ma'am, I'm losing everything," the young man said, glancing around his shelves and looking sad.

"Excuse us," Hudson said, taking Caitlin's arm and pulling her outside. "What the heck are you doing?" he whispered.

"Tyler needs a bookstore," Caitlin said. "I've heard at least a dozen people complaining about waiting weeks to fill a book order through the mercantile. We can move Mr. Bennett and his store to Tyler."

"This is not how business is conducted. We don't know this man from Adam," Hudson whispered.

"That's easy to fix," Caitlin said. "Ask the owners of the other businesses in town if he is a nice person. They will know. If they think well of him, we can help him move and set up a bookstore in Tyler."

Hudson shut his eyes, shook his head, and sternly pointed his finger at her. "*Do Not* make any promises to him!" Then he took her arm, and they returned to the store and approached the counter.

"Mr. Bennett, my wife is a bit impetuous. Would you be interested in moving your store to Tyler, or do you want to sell the books, go out of business, and call it quits?"

"I don't have the money to relocate," the young man said.

"If the money wasn't a problem?" Caitlin asked, and Hudson shot her a disapproving look, but that didn't stop her.

"I'd move in a heartbeat," the young man said.

"I believe you," Caitlin said with a smile. "I love books, and I have three daughters who also love to read."

"Call me James, ma'am," the young man said. "What kind of books do you like?"

While James spoke of authors and book titles, Caitlin asked about his background. He said he had worked in a library in Chicago before moving to Texas.

Hudson listened as Caitlin talked to the young man as if she'd known him for years.

"You know your trade, James," Hudson said. "And Tyler does need a bookstore."

Caitlin clapped her hands and smiled.

"Not so fast," Hudson said firmly to his wife. "Mr. Bennett, are you in debt to anyone?"

James replied, "I owe the mercantile five dollars and sixty-eight cents."

"How much would it cost to freight the contents of the bookstore to Tyler?"

"I have no idea," the young man said, looking around the store. "The bookshelves are mine, in addition to the books. The cash register was a gift from a good friend before I left Chicago. It took me forever to figure out how it worked, and no one else in town has one."

"Would you like to relocate to Tyler and run a bookstore there?" Hudson asked. "Even if you have to give up part of the ownership until you can repay a loan to move there?"

"Yes, sir," the young man said. "I'm going under here. The rent is paid for two more weeks here. That would give me time to pack everything. I'd have to look into the costs of using freight wagons or the train."

"Think about it tonight. My wife and I have to discuss this before making a firm offer. We have tomorrow to talk it through from all angles," Hudson said. "Caitlin, let's go, please."

"I think he agrees," Caitlin whispered as she walked past Mr. Bennett.

Caitlin had to skip along to keep up with Hudson's long strides. Finally, she pulled away and stopped. "Why are you angry?" she demanded.

Hudson looked at two old men sitting in chairs outside a tobacco store. "I'm not angry. I don't have a word that fits how I feel. We will discuss this back at the hotel."

"Well?" Caitlin demanded when they were behind the closed door of the hotel room.

"What you just did is not how to make a business deal," Hudson exclaimed firmly. "Just because you have an inheritance doesn't mean you can throw it around without due diligence!"

"I don't know what that means," Caitlin said.

"And that is exactly why you shouldn't be making offers before you know what you're getting into," Hudson said.

"I wasn't offering to buy the bookstore," Caitlin said. "I was offering to move it to Tyler."

"You don't know him," Hudson said, sounding exasperated.

"No, I don't," Caitlin said. "But I can tell when someone is a liar or distrustful, and James Bennett is neither."

"And how do you manage to do that?" Hudson demanded.

"Twenty-one years of living a lie," Caitlin said.

Hudson felt his anger dissolve, and he pulled her into his arms. "I can't undo what you lived through, Caitlin, but I can protect you now. I may not have your intuition, but I've dealt with crooks and swindlers for years. You can't make instant decisions based on feelings. It's a good way to go broke. I hope you bought enough books to read tomorrow because I will be busy doing due diligence."

"You still haven't told me what that means?"

"It means if you really want the bookstore moved to Tyler, I'm going to be busy checking his books, and I don't mean the reading books. I mean the business books. I'll talk with his banker and the train agent for an estimate of the freight costs for relocating. Meanwhile, I'll telegram Ben to find out who owns the storefront next to his office and see about buying or renting it."

"What will I be doing?" Caitlin asked.

"You're going to be resting," Hudson said. "Because when I get through with you tonight, you will be exhausted and mindful that you now have an equal partner and that you need to discuss financial matters before jumping the gun!"

From his words, Caitlin hadn't known what to expect that evening after a late supper. They'd retired to the hotel room, where another bathtub of heated water awaited.

After their baths, she was enjoying the sex until the unexpected happened. Hudson turned her over and positioned her on her knees. She had already learned that was one way to have sex. She hadn't expected to be spanked while he was thrusting into her, but his hand smacked her bottom hard enough to make it sting.

When she protested, Hudson had stopped, sat back against the headboard, and pulled her across his lap. He began to scold her again, and the sex was postponed as he spanked her. He explained the discipline was because of her actions that afternoon. He would lose two days of their honeymoon because of her efforts to help a stranger. While he agreed that Tyler needed a bookstore, he wasn't happy about her jumping into a situation without first talking to him.

Later that evening, he'd initiated sex again and positioned her on her knees again. This time, when he spanked her bottom, it was already tender. She was about to cry when her body reacted with the most amazing orgasm she'd felt so far.

Hudson's smug and satisfied smile told Caitlin he knew what he was doing.

Caitlin wasn't sure what to make of the development, but her husband, over the evening and into the night hours, had initiated sex and spanked her repeatedly. He'd explained that spanking was going to be part of their marriage, both during sex and disciplinary when warranted.

What surprised Caitlin was those few minutes during sex

when her body was out of her control. She could feel the tension building, and then wave after wave of shivers made her gasp with pleasure. She knew Hudson liked it because he usually groaned when the contractions started. Her insides tightened around him, and the shivers traveled from her body to his.

They dressed for breakfast, and they went downstairs to the restaurant. When Caitlin sat in her chair, she took a deep breath.

"Tender?" Hudson asked in a whisper.

She nodded, closing her eyes.

"Good," he said simply, pulling out his pocket watch. "I don't know how long it will take to deal with James Bennett. I need to talk to the local banker and anyone else he has been dealing with. We will discuss the finances if I decide his relocation makes sense."

"Shouldn't I be there?" Caitlin asked. "It was my idea, and I can afford the costs."

"We won't be using your money," Hudson said. "Overall, I think it's a good idea, but I will finance it as a loan. If he follows through and repays the loan, the bookstore will revert to his ownership."

"Why won't you use my money?" Caitlin asked.

"Because it's yours," Hudson said. "I didn't marry you for your money, and I will support my family."

"What about the costs for fixing the barn roof?" Caitlin asked.

"That we may split," Hudson said. "Because the barn isn't getting just a roof. It's being rebuilt with a separate room for feed, more horse stalls, a loft to store hay, and an overhang to store the buggy and a wagon."

"You could have told me you were doing all that," Caitlin said.

"Not at the time," Hudson said. "I was too angry! I'm still

having nightmares, hearing you scream and disappearing through the roof. Take it easy today because we're going home to four high-strung girls tomorrow afternoon."

"We only have three daughters," Caitlin said, confused.

"I was counting my sister in the lot," Hudson said with a grin.

Caitlin returned to the hotel room after going across the street and purchasing gifts for the girls and Nell. She figured she owed Nell for watching the children while they were away.

She caught a glimpse of Hudson going into the bank with James Bennett. Her life was going to be different now. Before Florence died, the only money she was given was to pay the grocer, although she had managed to skim off enough to pay for her art supplies. She'd had months of enjoying her status as an heiress and had never felt guilty for her purchases. Now, by Texas law, her money was under the control of her husband, although Hudson had reminded her several times that he was not interested in her money. He'd already told her that he would be their family's primary source of income.

As the day dwindled away, Caitlin's bottom stopped being tender and only gave her a twinge when she sat down. She had packed their bags and was reading when Hudson entered the hotel room.

"How did it go?"

Hudson crossed the room and kissed her. "Your instincts are good. No one had anything negative to say about James or his business skills. Ben sent me a telegram. He owns the building where he has his law practice. He will draw up a lease, and I'll sign it for the year. The books and cash register will be packed in containers and shipped by train to Tyler. The shelving will be moved by freight wagons, and I've already talked to Phil Dennesin, who owns the local livery. He has enough wagons to move the rest. His men will remove the shelves as soon as he gets the word, and the shelves should be in Tyler by the next day. James will come with the wagons. He's been sleeping upstairs over the shop and has some furniture that will come with him. All this planning is dependent on the good weather holding. If we're lucky, Tyler will have a bookstore in a few weeks."

"Did you eat dinner?" Hudson asked.

"No, I forgot," Caitlin said.

"How do you forget to eat?"

Caitlin shrugged. "Jilly was always chasing after me to eat. Now it's the girls reminding me because I have to feed them."

Hudson looked around at the four valises and checked the time on his pocket watch. "Our luggage has grown."

"Books and gifts for the girls and Nell, Ben, and the baby," Caitlin said.

"We have time for a quick dinner, and I'll tip Clarence to take the two heavy bags over to the train station ahead of us."

"We didn't go far, but it was worth it," Hudson said, leaning down for a kiss.

The town of Tyler hadn't changed while they were gone, except the sun was now shining, and mud was drying, as it was in Thedford.

There were hugs all around when Nell opened her door. The girls screamed and hugged them with delight.

Hudson thanked his sister for watching the children and then hitched his horse to the buggy they'd left at the livery to run his errands. He talked with Ben and signed the lease for the new bookstore. Hudson returned to the train station for their luggage. His next stop was to the bank, where he opened a bank account for James Bennett, explaining that the young man was opening a business in town.

The banker, John Bones, informed Hudson at the bank that he had missed Angus Ballard's return to Magnolia Ranch three days earlier. Hudson expected Angus would be angry that the Henasee's property deal hadn't been finalized in his absence.

"I'll deal with him," Hudson said.

"Better you than me," John said.

Hudson knew there would be an explosion when he returned to the ranch, but it couldn't be avoided. Angus had gotten his way for so long that he'd forgotten the meaning of the word no.

With all his errands completed, Hudson returned to Nell's house to pick up his family and headed home.

The barn reconstruction was finished, and now it was twice the size it had been originally. He backed the buggy under the overhang, unhitched the horse, but tied it to a post.

Caitlin stood back from the barn, holding hands with the girls, when he joined them. "You even had it painted to match the house," Caitlin said.

"I'll inspect it after I bring the luggage in," Hudson said.

"Are we married now, Papa?" Charlotte asked, tugging on her father's arm.

"Yes, we are married," Hudson said.

"Is Caitlin my new Momma? Can I call her Momma now?"

"Yes, you can," Caitlin answered.

"Does that mean you're our Papa now?" Naomi asked.

"Yes, it does," Hudson said. "We are a family now, and you girls are sisters. We are the McFarlanes. Does everyone agree with that?"

"Yes!" Naomi exclaimed, and she was jumping up and down with Charlotte."

Maisey started crying, and tears were running down her face.

Caitlin reached for the girl and pulled her into a hug. "What's wrong, sweetheart? We won't insist if you don't want to take the McFarlane name."

Maisey shook her head. "I was afraid you'd send us back!"

"No," Hudson said, joining the hug. "We are a family now, all of us."

"Most people don't want orphans," Maisey cried.

"We're not most people," Caitlin said, kissing Maisey on the forehead. "I lived in an orphanage until I was five."

"I was almost sixteen when my parents died," Hudson said. "My sister was only eight. Do-Gooders tried to put her in an orphanage, but I wouldn't let them. We are all family now."

"Is Mr. Henasee part of our family?" Charlotte asked.

"I'll have to give that some thought," Hudson said, and Caitlin burst out laughing.

"All right, ladies, it's time to go inside now," Caitlin said. "With all the building that was going on while we were gone, everything must be covered in dust. We brought gifts back for you and will give them to you as soon as we settle in."

The girls ran into the house giggling, and Hudson wrapped his arm around Caitlin. They looked at the new barn. "Well, let's see if my guys did the job right," he said.

While Hudson put the horse in a new stall, Caitlin looked around. Except for the tack room, the barn had been rearranged. Fresh hay had been stored in a loft that hadn't been there before, and instead of two stalls, there were six. There was a separate feed room for bagged forage. In addition to rebuilding, the stalls were gated to open to a fenced corral behind the barn.

"I didn't expect all this," Caitlin said.

"It's the standard layout for the barns on Magnolia Ranch. I need to bring my horses here if I'm going to ride to Magnolia Ranch or the Farm daily. Luckily, a back way to reach both from here cuts off about three miles."

"I was afraid you'd want to move the ranch," Caitlin said.

"I gave up a large cabin after I lost my wife, and then Nell married," Hudson said. "A family with kids needed it. My cabin is not big enough for five, and you are already settled here. Bert would probably come after me with a shotgun if I tried to take you away."

"I'm very fond of Bert," Caitlin said, teasing. "Don't tell him I repeated this, but he has a high opinion of you."

Hudson let out a whoop that echoed in the nearly empty barn. He whirled her in a circle and then kissed her. "We're going to get along just fine!"

CHAPTER 9

*W*hen Hudson knocked on the door, he already knew his boss was home.

"Where the hell have you been?" Angus Ballard growled, opening the back door to his office.

"I could ask you the same," Hudson said. "You were supposed to be gone a month, and it stretched into damn near four months during some of the worst weather we've had in the last sixteen years. We had flooding, hail storms, lightning strikes, and tornados!"

"I heard," Angus said. "The bottom line will be thinner this year because of all the damage."

"I sent you telegrams," Hudson said, sitting across from the desk. "Some you answered, and some you didn't. If you didn't, I used my judgment."

"You lost the Henasee land!" Angus growled. "I had that land tied up before I left."

"Apparently, you didn't have it in writing, and Bert was stringing you along," Hudson said. "By the time I heard about what was happening, Bert had already sold the property."

"I heard," Angus said, his eyes narrowing to a squint. "Why didn't you buy it back!"

"She made a deal with Bert, and she's not willing to sell," Hudson said.

Angus stood up from his desk and walked over to a window. "I also heard you married her!"

"I did," Hudson admitted with a smile.

"Good," Angus said, nodding his head. "Then the property belongs to you, and we can continue with our plans."

Hudson shook his head. "That's not going to happen, Angus. I didn't marry Caitlin for her property. What she does with it is her business."

"Damn it," Angus cursed. "You listen to me..."

"No," Hudson said, getting to his feet. "You listen to me! I made promises to my wife, and I don't intend to break them."

"What about loyalty to Magnolia Ranch and me?" Angus growled.

"You've had my loyalty for sixteen years, and we've been through some rough times together. I have never interfered with your personal life, and I expect the same respect from you!" Hudson turned to leave.

"Wait," Angus said.

Hudson stopped and turned to face his boss.

"Sit down," Angus said, returning to his chair.

There was a long silence before Angus spoke. "Magnolia Ranch and the Farm have been in my family for four generations. I thought there would be a fifth, but I finally gave up on the idea. Emma and Abigail have married well and are not interested in returning to Magnolia. I'm fifty-six years old, and most of the males in my family don't live past their mid-sixties.

"I have changed my will and informed my daughters of my actions. It is an understatement to say they are unhappy with my decisions, but I won't change my mind. When my time is over, Magnolia goes to you. I made the will unbreakable. If those paper-pushers Emma and Abigail married try to claim ownership, they will lose their inheritances altogether."

"I don't know what to say," Hudson said.

"You're the son I never had, and you've earned it," Angus said. "If I make any modifications again, most likely, it will be in your favor. That doesn't mean we won't go head-to-head occasionally in disagreement. We've been butting heads for a long time, and I don't expect that to change."

"Did Emma and Abigail agree with your plans?" Hudson asked.

Angus shook his head. "Hell no, and I don't need their agreement. They have shown no interest in Magnolia for the last twenty years except for demanding money. They have treated me with disrespect, and truthfully, they don't deserve anything. The documents are in the hands of Judge Harrison. I apologize for assuming I would have anything to say in your marriage. Where's our baby girl?"

"Charlotte is with her new mother in the old Henasee house. She's made the place livable and renamed it Rose Hill. You wouldn't recognize it," Hudson said, pulling out his pocket watch. "I've been gone nearly a week and need to speak with the foremen. Are you coming?"

"Yeah," Angus said. "Give me a few minutes."

"I'll meet you in barn one," Hudson said, but he detoured to the kitchen.

Mrs. Brimmer looked up from peeling potatoes. "How is the new marriage going?" she asked.

"It couldn't be better," he said. "Don't tell Angus about Charlotte being able to talk. I want to surprise him if possible."

"You know he dotes on her," Mrs. Brimmer said with a smile. "I'll spread the word, but you'd better bring that child back here soon, or someone will spill the beans."

"I'll bring her tomorrow, but you'll have to watch her as I

haven't hired a nanny and have no intentions of doing so," Hudson said, smiling.

"Why would you? You've given her a mother," Mrs. Brimmer said with a smile.

The rest of the day went well. There was no more talk of Angus' will. Most of their discussions were Magnolia Ranch or Farm-related. There had been a few remarks from Angus about how disappointed he was that neither of his daughters had children or wanted them. It was doubtful they would produce grandchildren as both were in their mid-thirties. It was also unlikely that they would return to Magnolia again. They had no interest in returning to Texas.

Charlotte greeted Hudson as soon as he came through the door. She was wearing dirty overalls, as were Maisey, Naomi, and Caitlin.

"I'm the one who should be dirty," he said, backing away from them.

"We were planting rose bushes," Caitlin said, showing her dirty hands. "We're waiting for the stove reservoir to heat the water. How did your day go?"

"Really good," Hudson said. "I brought two of my horses back with me. Did you see Bert today?"

"Yes, he brought the rose bushes back with him from the train depot," Caitlin said.

Charlotte tugged on her father's trousers. "Did you see Grandpa today?"

Hudson knelt down in front of her. "Yes, Angus has come home, and he asked about you."

"Did you tell him I can talk," Charlotte asked.

"No," Hudson admitted. "I want you to surprise him."

Caitlin dipped hot water from the reservoir into the basins and added cold water, testing the temperature. "Girls, the water is warm enough to wash. I want you to take off the overalls in the butler's pantry. When you are clean, put the overalls in the tub to soak. Use the back stairs to your room, and get dressed. Maisey, will you see that Naomi and Charlotte are clean before they go upstairs?"

"Yes, ma'am," Maisey said, following Charlotte and Naomi with a bucket of hot water.

When the door closed, Hudson leaned over and kissed his new wife. "Did you have a good day?"

"Reasonably," Caitlin said. "How was yours?"

"Argumentative," Hudson said. "But that's normal when dealing with Angus. I have news, but I'll share it after the girls go to bed. What's for supper?"

"Baked chicken," Caitlin said. "Bert is going to build us a chicken coop out back."

"I can do that," Hudson said, frowning.

"You don't need to," she responded. "Bert is old and lonely. It will give him something to do and make him feel needed. You can check on the chicken roasting in the oven while I bathe and get some clean clothes on."

Later that evening, after the girls were tucked into bed, Hudson sat on the parlor couch with his arms around Caitlin, explaining his day.

"I've only met Emma and Abigail once, and they weren't interested in the ranch. Still, I didn't expect them to abandon the family legacy. Angus didn't tell me what happened, but I don't think his daughters treated him well."

"Did they marry into wealth?" Caitlin asked.

"Yes. From what I understand, Emma left first. She was supposed to be going to college, but she married a lawyer with a political bent in her first year and quit to marry him. He's been a California senator for about five or six years now. After Emma married, Abigail visited her sister and telegrammed Angus that she had also married a lawyer.

"I've worked for Angus for sixteen years, and they've only

returned once. They only stayed a few days, and I suspect money was exchanged."

"Did you tell Angus that you married?" Caitlin asked.

"Of course I did," Hudson said. "He was a little surprised, but he got over it quick enough. I'm going to take Charlotte with me tomorrow. Angus loves Charlotte, and she'd just started calling him Grandpa when she lost her voice. He will be overjoyed when he realizes she can talk again, and I give you the credit for that."

"I didn't do anything," Caitlin said.

"Yes, you did," Hudson said. "You protected a little girl and enabled her to break free from whatever kept her silent. Because of your upbringing, you don't want to see children used or abused, and I admire that strength in you. But, there is something that you need to face."

"Angus," Caitlin said, nodding her head. "Tomorrow, take Charlotte with you, and I'll ask Bert to watch over the girls the following day."

"He's going to love you," Hudson said.

"But, will I love him?" Caitlin asked.

* * *

"Papa, when can I have a horse?" Charlotte asked on the way to Magnolia Ranch.

"I think we might have to start with a pony first," Hudson said.

"When?"

"I'll have to talk it over with Caitlin," Hudson said.

"Maybe Grandpa will give me a pony," Charlotte said.

"Angus doesn't have any ponies," Hudson said. "He only has working horses, and you're not big enough for a horse."

"I'm big enough for a pony," Charlotte said.

"That's a decision we'll spend some time discussing," Hudson said.

When Hudson rode into the Magnolia Ranch, he dismounted and tied his horse to the fence.

Knocking on the office door, Angus shouted from inside. "Come in!"

Hudson opened the door, and Charlotte ran ahead of him.

"Grandpa!" Charlotte exclaimed, running to Angus.

Angus turned a stunned look to Hudson as he gathered Charlotte into his arms. "She's talking!"

"She has been for a couple of weeks," Hudson said.

"Baby girl!" Angus exclaimed, setting Charlotte into his lap. "What made you talk after all this time?"

Charlotte shrugged. "My new Momma showed me how to see angels in the clouds. She said my other Momma was in the sky and clouds with God, and he was taking care of her. I can talk to her anytime I want, but she can't answer."

"That's true," Angus said.

"I'll leave you two to chat," Hudson said. "I'll go check in with the foremen."

Angus caught up later with Hudson in one of the six massive barns. "When do I get to meet this miracle worker you married?"

"Tomorrow," Hudson said.

"Mrs. Brimmer told me what happened with the nurse. You married that woman pretty darn fast," Angus said.

"She's a beauty inside and out. I couldn't take a chance of some other man courting her. I knew she was going to be mine after our first meeting. Caitlin is beautiful, but she hasn't had an easy life until recently."

"I'm looking forward to meeting her," Angus said. "Not living on Magnolia will make your job more difficult."

"I'm close enough," Hudson said. "I have the cabin for when I need to spend the night."

"I heard your wife is a city girl," Angus said.

"She was, and she's adjusting," Hudson said with a smile. "It hasn't helped that we've had the worst weather in decades. Bert has been a big help to her."

"That old coot?"

"Yeah, and they are best friends," Hudson admitted. "He looks out for her, and she looks out for him. He tolerates me, for her sake."

"What's she going to do with that thousand acres?" Angus demanded.

"We haven't discussed it beyond her promise to Bert not to sell it to you," Hudson said. "Caitlin is settling into country living and seems to be enjoying it. She's been planting rose bushes and flowers, and Bert has promised to build her a chicken coop. She's also looking for a good milking cow."

The following morning, Caitlin wore one of her favorite dresses. The soft blue color looked good on her, but she was shaking.

"There's nothing to be afraid of," Hudson said as he lifted her into the buggy's seat.

"I'm not afraid," Caitlin lied.

"Then stop trembling," he said. "Angus doesn't bite."

"He might after he hears what I have to say," Caitlin retorted. "Is Bert here?"

"Yes, with a cart of lumber to build the chicken coop," Hudson said. "You don't have to do this today if you're not ready."

"Yes, I do. I came to Texas to confront Angus Ballard. I need to face him, and I can't run scared now," Caitlin said.

"Come on," Hudson said. "Are you sure Bert can handle three little girls?"

Caitlin laughed. "Naomi and Charlotte might think they can get away with misbehaving, but Maisey won't let them. She's been looking out for Naomi for years."

Pulling into the Magnolia Ranch compound was amazing. The main house was huge, built of logs, but it wasn't a log cabin by any means. Hudson drove to the end of the house, clearly marked by the Magnolia Office sign burned into a wooden plaque.

Lifting Caitlin to the ground, Hudson gave his wife a hug. "I'll stay with you if that's what you want. There's no reason to be afraid."

"I'm not afraid," Caitlin said, shaking her head. "I'm terrified!"

"No, you're not," Hudson disagreed with a squeeze. "One word out of place, and you'll hang Angus on one of his trophy heads."

Hudson knocked on the door, and they heard a shout, "Come in!"

Entering the office, a tall, stocky man stood at the window with his back to them.

Hudson and Caitlin walked over and stood in front of the desk.

Angus turned around and grasped the left side of his chest. "Florence?" He stumbled forward, and Hudson ran to his side and shoved him into his desk chair. Angus had gone pale, and beads of sweat appeared on his forehead.

"Florence?" he repeated.

"No, I'm not Florence. My name is Caitlin Ridgeway McFarlane. I am Florence's daughter, and according to her diary, will, and other legal papers she left behind, you are my father."

"Florence had my child?" Angus questioned. "Why didn't she contact me? If I'd known, I would have married her. I loved her. She wouldn't leave Philadelphia or her sister, Beaula. I tried to convince her to marry me, but she wouldn't."

"According to Florence's diary, she tried to contact you with no results," Caitlin said. "She was devastated when you didn't respond to her letters."

"I never received any letters," Angus exclaimed. "I wrote letters for months and finally gave up. Beaula hated me, and I thought she was why Florence wouldn't marry me! She constantly lied to Florence, telling her that I wanted to take her into the wilderness and that I was lying about owning Magnolia."

"I can believe that," Caitlin said. "It's possible that Beaula intercepted your letters. Beaula was totally dependent on her sister, although she would never allow anyone to know. Florence was the inheritor of the entire Ridgeway Estate and holdings from their father. I didn't know Florence was my mother until the Ridgeway attorney presented me with the will. It explained a lot in my life. I didn't know my father's name until I found and read her diaries and personal papers. I discovered she hid the truth about many things."

Angus pushed back his chair and walked around the desk. He opened his arms wide and hugged Caitlin to him. "I am sorry. I had no idea. You look just like Florence, and she was a beautiful woman."

Hudson looked from one to the other. "I don't think this reunion will end in bloodshed, so I will get some work done. I'll see you later."

Angus looked over the correspondence that had taken place twenty-two years before between himself and Florence. She had saved every note and letter until they had stopped. Angus listened as Caitlin described her childhood abandonment to a convent-run orphanage and her years of servitude in the Ridgeway Estate and to Beaula.

"I don't understand why Florence wouldn't stand up for her own child," Angus exclaimed.

"She was terrified of Beaula," Caitlin said. "In her diary, she wrote that Beaula threatened to put her in a mental asylum. As a child, I only knew what I was taught, and that was that I was an adopted orphan.

"I was hidden as an illegitimate mistake that would ruin Beaula's status in Philadelphia society. I was raised in the convent until I was five, and that's too young to have memories. Then, I was kept out of sight in an upstairs room at Ridgeway with a caretaker until I was ten. Publically, the aunts claimed they had adopted me.

"Florence visited me in the playroom, and I always considered her the nice aunt." Caitlin smiled. "We played with the doll house my girls are playing with now. Even as a small child, I knew she was frail.

"When I was ten, the nurse disappeared one day, and Aunt Beaula told me it was time for me to *earn* my keep. I was told I was responsible for Aunt Florence's care. I didn't mind. We became great friends, but she never gave me a hint that I was her daughter. As I grew older, the servants were fired, or they quit, and I took over their duties. Nothing I ever did was up to Beaula's standards."

"That was one hell of a big place for one small girl to maintain," Angus growled.

"My salvation was Jilly Mason, the cook. She stood up to Beaula for my sake. She refused to be fired and told Beaula she would take me if she left. She also threatened to tell her friends the truth about what went on in Ridgeway Estate. She knew many of the servants in that area.

"It was important to Beaula to put on a show when her so-called friends visited, although that wasn't very often."

"What about your schooling?" Angus asked.

"Florence took that on, even though she was bedridden," Caitlin said. "She would have made a good school teacher. It was a secret we kept from Beaula. We kept a lot of secrets from Beaula with Jilly's help. Florence also taught me to draw and paint, both of which I love to do. Ridgeway Estate was full of secrets. Beaula pretended to be a dutiful sister, although she was far from it. I overheard her once berating Florence for refusing to sign a document. I discovered from Mr. Deveraux, the family attorney, much, much later, that she was trying to force Florence to give her the family inheritance. Florence refused, and there was hell to pay from Beaula.

"I raised the question with the doctor if Beaula might have poisoned Florence, but he said I shouldn't suggest such things. But, then, he didn't know Beaula like I did."

"Did she get the estate?" Angus asked.

"No, she got nothing," Caitlin said. "Three days after the funeral, Mr. Deveraux, the Ridgeway attorney, delivered several letters from Florence and her will. That's how I discovered I wasn't her niece but her daughter. I inherited Ridgeway Estate and everything. Beaula didn't get a penny.

"'The first thing I did was banish Beaula from the house. I arranged for her to rent a small brownstone. Very small, with only a front room, a bedroom, and a tiny kitchen. It's not up to the standard she would have preferred. She, and she alone, was behind my being orphaned and used as a nurse and servant. Mr. Deveraux arranged with the bank for her to receive enough each month to survive. I wasn't feeling very generous that day, and if I had known then what I know now, I might not have done that for her."

"I didn't want the house. It was a beautiful house, but it held fifteen years of good memories of Florence and horrible memories of Beaula. I didn't want to stay in Philadelphia either. When the people in Beaula's circle thought I was a servant, they treated me disdainfully. When the news of my inheritance became known, suddenly, I was receiving invitations to parties and suppers. They might have thought they were making a grand gesture, but I thought they were horrible, snobby hypocrites."

Angus laughed. "Now you're sounding like a true Ballard!"

"I sold the house and the property, and Jilly and I came west to Tyler."

"Jilly was the cook?" Angus said, trying to keep the names straight.

"Yes. Jilly has been my best friend, protector, and personal caretaker since I was a child," Caitlin said. "She's always been there for me. She came to Tyler with me, but her son was ill, and she had to return to help him and his wife."

"She's older?" Angus asked.

"Jilly is in her late fifties or early sixties. She won't tell me her age. She's been there for me since I was twelve. When Beaula tried to break my spirit, Jilly was behind me, helping me plan revenge."

There was a knock on the door, and Angus yelled, "Yeah!"

A woman opened the door. "Hudson sent Jerry to tell you Lightning is foaling."

"Damn," Angus swore. "Mrs. Brimmer, this is Caitlin McFarlane, my daughter and Hudson's wife."

"Don't let me keep you from something you need to do," Caitlin told Angus. "I can't leave until Hudson comes for me. I don't know the way back home."

"Then excuse me," Angus said, grabbing his hat. "Lightning is a full-blooded Arabian!" He ran out the door.

"Did that make any sense to you?" Mrs. Brimmer asked.

"Not much, but I wasn't raised on a ranch."

"You'll learn," Mrs. Brimmer said. "You might as well come into the kitchen and keep me company. Angus may be gone an hour or two days. I don't get involved with anything beyond the house and the garden. The kitchen is my domain."

CHAPTER 10

"So, you are Angus' daughter," Mrs. Brimmer said.

"It seems so," Caitlin said.

"I was originally hired by Mr. Andrew Ballard, Angus' father," Mrs. Brimmer said. "He was a bitter old man. I remember when Andrew sent Angus to Pennsylvania. Although I don't remember the details, Angus was supposed to handle the finances of a family member who had died. Angus was only supposed to be gone a few weeks, but it stretched into several months. Mr. Andrew had a swearing fit every time he received a letter because Angus was involved with a young woman back east."

"My mother," Caitlin said.

"It was a long time ago," Mrs. Brimmer said. "When Angus did return, he wasn't happy. There was a lot of shouting and arguing in those days, but I kept my head down and out of their business. Mr. Andrew was a hard man and only had one son to take over Magnolia.

"When I started working here, I thought Angus was a widower. I found out later that his wife, Louise, had abandoned him with two small girls to raise. Angus tried to divorce her, but he discovered she was already married and hadn't bothered to divorce her first husband before marrying him. She also admitted that the girls weren't fathered by him, but he took and raised them as his own.

"Mr. Andrew tried his best to get one of his granddaughters to marry and give him a great-grandson, but that wasn't happening. Neither of those girls was interested in being a rancher's wife. They took off supposedly to go to college, but it turned out they were living with their mother until they married.

"It was shameful how Mr. Andrew berated Angus for not remarrying. The older Mr. Andrew got, the worse he treated everyone around him." Mrs. Brimmer quickly made the sign of the cross on her chest. "It was a blessing when he passed."

"You still work here, so Angus must treat you well," Caitlin said.

"That's true," Mrs. Brimmer agreed. "Angus is not like his father. He has done with Hudson and Nell, as you have done with the young ones you adopted. Family is more than a blood-line." The housekeeper handed Caitlin an apron. "The men could be hours, and today I'm making apple pies."

"I haven't tried making pies," Caitlin admitted. "But I'm willing to try!"

It was several hours before Angus returned. He stood in the doorway, covered in who knew what. Mrs. Brimmer pointed a finger at him, stopping him in his tracks.

"The foal was a colt," he announced with a grin. "And we're starving."

"No one starves at my table," Mrs. Brimmer snapped. "No one comes to my table filthy either. Get yourselves cleaned up!"

"Yes, ma'am, we're heading that way," Angus said, but he turned to Caitlin. "Hudson went to his cabin. He'll be back in a few minutes."

Caitlin had already learned from Bert that dinner was the

largest meal served. Ranchers were awake at dawn and burned off a hearty breakfast long before noon. The Magnolia Ranch mid-day meal could have graced any holiday meal for most families. There were steaks, dressing, potatoes, beans, biscuits with churned butter, and apple pies. Hudson and three other foremen sat at the table. Caitlin was introduced to the foremen as Hudson's wife and Angus' long-lost daughter.

"Gentlemen, please remember there is a lady present," Mrs. Brimmer warned the men sternly.

"I can eat in the kitchen if you want to talk freely," Caitlin suggested. "I know all the swear words. I'm just not allowed to use them. I also know they are part and parcel of most men's vocabularies."

"I think we can hold our tongues," Hudson said with a grin

The mid-day meal was a time for all the foremen to discuss various problems or difficulties in the different sectors of the ranch for which the men were responsible. Caitlin didn't understand most of what the men were discussing, but she listened.

There seemed to be a diverse separation of responsibilities. The men discussed tending to the livestock and the land that supported the cattle. Ranchers were rugged men, but they remembered their manners because a woman was present.

When the men finished, they pushed back their chairs to leave but didn't forget to thank Mrs. Brimmer, tipping their hats and mumbling, 'Thank you, ma'am.'

Angus remained behind and asked Hudson if it was all right to give Caitlin a look around the property.

"Sure," Hudson agreed, but he took Caitlin aside. "If he asks questions you aren't comfortable answering, don't hesitate to tell him so."

"He's already accepted that I'm his daughter," Caitlin said.

"You don't owe him anything, and Angus can be a cunning old bastard when he wants to be," Hudson said. "Sooner or later, the Henasee property will come up. He's good at manipulating people into making promises."

"I've already been warned by Bert," Caitlin said.

Hudson leaned down and kissed her. "I'll see you later."

Angus started his tour of Magnolia with the house. It was large and spread out. He explained that part of the central room was the original cabin. Each generation of Ballards had expanded the ranch and the house. The largest expansion had been during his grandfather's regime. Edwin Ballard had four sons, one daughter, and a dream of owning the largest ranch in eastern Texas. He'd lost three sons to the war and a daughter to illness. Andrew Ballard, Angus' father, had taken on his father's quest and passed that quest down to his only son, Angus.

The house was impressive but masculine, with a lot of the furniture covered with leather or animal hides. Rugs were the skins of mountain lions and bears with their heads still attached, and most of the fireplace mantles held racks of rifles or the stuffed heads of elk or bison.

Angus laughed when Caitlin looked at an elk head with antlers four feet wide with dismay. "You're a city girl," he announced and frowned. "You'll have to get over that."

"I am what I am," Caitlin said. "I took down a head like that in my house. Bert didn't have room for it, so he gave it to Daniel Foster. It's hanging in his hotel now."

"Be careful of that old man," Angus warned.

Caitlin looked straight into Angus Ballard's eyes. "He gave me the same warning about you! I don't need either opinion about who I make friends with. I may be a city girl, but I wasn't raised sheltered, and I've been fending for myself for a while."

"I'm your father," Angus said gruffly.

"Yes," Caitlin agreed. "But that relationship is only on paper now. You took a young girl's innocence and left her with a child. You didn't stay around to see if there were any repercussions of your actions."

"I wrote her," Angus growled.

"You said you hated Beaula," Caitlin said. "That means you knew her. She was, and still is, a horrible woman. Florence wasn't strong enough to stand up to her. If you knew Florence, you should have been her strength, but you weren't. My mother was a weak, sickly woman, but she was the one who took me out of the orphanage when I was five. She was the one who insisted that I be her caretaker, and she did that so I could be educated and learn to stand on my own. She also gave me the gift of art. I know now that it passed through her to me. I haven't forgiven Florence for failing me as a mother. But I know she tried to keep me out of Beaula's clutches. When she failed, Jilly Mason stepped in to protect and support me.

"You, on the other hand, chose to leave, and you must have known Florence was a frail woman."

"I had to return to Magnolia," Angus said. "My father was dying, and my daughters were too young and sheltered to deal with the ranch."

"I understand, but it doesn't change the facts for either of us and although your blood runs in my veins, you are still a stranger."

"You and Hudson will inherit Magnolia," Angus said.

"No," Caitlin said, shaking her head. "Hudson will inherit Magnolia. It's his legacy because he's earned it. He is the son you didn't have and has earned Magnolia." She smiled with amusement. "As much as it pricks his pride, Hudson has married a woman of wealth. Florence got her revenge in the end, and she knew exactly what she was doing. Would you show me the new colt now?"

Effectively changing the subject, Angus knew he'd met his match, at least for this day. He crooked an arm, and Caitlin took it as he escorted her to a large barn.

"I'm thinking about getting Charlotte a pony," Angus said.

"Don't," Caitlin said with a shake of her head. "Charlotte

was told no by Hudson, and it's his decision. Besides, Maisey is the oldest of our girls. If anyone gets a pony or a horse, she will be first. Hudson and I have agreed that the girls will not be treated differently. Maisey and Naomi are part of our family, as much as Charlotte, and that goes for everything. There are privileges Maisey will earn before the younger girls simply because she's older. The next time we come to Magnolia, we'll bring all the girls, and I'm giving you fair warning. My two girls will not be treated any different than Charlotte."

Angus gave Caitlin a one-finger salute. "I hear you loud and clear. Is there any chance of you moving to Magnolia?"

"It would be easier for Hudson," she admitted. "But we need the time and separation because we have to blend our two families into one. It's up to you to decide if you want to notify your daughters."

"I don't consider Emma and Abigail my daughters anymore," Angus said.

"That's your decision to make," Caitlin said.

On the trip back to Rose Hill, Caitlin and Hudson discussed her day with Angus.

"I thought finding my father would give me a sense of belonging, but I don't feel anything for him yet. He's a stranger who supposedly loved my mother twenty-two years ago. He was nice enough, but he is still a stranger."

"Of course he is," Hudson said. "You reopened his past and brought it into the present. He has to accept the consequences of his actions, and you made him face a past where he didn't get what he wanted. Angus is not a man who likes to fail. Don't worry about it because I'm here, and I won't let him pressure or take advantage of you."

Hudson drove the buggy to the new barn. He lifted Caitlin to the ground and began to unharness the horses. She was immediately surrounded by the girls, all talking at once.

"Whoa, ladies," Hudson ordered, guiding them out of

kicking range. "What have I told you about being quiet around the horses? Take this hen party inside."

Caitlin sent the girls ahead of her and followed them into the kitchen. All three girls were talking at the same time.

"One at a time, please," Caitlin exclaimed. "Maisey?"

"We worked with Mr. Bert most of the day," Maisey said. "We built the chicken house, and he said he'd bring us hens and a rooster tomorrow. He said we'll have all the eggs we can use in a few days."

"That's good news," Caitlin said. "I hope all of you behaved today. Now, I'm going to start supper. I want you to play outside until I can get some water heated. When I call you in, I want you to bathe and change into clean clothes. Leave your overalls soaking in the bathwater, and I'll scrub and hang them up to dry later."

The girls ran past Hudson as he was coming inside.

"Bert must have taken care of all the chores before he left," Hudson said.

"He does that a lot," Caitlin said. "Bert has been a sweetheart ever since I arrived."

Hudson made a face and grimaced. "The words Bert and sweetheart in the same sentence doesn't sound right."

"Jealous?" Caitlin teased. "Bert has been a father figure to me ever since I arrived. I owe him a lot."

"I know," Hudson agreed. "And I may have to change my opinion of him because he has been so helpful to you." He leaned down and kissed her, and one kiss led to another until they backed away. Now wasn't the time or place. They had three little girls who could burst in on them at any second.

Maisey was the quiet child, while Naomi and Charlotte were non-stop chatter. Charlotte wanted to know when they were going to see her grandpa again.

The evening was much like the previous day. Caitlin had established a routine for the girls. After supper, the dishes were washed, and the kitchen was cleaned. Then, there was quiet time for the girls to settle down for an evening of reading or playing games while Caitlin washed whatever clothing needed to be scrubbed and hung it on a clothesline she strung up on the back porch before joining her family.

Hudson caught Caitlin's eyes a few times, and he could only guess what she was thinking as a shy flush of color rose in her cheeks.

When it was bedtime, Caitlin sent the girls upstairs and let them run ahead. Then she went over to her husband and kissed him.

"I read them a story or a book chapter at night when they are tucked in. I'll only be a few minutes."

Hudson checked the doors to ensure they were locked before going upstairs. There were empty bedrooms upstairs, but the girls occupied one large bed together by choice. He pulled off his boots and clothing and pulled on a robe. He hadn't owned a robe before marrying. It had been a gift from Caitlin on their short honeymoon, and it had come in handy when someone in the hotel knocked on the door. He would have to take more precautions with three small girls in the house.

Caitlin gave a quick knock on the door before opening it. After leaving the girl's bedroom, she'd gone to another bedroom and prepared herself. She wanted to look her best for her husband.

She'd let her hair down, and it hung in a stream of golden red to her waist. She was blushing again and wondered when she would be able to face her husband as freely as he was with her. Maybe men were more comfortable with being naked. She was getting used to their nudity once they began to make love.

"Are they asleep?" Hudson asked, leaning over and kissing her.

"Yes!" Caitlin said as he kissed her again.

"Good," Hudson mumbled, untying her wrapper. "It's my turn."

Hudson smiled as the wrapper fell to the carpet and exposed the beautiful woman he now called his wife. He was a lucky man, and Caitlin was a woman learning to enjoy intimacy. She wasn't experienced, and it was his job to teach her. So far, she had eagerly responded once he nudged her in the direction he wanted. She was neither afraid nor embarrassed by the act of lovemaking. She lost her inhibitions in the pleasure, and making love to a responsive woman was indeed a gift.

Hudson moved downward, taking her small breasts in his mouth, suckling them, and teasing them with his tongue. Caitlin's mind clouded over with pleasure and need. She was eager with anticipation when she spread her legs apart, giving him more access and encouragement. She trembled when he shifted himself further downward in the bed. She knew what to expect now as he trailed a line of kisses down and across her belly. Hudson scooted down even further, taking one of her legs and then the other, bending her knees and pushing them gently aside to expose all of her womanhood.

Caitlin closed her eyes. Her husband was seeing what she hadn't seen herself. Then, her eyes flew open as he began to tease her private parts with his tongue. She really liked this part of making love. His thumb circled her most sensitive place, and she closed her eyes again.

Hudson played his wife's body like a fine instrument. She'd come close to a full orgasm before under his tutelage, but she hadn't made it yet. This time, he was determined to push her into a full orgasm.

Caitlin gave herself to her husband freely, with total trust that he wouldn't hurt her. She loved how he made her feel, but Hudson claimed she still hadn't experienced a goal he'd set for her. She couldn't imagine feeling more, but he claimed it was yet to happen.

Hudson gave Caitlin more time, letting the sensations build slowly and then pushing her over the edge into near delirium. First, it felt like a tickle, then something seized and shook her insides. Arching her back, whatever was happening inside her made her feel giddy and weak. She was gasping, nearly sobbing, and aching with desire. She pulled a pillow over her mouth because she couldn't contain the noises escaping her throat. Her entire body screamed silently with pure pleasure. When it was finally over, Caitlin was crying. Hudson inserted a finger inside her, then two, pumping and letting her know there was more to come. She responded and was an open invitation for his taking.

With her skin glowing from the after-sensations of passion, Caitlin thought she was exactly where she belonged.

Did you like that?" Hudson asked.

"It was amazing. I didn't know I could react like that!"

"Now you do, and I intend to make you feel like that several times tonight."

Caitlin looked down over their naked bodies and gave her husband a *come hither look*.

"I'm ready whenever you are."

Hudson rested his chin on the top of her head with a smile. "Sweetheart, it won't take me long!"

Caitlin was awake in the wee morning hours long before daylight. Neither she nor Hudson had slept much, but she didn't mind. Lying in bed beside her husband, who had awakened her to the joy of being a woman, she marveled at how much her life had changed in such a short time.

Sometimes, when she was alone, random thoughts flittered through her mind, such as... she should have known Hudson longer and better before marrying, but she wasn't second-guessing her decision.

She was second-guessing her responses to some of the new men in her life now. Bert, who was what she thought a grandfather would be like. He had become an instant friend, helping her with whatever she needed to learn about living in the country. Bert had been there for her and the girls from the beginning. Now she had Angus, although she'd only spent a few hours with him.

Hudson returned to his job as manager of both Magnolia Ranch and Magnolia Farm. The farm was on the other side of his wife's property, and when he had to ride from one property to the other, it was natural for him to stop in to see his family.

The first week back from their honeymoon, nearly every day, there were projects that Hudson had to check on. Hudson and Angus alternated on who was in charge of what. There was still a barn at the farm that needed to be rebuilt. It had burned down from a lightning strike. The men had gotten all the animals out, and no one had been hurt.

Hudson used some of Magnolia's younger manpower to help James Bennett set up his bookstore in Tyler. The storefront had to be cleaned and painted before the shelves were anchored to the floor and walls so they wouldn't turn over. Caitlin spent part of a day introducing James to the various store owners and other businesses in town. She and Maisey helped unpack crates and store the books on shelves while Naomi and Charlotte were at Nell's house. Every time they helped James Bennett, they came home with an armful of books.

Hudson was a little jealous of Caitlin's time with their new friend, but he knew how important books were to her. The library at Rose Hill was growing, and the new store was rarely empty of customers.

Caitlin was busy and hadn't returned to Magnolia Ranch, and Angus was getting angry. He called Hudson to his office and complained.

"How the hell am I supposed to have a relationship with my

daughter when she's not around! Tell her to get her ass up to Magnolia Ranch!"

"First, you are speaking of my wife, and you will do so with respect," Hudson said. "Second, ordering her to come here won't work. She's the mother of three little girls, and her days are full. She's home-schooling the girls."

"Two of whom I've never met!" Angus swore.

"Then get your butt down to Rose Hill to meet them," Hudson said. "Ordering Caitlin to do something is the wrong tactic, Angus. Making yourself useful is the best way to get to know her. She knows you are her father, but you've never been in her life and haven't tried to seek her company. Why should she disrupt her plans for you?"

"What does she need?" Angus demanded.

"She doesn't need anything, and you can't buy her affection," Hudson said. "When she told me her worth, I damn near had a heart attack. Even so, I've put her on a budget. She treats her inheritance almost like play money. This isn't about your wealth or Magnolia Ranch. You need to find some common ground."

"What would that be?" Angus growled.

"The girls are one way," Hudson said. "If they accept and like you, she'll find a place in her heart for you. But don't start a feud with Bert because Caitlin and the girls consider him family."

"I'm not sure I can bend that far," Angus complained.

"It's your choice," Hudson said. "As far as I know, Caitlin isn't going anywhere tomorrow. If the sky remains overcast, she'll stay home. She doesn't like being out in bad weather. Now, if you're done bitching, I need to ride over to the farm and talk with Henry before I go home this evening."

CHAPTER 11

*W*hen Hudson awakened, Caitlin wasn't beside him. He was in bed alone, and he'd slept hard. Tossing off the blankets and looking through the window, he saw Bert trying to teach Caitlin how to milk a cow.

He'd been late getting home the previous night because he'd brought a milk cow from Magnolia farm, and cows didn't travel as fast as horses or cattle.

Maisey and Caitlin were watching Bert's every move. Caitlin took his place when he stood up from the stool, but she hadn't followed his instructions correctly. She couldn't get the milk to come out of the udder. Maisey sat on the stool, and it was apparent that she had milked a cow before, as squirts of milk were going into the bucket.

Caitlin clapped her hands at Maisey's success, where she had failed. Naomi and Charlotte were clapping their hands. His wife tried three more times before Bert shook his head and said something that made his wife and daughters laugh.

Pushing the curtains aside, Hudson looked upward at dark rolling clouds again. The only person he knew who wanted more rain was his wife with her newly planted rosebushes.

There was a rumbling of thunder, and rain splattered on the window. Looking down again, Bert handed Caitlin a bucket, and she carried it behind the girls who were running for the back door. Bert grabbed the milking stool and led the cow back into the barn.

Hudson got dressed and went downstairs to face his wife and daughters. When he entered the kitchen, Caitlin gave him a look that clearly said the spanking he'd given her the night before wasn't forgotten. She'd deserved it for ignoring his warning about going to Tyler alone. Luckily, she hadn't been hurt until he'd set her bottom on fire.

He bent down to kiss Charlotte on the cheek, but she jumped out of the chair. "I'm mad at you!" she yelled.

"Stop!" the sharp tone of Caitlin's voice stopped the seven-year-old in her tracks.

"I'm mad at Papa!" Charlotte wailed. "He won't let us keep the ponies!"

"*We* won't let you keep the ponies," Caitlin said firmly. "That's a decision your father and I agreed on as your parents. Now, you will apologize to your father and stand in the corner of the dining room for fifteen minutes."

"I won't!" Charlotte screamed and stomped her foot.

"One more disrespectful word and you will sit in the corner until supper. If that doesn't change your attitude, you will be there every day until you apologize," Caitlin said firmly.

"Papa!" Charlotte screamed.

"In the corner," Hudson said firmly.

Charlotte began to cry and wail, but she obeyed, and Caitlin closed the door between the two rooms.

"Girls, would you go to the classroom and read for a few minutes? I'll call you when breakfast is ready," Caitlin said.

"Hey, not before I get my morning hugs," Hudson said, and Maisey and Naomi hugged him before leaving the room.

Caitlin turned to Hudson when the door closed behind them. "Thank you," she said.

"She deserved it, just as you did last night," he agreed. "I told you not to drive to Tyler by yourself, and I meant it. If Bert can't drive, you'll have to wait until I can take you there."

"I said I was sorry," Caitlin said.

"Saying you're sorry doesn't undo deliberate disobedience," Hudson said firmly, rubbing her bottom. He could still hear Charlotte crying in the next room. "I told Angus we hadn't decided yet about teaching the girls to ride. He had no business sending those ponies over here without our permission."

Caitlin nodded. "I fixed you a basket breakfast, hoping the rain would hold off until you got to Magnolia. Since you'll get wet anyway, sit down, and I'll fix you a hot breakfast."

"The basket breakfast will be fine," Hudson said. "Are you sure you want the ponies returned? Angus has no use for them."

"I won't be bribed or bought," Caitlin said firmly.

"I tried to tell him," Hudson said. "Has Charlotte gotten sassy like this with you before?"

"She's been spoiled and pampered most of her life, except for that horrible Campbell woman," Caitlin answered. "Charlotte has turned on the tears before, but she'll learn I won't tolerate bad behavior."

"What about Maisey and Naomi?" Hudson asked.

Caitlin shook her head. "They come from a different background. Trust me, they have never been spoiled. I'm not saying they won't get into trouble occasionally; all children misbehave, but I don't expect them to pout and be disrespectful. If they are, they will be punished accordingly. Maisey keeps a firm rein on Naomi. I think she's still afraid of being sent back to the orphanage."

"What makes you do things I tell you not to do?" Hudson asked.

Caitlin flushed. "Stubbornness?"

"Next time, give it a little more thought before crossing me," Hudson suggested.

* * *

HUDSON KNOCKED on the office door and heard Angus' growl before entering.

"Why the hell did you bring those ponies back!"

"Because Caitlin and I had already discussed it and told Charlotte and Naomi that they were too young for ponies or horses. Maisey will get a horse first because she is the oldest," Hudson said.

"How is that fair?" Angus demanded.

"There's a three-year difference, and yes, it's fair," Hudson said. "You tried to override Caitlin and my decision on the matter. If you want to get to know your daughter, interfering with our decisions on how to deal with our children is not the way to do it."

"Hell," Angus exclaimed. "Charlotte told me they were getting ponies, but you hadn't had time to find them yet. I thought I was doing you a favor."

Hudson shook his head. "If she told you that, it was a lie, and I'll attend to her later."

"My intention wasn't to interfere..."Angus said.

"The ponies are in barn three," Hudson said.

"What the hell am I supposed to do with ponies?" Angus swore.

"That's not my problem," Hudson said with a chuckle. "And I don't think today would be a good day to visit Caitlin. It's best to put it off until she cools off. She's a little angry with me, too!"

"What did you do?" Angus asked.

"That's between me and her," Hudson said.

The storm didn't last long and wasn't as dangerous as the previous storms. A simple rain, Caitlin could handle. She kept the girls busy with school lessons, reading, and baking cookies. Caitlin also talked privately with Charlotte about misbehaving, and the child cried when she was told the ponies had been returned to Angus. She wouldn't get a pony or a horse until her ninth birthday, and only if her father and Caitlin thought she was responsible enough to care for it.

Angus saw Hudson daily but still hadn't decided how to handle Caitlin. He did recognize that she wasn't like either of his older daughters. Emma and Abigail had been easy to raise. All he had to do was buy whatever they wanted to keep them happy. Angus hadn't heard from either of them since he broke the news that Magnolia wouldn't go to them when he passed.

He couldn't bribe Florence's daughter... his daughter, and he did want a relationship with his only blood offspring.

"Is there a problem?" Mrs. Brimmer asked.

Angus turned from the window. "Why would there be?"

"Something is bothering you," the housekeeper said. "You've been looking out that window for the last half hour."

"What would a wealthy young woman want that she couldn't buy herself?" Angus asked.

"You're an old fool," Mrs. Brimmer said honestly. "Caitlin ain't after your money, Magnolia, or anything else. She's building a family. That's why she took to Bert Henasee, Charlotte, and those girls she's adopted. Now Hudson is part of it because he doesn't ask anything of her except love. If you want to bond with that gal, be upfront and honest. She's already had too much conniving and dishonesty in her life. She's got a good man with Hudson, and that's all she needs. She ain't going to accept you as a father unless you're honest with her. All she wants or needs is people around her that ain't trying to use her."

Hudson stopped by the office as he did every evening

before going home. Angus liked to believe that Magnolia couldn't run without him, but everyone in his employment knew better. Hudson ran down a long list of projects and their status and then tipped his hat. "I'm heading home."

"Would Caitlin mind if I joined you?" Angus asked.

"I don't think she'll mind," Hudson said. "And there's going to be a full moon tonight, so riding back won't be a problem."

Riding alongside Angus, Hudson was reminded of his youth when his job was to follow his boss, keep his mouth shut, and learn. He had no idea that Angus was training him to be his second in command. He'd caught on years later but had never expected that Magnolia Ranch would be turned over to him sometime in the future. They spent most of the ride talking about the ranch and the farm.

"How are you and my daughter getting along?" Angus asked.

"Well, considering that we've only been married for a couple of weeks, we're doing well," Hudson said.

"Is Bert still hanging around?" Angus growled.

Hudson grinned. "I'm getting used to him," he admitted. "He's helpful and thinks the world of Caitlin and the children. Bert goes to town several times a week, saving Caitlin from going, although she likes to get out and visit her new friends and the new bookstore."

"I heard the women in town are trying to stir up trouble by wanting to vote," Angus said. "If Caitlin gets involved with those radical women, you'd better put your foot down."

"My wife has a mind of her own," Hudson said firmly. "She's intelligent, and I don't need to tell her what is right or wrong."

"In my day, women did what they were told!" Angus grumbled.

"Do you think that might have had something to do with why Louise abandoned her daughters and divorced you?" Hudson asked.

"Louise didn't divorce me because she wasn't my legal wife," Angus snapped. "I tossed Louise out on her ass because I caught her with another man. She tried to extort money from me, but I stopped that real quick. I threatened to file charges against her for bigamy. It turned out that she was already married."

"I didn't know that. Do you ever hear from her?" Hudson asked.

"Louise has been dead for nearly a decade. She got to the girls, though, and turned them against me. My father arranged our marriage, but it wasn't a good match from the start. She was a liar and a cheat. Texas was different then. The town of Tyler was a mercantile, a blacksmith, and a saloon. If you wanted a woman, you had to pay hard-earned cash for her at the saloon.

"Good women were as scarce as hen's teeth, and most girls were married as soon as they turned twelve and were legal. We only lived together for three years. I came home one day to squealing young'uns and their mother gone. I had her tracked down and discovered she was already married, didn't get a divorce, and was still sleeping with the bastard the whole time she'd been with me. I didn't want to deal with her anymore, and I paid her to disappear but to leave the babies behind.

"Louise admitted later that I wasn't the girl's father. I should have known. There ain't been a baby born to a Ballard that wasn't a redhead in over a century. My father wanted me to marry again. He was determined to get another male heir, but I was just as determined not to tie myself into that mess again. The only woman who ever tempted me was Florence. I did love her, but there was no way I would stay in Philadelphia."

"Caitlin would probably like to hear that last bit. You should probably try to forget the rest. You told me a long time ago, when I lost Malinda that mourning wouldn't get me anywhere, but you were wrong. I did mourn her and had no thoughts of marriage until I met Caitlin. Meeting her was like being kicked in the head. I'm a blessed man to find another woman that suits me so well. My wife wants to know you, Angus. She came to Tyler to meet you, but you've got to put some effort into knowing her."

Angus followed Hudson into the barn, approving of the changes made. Hudson took care of his horse, but Angus left his horse saddled for the return trip to Magnolia.

"Grandpa!" Charlotte squealed when Angus followed Hudson into the kitchen. He lifted Charlotte in his arms and gave her a kiss.

Hudson walked over to Caitlin and gave her a kiss. Then he walked over to the table and put an arm around the girls. "Maisey, Naomi, this is Angus Ballard, the man I work for at Magnolia Ranch. Angus, these are our other two daughters. Maisey Jean is ten, and Naomi is seven like Charlotte."

"I'm glad to meet you girls," Angus said.

"Why don't you girls come with me and show me how your schoolwork is progressing?" Hudson asked, leading the girls out of the kitchen.

"Well, that was pretty obvious," Caitlin said, turning to her father.

"Obvious or not, I'd like to get to know my daughter," Angus said, handing over a large packet. "I've read everything you gave me. Florence's diaries were an eye-opener, and the copies of her letters showed me another side of her. The thing is, I never got the letters. Maybe Beaula stopped them, or maybe it was my father. I don't know. But, if I had received them, I would have returned to Philadelphia. I would not have abandoned her or my child."

"I believe you," Caitlin said. "I was angry with you at first. I hated that you left Florence in a horrible situation. She wasn't a strong person. I've had time to think and guess at what really happened. Beaula's interference was probably behind most of

Florence's bad decisions. I can't blame you for something that was out of your control. Even in Florence's diaries, she suspected that Beaula wasn't mailing her letters. Beaula needed to keep Florence under her control. It was the only way she could have access to the Ridgeway inheritance.

"When Florence died, I was already planning to leave the Ridgeway Estate. I wasn't staying around to put up with Beaula's manipulation any longer. I only stayed because I loved Florence. When Mr. Deveraux, the attorney, told me the truth. I was so mad that I threw Beaula out of the house and wouldn't let her return. I don't know where she went, but she kept trying to come back. Jilly and I spent days in Florence's room, going through her things."

"Beaula deserved it," Angus said.

Caitlin shrugged. "It was Mr. Deveraux's idea not to stoop to Beaula's level. That's why I rented the brownstone for her and gave her an allowance to live on. I don't expect to ever see her again."

"Do you like living in Texas?" Angus asked, looking around the kitchen.

"Very much," Caitlin said with a smile. "Bert wasn't happy when he found out you are my father."

"I'll bet," Angus laughed. "His battle was with my father, not me. He forgets that."

"*We* love him," Caitlin said firmly. "I'm hoping in time, we'll love you too."

"He got a head start on me," Angus complained.

"We'll give you a fair chance," Caitlin promised. "But there will be no playing favorites. If you want to treat the girls, it can't be more than three cents worth of candy without discussing it with me or Hudson."

"I'll remember that," Angus promised. "It was an expensive lesson I've already learned. What the devil am I going to do with three ponies?"

Caitlin laughed. "Give them to the smaller children on Magnolia. Charlotte has to write, 'I will not lie' twenty-five times a day for a week for telling you that lie."

Supper went well, with Angus asking all the girls questions. He rode away from Rose Hill before the sun went down.

"Well?" Hudson asked when the girls were sent upstairs to bed.

"I think it went well," Caitlin said. "I think we can be friends, although I'm not sure about him becoming a father figure."

"Give him a chance," Hudson said, pulling his wife into a hug. "Emma and Abigail don't give a damn about him. He hasn't told me the full details of what happened on this trip, but he did tell them they wouldn't inherit Magnolia."

Hudson left early the following morning but promised to return before supper.

When Bert pulled up beside the barn, Caitlin and Maisey had just finished milking the cow.

"Have you got the hang of it yet?" Bert asked from his wagon seat and motioned to the milk bucket.

"I'm not as good as Maisey yet, but she says I'm learning," Caitlin admitted.

"Well, I'm heading over to the Brokehalls' place," Bert said. "I thought the youngsters might enjoy playing with their children their age. They have three girls, like yourself, and about the same ages. The girls have met them already over at my place. I'll have them back before dinner time."

"Maisey?" Caitlin questioned.

"They are nice, and we had fun that day," Maisey said.

"I don't have any objections, as long as you keep an eye on them," Caitlin said to Bert, and a few minutes later, she was waving to her girls and reminding them to behave.

Caitlin had very little private time to herself now that she was married and a mother. She roamed around her empty house for a few minutes before going upstairs to change into an old dress and went into the rose garden to trim her bushes.

When Hudson returned home, he wasn't met by excited little girls or his wife. The doors weren't locked, and there wasn't a note. He went upstairs, looked out the window overlooking the rose gardens, and smiled. Caitlin was carrying a basket full of roses and other flowers he didn't know by name. She was playing in the flowers with a look of pure happiness. Hudson watched her, wanting to preserve the memory. Her joy in something so simple amazed him. His wife was wealthy but she didn't want diamonds and expensive clothing. It was the simple things in life that she craved. He'd seen the fancy dresses in the chifferobes in the empty bedrooms. Caitlin admitted to being embarrassed by her extravagant spending immediately after she received her inheritance. She didn't wear the dresses because she said they were too fancy to wear in Tyler. She called the fancy dresses silly and said she would reuse the fabrics someday.

Hudson went downstairs and looked for his wife among the many bushes. He called her name, and she appeared with her basket of cut roses.

"Where are the girls?" Hudson asked.

"Bert took them to the Brokehall's place. They have children the same ages as ours, and they'll have fun playing with them. They'll be back before dinner time," Caitlin explained.

"We are alone?" Hudson asked.

"Very much so," Caitlin said, looking into his eyes. She saw pure desire before he bent down to kiss her. She leaned into him, and the next minute, she was swept into his arms and carried to their bedroom. Hudson kicked the door shut.

Hudson began to unbutton her blouse. "How about us having some fun?

"That sounds good to me," Caitlin agreed happily.

Hudson removed her blouse to let his fingers wander under

her chemise. She unbuttoned his shirt, and it only took seconds to remove it. Piece by piece, their clothing was tossed aside until they were both naked.

Upon revealing her body, Hudson visually worshipped every part of her. He was entranced and wanted to see, touch, and kiss all those beautiful parts that were usually covered.

Hudson thrust his fingers inside her, pumping them deep into her and preparing his wife for his entry.

Caitlin opened herself to her husband and was in the mood to play, and so was he. Hudson lowered his mouth to her sex. Caitlin loved this kind of play and soon begged him to take her. Then Hudson thrust into her deep and demanded more from her.

Caitlin moaned with relief after a prolonged orgasm. But Hudson wasn't through yet. His work rough fingers went to work on her clitoris again while his tongue circled her breasts. He brought her to orgasm a second time and a third.

Then Hudson positioned Caitlin on her knees. She knew what was coming and sucked in her breath as his hand spanked her naked bottom. He stroked her buttocks and her clitoris until she was gasping. Her husband repeated the cycle of spanking. It was pain and pleasure.

"Hudson!" Caitlin cried, and he was there, thrusting into her deeper and riding her. She wanted to let go, and when his hand spanked her bottom again, she came with a flood of relief, while at the same time, she could feel her husband becoming wet and hot. Caitlin felt goosebumps rising all over her from the intensity of the joining of their bodies.

They collapsed together, breathing hard and letting their bodies recover.

A few minutes later, Caitlin slid from the bed and went to the water basin to clean herself. Hudson raked his eyes over his wife's body. God, she was beautiful. He jolted as his organ hardened again, and he turned her around and bent her over the footboard of the bed.

Caitlin spread herself and braced for what she knew was coming. She could feel herself dampening in preparation. When he thrust into her, she gasped but planted her feet firmly and bent over further to accommodate her husband's needs.

Hudson drove into her hard and deep. He'd been walking around with hard-ons long before he'd married Caitlin. She seemed to read his mind, knowing when he needed a quick slap and tickle and when he wanted long, nearly violent sex. He loved every second of connecting their bodies together. He loved it when her body responded to a woman's needs. When he came, he gave a guttural groan of satisfaction, but he kept pumping and reached around her and stroked her clitoris. She didn't need much attention as she shuddered and held tight to the footboard.

"Are you good?" Hudson demanded.

She nodded and turned in his arms. She wasn't surprised by her reaction to him. Sometimes, her body responded when her husband just looked at her. Caitlin didn't know if other women responded to their husbands the same, and there was no one she could ask.

Hudson took Caitlin's hand and led her around the bed, but she pushed him to sit.

Giving him a glance over her shoulder, she returned to the basin. "Don't go anywhere. I want to clean up a bit."

Hudson nodded because he knew sex could get messy. When she returned, she was hot and needy again.

Caitlin glanced at the clock as she was rocking on top of Hudson. It was her turn to be on top, and she rode him with the same rhythm as riding a horse. He groaned under her rolling hips, thrusting upward into her. She had learned that sex was not just lying still and waiting for her husband to finish. When he rolled her over and pulled her to her knees, she knew what was coming. It had been shocking at first, but any time she was positioned in front of him, sex included his spanking her bottom. At first, she'd thought it was weird, but she had begun to anticipate and strangely enjoy the smacks.

Suddenly, Hudson flipped her over and took control. He sank into her repeatedly. When she gasped, he groaned, and they rode their bodies together to the very end.

Later, Hudson kissed Caitlin and helped her button into a clean dress. They were expecting the girl's arrival, and they couldn't be seen naked. They'd spent the better part of the day making love and were physically spent. Still, they would have continued their grown-up play if they hadn't expected the girls to arrive.

CHAPTER 12

*C*aitlin went to complete the chores that had been ignored most of the day while Hudson went into the barn to do the same.

She separated and trimmed the roses she had cut earlier, divided them into vases for the parlor and the dining room, and carried a vase upstairs to their bedroom. Returning to the kitchen, she began fixing a supper of quiche made of fresh eggs, cheese, milk, and vegetables.

"What smells so good?" Hudson asked, coming into the kitchen.

"It's called quiche," Caitlin said. "Eleanor gave me the recipe. She got the recipe from Mrs. Schmidt, the German woman who works at the hotel. It's become very popular at the Rusty Pot. We have too many eggs and can't give them to Bert because he has his own.

"If we have extra, I can take them to Mrs. Brimmer. What she doesn't use will be given to the other wives," Hudson offered. He kissed Caitlin and then raised his head at the sound of giggling girls.

The girls ran through the door, followed by Bert. He

hoisted a string of fish and set them in the sink. "Best get these cleaned and into the spring house," Bert advised, nodding toward Hudson. "She's squeamish about cutting off the heads."

"We'll have them tomorrow for supper, and you're invited," Caitlin said quickly.

Bert gave Hudson a sour look, but he nodded. "I'll be here."

"When are you going into town this week?" Caitlin asked.

"Probably the day after tomorrow," Bert said. "What do you need?"

"I would like to look through the Ellisons' catalogs," Caitlin said.

"What are you looking for?" Hudson asked.

"I want to see what a sewing machine would cost," Caitlin said. "I'm not very good with hand sewing, and I thought a machine might help."

"We can do that Saturday," Hudson said.

"Why can't you use the one you've got already?" Bert grumbled.

"I don't have a sewing machine," Caitlin exclaimed.

"Yes, you do," Bert said. "It's in the office."

Caitlin and Hudson gave the old man a look of confusion.

Bert stomped through the house, shaking his head and grumbling as he was followed to the office. He went straight to a cabinet and opened several drawers. They watched as he opened compartments and displayed a Minnesota Sewing Machine. "I bought this for my Pansy a year before I lost her. It's a top-of-line deluxe drophead model and probably still is. The instruction books should still be in one of the lower drawers. Pansy was right proud of owning this machine!"

"I can see why," Caitlin exclaimed, opening the drawers. I thought it was a beautiful piece of furniture." She found an instruction pamphlet in the bottom drawer. She turned around and hugged Bert. "I didn't know it had a sewing machine hidden inside! Thank you! Now I need to figure out how to work it!"

"I'll leave that for you," Bert said. "Before you arrived, I carried a trunk to the attic. It was full of cloth goods and women's do-dads. You're welcome to it. It used to be right there by the machine. Like I told you when you bought the house, it came with everything in it."

"Thank you," Caitlin repeated, giving Bert another hug and kiss on the cheek. "You're so sweet to me!"

"Now, don't get all mushy with me," Bert grumbled. "I'll be here tomorrow for supper. Tell me if you need anything from town so I can get on about my business."

"He's the sweetest man," Caitlin said when Bert was out of hearing range. She grabbed Hudson's hand and dragged him to the stairs. "Help me find the trunk!" She checked the time on her brooch watch and thought she had plenty of time before the quiche would be ready.

Hudson dutifully followed and shook his head at his wife's enthusiasm. He hadn't been in the attic before, and it was crowded with trunks, crates, and boxes. "What the hell?" Hudson exclaimed when he saw a rack of rifles leaning against some boxes.

"There were guns everywhere!" Caitlin complained, opening a small trunk and then closing the lid. "The bullets, for them, are in that green box."

"You've got to be kidding me!" Hudson said, walking over to the small trunk and opening it. With a heave, he picked up the trunk to carry downstairs. He turned to his wife before leaving the attic. "Don't touch those rifles!"

"I wouldn't," Caitlin said. "Bert was trying to teach me how to shoot, but I haven't had the time to practice since I got the girls and then married."

Hudson reached over, checked a rifle, and found what he

suspected. The rifles were loaded. He shook his head again. "Did Bert tell you to store this arsenal up here?"

"No," Caitlin said, opening another trunk and closing the lid when she didn't find what she was looking for. "Bert said to put them somewhere safe. I thought the attic would be safe. I didn't want them around the girls."

"So you stored explosives in the attic in the heat of summer?" Hudson exclaimed.

"Oh! This must be the trunk Bert was talking about!" Caitlin exclaimed with a smile over her shoulder, ignoring her husband's words. "Aren't these fabrics pretty!"

"I'm more concerned with explosives," Hudson said, realizing that his city-bred wife had no idea of the danger she'd put herself and the girls in. He reopened the trunk she had closed and felt through the layers of cloth before closing the lid. "Downstairs!" he barked. "I'll take care of this mess. Are there any more guns in the house?"

"Only the rifle behind the coat tree in the foyer, a revolver hidden in the closet, and my little Derringer in the drawer of the table in the parlor," Caitlin said. "Bert was teaching me how to shoot, but I wasn't very good at it. Since we married, I think he forgot about teaching me."

"Downstairs," Hudson ordered, lifting the trunk filled with fabric.

"I wanted to check the other trunks," Caitlin protested.

"Not until I check and double-check the munitions," Hudson said firmly. "When I finish with that, we're going to have a discussion about weapon safety."

"I did something wrong, didn't I?" Caitlin asked.

"Yes, but I'm not blaming you," Hudson said. "This is Bert's fault!"

"He told me to put the guns somewhere safe," Caitlin said again, following Hudson downstairs. "I thought the attic would be safe."

"Honey, I'm not blaming you," Hudson said. "Don't worry about it, and save me some supper."

"Where is Papa?" Charlotte asked at the table.

"He asked to be excused, and he is doing something upstairs," Caitlin answered. "Tell me about your day at the Brokehalls'."

Caitlin listened to the girls describing their day, but she also heard Hudson making trip after trip, up and down the stairs. He was using a side door and carrying rifles and crates into the barn.

After supper and washing the dishes, Caitlin asked the girls to spend extra time on their school lessons.

Hudson made a final trip to the barn, and Caitlin heard him hammering on something. Then he returned to the house through the kitchen door and washed his hands at the sink pump.

"Finished?" Caitlin asked while she plated a large portion of quiche for him.

"That was quite an arsenal of weapons Bert left behind," Hudson said. "I stored them in the tack room and nailed the door shut. He and I are going to have a talk about him leaving them behind. We don't need that many weapons in the house, especially in a house of curious little girls. You need one or two rifles and one handgun for protection, and it won't be that pitiful excuse you call a weapon. I'll teach you how to use them."

"My little Derringer is a real gun," Caitlin said.

"Not in my opinion," Hudson said sternly. "Since you won't be going to town by yourself, you don't need to carry a pistol in your handbag."

"I'm not going to be a prisoner in my own home," Caitlin protested.

"I agree, and Bert can't be around all the time either. I've given this problem some thought. One of our foremen has a son, and he's about fourteen or fifteen. He's finished schooling, but Magnolia doesn't hire boys under sixteen. Jesse is big for his age, and I'll talk to his father about him working here, doing the chores, driving you and the girls into town, and keeping an eye on the place when I'm gone. I went hunting with Jesse and his father last fall. The boy is a damn good shot."

"I haven't had any trouble since I moved here," Caitlin protested.

"That's true, but trouble usually rides in unexpectedly," Hudson warned. "Sheriff Benson rode out to Magnolia last week with a warning. There have been several hold-ups in the last couple of weeks. Except for strangers, he's dropped his rule about guns in town."

"So, it's acceptable for a boy of fourteen to carry a weapon, but it's not acceptable for a grown woman?" Caitlin said.

Hudson nodded. "Now, you're getting the idea, and I'm not saying I won't teach you how to shoot a gun. I will, but you're not a man. You're a small woman, and you look younger. Even if you were holding a weapon, you're not much of a threat. A good-sized boy like Jesse Cole carrying a rifle would give a drifter second thoughts before trying to rob a house full of females. It's either hire Jesse, or you and the girls come with me in the mornings to Magnolia Ranch, where I know you'll be safe."

"All right, but if I don't like this boy, you'll have to find someone else."

"He's a good kid. Give him a chance," Hudson said.

* * *

THE FOLLOWING EVENING, Hudson showed up with the boy he introduced as Jesse Cole. Caitlin looked upward in surprise. The so-called boy was a broad-shouldered young man, nearly level with her husband's height of six feet, four inches.

Hudson showed the boy around the property, explaining his chores and duties, the most important being a driver and guard for his wife and daughters. The boy was settled in an unused room off the kitchen.

When Bert showed up for supper the following evening, Hudson took him outside to the barn for a man-to-man conversation about the guns.

Bert was surprised. "I didn't tell her to store them in the attic! I told her to put them in a closet out of sight when she took down the gun racks."

"We're dealing with a city-bred woman here, Bert. The only gun she'd ever touched before was a little palm pistol. That little two-shooter is so poorly made that it might have blown up in her hand if she had fired it. I emptied the damn thing and threw it in the burn barrel!"

"I didn't know," Bert said. "I used to be a collector, but now I don't have any use for them. It ain't like the old days when a man was always packing."

"I have my own collection, and according to Sheriff Bensen, those days might be back," Hudson said. "Talk to Rob Ellison. He might either buy them from you or sell them for you."

"I'll see about it," Bert promised. "Keep them under lock and key until I can move them."

"I nailed the tack room door closed," Hudson said.

It only took a few days for Bert to remove all the weapons. Rob Ellison bought the lot for what he considered a reasonable price. Jesse Cole was working out well. He was well-mannered and taking on the chores around Rose Hill. He also helped teach Caitlin how to use a revolver and a rifle. After several sessions, she could hit the target. It was not a bulls-eye, but she did manage to hit the target.

Caitlin and Maisey were learning how to operate the sewing machine.

Rose Hill was settling down with daily routines. Monday

through Thursday were regular school lessons for the girls. If the weather was good, Caitlin would take her paints and easel outside to work on her paintings. She would also encourage the girls to draw. Fridays had become a day to go into town to visit friends and shop, and the last two days of the week had become days to visit Magnolia Ranch or invite friends for dinner. When they went to the ranch, Jesse visited with his family. The boy was so large that it was sometimes hard to remember that he was just a youngster himself.

Angus made himself available to spend time with Caitlin and the girls. He learned quickly that any discussion that included bad-mouthing Bert or suggestions about using the Rose Hill property would shorten the time spent in his company. One thing his daughter had inherited from her Ballard parentage was stubbornness.

One evening, when Hudson came in from work, the first thing he did was have a whispered conversation with Jesse. Then he suggested Caitlin and the girls go into Tyler the next day because he'd be at the Magnolia Farm trying to defuse a worker/supervisor problem.

"Can we go to the bookstore?" Maisey asked.

"I don't see why not," Caitlin said.

"I've got some errands to run for my Ma," Jesse said. "She gave me a list for the next time we went to town. Getting my Pa off Magnolia is like pulling teeth!"

Caitlin smiled at the boy. "You'll have plenty of time to shop while we visit."

"I'd like to be there, but I'm needed elsewhere," Hudson said.

Jesse dropped Caitlin and the girls off at Nell's house. The girls played with the baby while the women exchanged news with each other. When baby Benjamin was put down for a nap, Caitlin suggested it was time for them to go to the bookstore and the mercantile. They would visit Eleanor at the Rusty Pot for dinner.

James Bennett was glad to see his sponsor, and he pulled out three books from under the counter he'd been holding for Caitlin.

"How is business?" Caitlin asked.

"So far, so good," James Bennett said with a smile. "I have regulars, like yourself, who stop in whenever they are in town. I'm not making a fortune, but I'm not going broke. It helps that I'm across the street from the train station. Instead of milling around and stretching their legs, the passengers come here to buy a book to read while traveling."

"I'm glad it's working out," Caitlin agreed. "Come along, girls, we have other stops to make."

The next stop was the mercantile, where they were greeted as friends by the Ellisons, and Caitlin left a list of supplies they would pick up on their way out of town.

Walking next door to the Rusty Pot café, Caitlin was holding the door open for the girls when she caught sight of a woman in mourning black. She paled and shuddered, looking over her shoulder.

"What is it? Eleanor asked.

"Nothing," Caitlin denied. "I thought I saw someone, but it can't be her."

Eleanor stepped outside and looked across the street. "I don't see anyone but old Mrs. Yates."

"A woman wearing mourning black?" Caitlin asked.

"That's her. She lost her husband a few years back," Eleanor said. "She's probably on her way to the cemetery. She goes there almost every day, although she usually goes early in the morning. Go on in and take the big table at the window. If anyone else comes in, tell them I'll be back in a few minutes."

Caitlin guided the girls to a table and assigned Naomi to read the chalkboard with the menu of two meals listed. Today's choices were beef or lamb, and there were plenty of vegetables offered. She kept looking out the window and realized she'd been scared by the woman in black. Just seeing her had brought up bad memories of Beaula.

The bell over the door rang, and Caitlin looked over, expecting it to be Jesse.

"Jilly!" Caitlin exclaimed, jumping to her feet and running into the arms of Jilly Mason. She burst into happy tears.

"Now, now, calm down," Jilly exclaimed, hugging the young mistress.

"I didn't expect you to return, but I was praying you would!" Caitlin exclaimed. "Oh, come meet my family."

The bell over the door rang several times, and Caitlin pulled Jilly aside. "Come meet our girls, and we'll get our dinner ordered."

There were quick introductions, and their dinner orders were given to Eleanor. Caitlin hugged her friend again. "Tell me what you've been doing?"

"I've been busy," Jilly reported. "Now that Lincoln has recovered, he doesn't need me hanging around. He's working at a bank now as a security guard. Della is working in a bakery. Now that their lives are back to normal, I figured it was time to see what trouble you've been getting into."

"When did you get here?" Caitlin asked.

"Yesterday," Jilly admitted. "That nice Mr. Daniel Foster at the hotel sent a message to your husband that I was here."

"And he never said a word to me, but he sent us to Tyler today, and you are my surprise," Caitlin exclaimed, hugging the only true mother figure she'd ever had. "You'll meet Hudson later."

"Oh, you've written enough to me about him! I think I could pick him out of a crowd," Jilly exclaimed. "I've only been gone a couple of months, and you've already snagged a husband and three daughters!"

"Along with a father, a grandfather figure, and many good friends," Caitlin bragged.

The bell over the door rang again, and this time, Jesse walked to the table.

Jilly turned to Jesse. "And, who are you, young man?"

"I'm the hired help, ma'am," Jesse admitted. "I do whatever needs to be done around Rose Hill; that ain't women's work, and keep these ladies safe."

"A jack of all trades," Jilly announced with a smile. "I like a young man who stays busy."

"Have you got a spare room for one more?" Jilly asked Caitlin.

"We have plenty of rooms," Caitlin said with a smile. "We have a six-bedroom house and only use two of them."

* * *

"So, we've added another person to our family?" Hudson said later that night when the girls, Jesse and Jilly, had all gone to bed.

"Maybe," Caitlin agreed, snuggling into her husband on the parlor sofa. "Jilly was my protector from Beaula for many years. She's the closest I've ever had to a mother. She's already said she'll go home once she is assured that I'm happy, but as far as I'm concerned, she can stay forever. Not only did her son Lincoln recover, but his wife Della is expecting a baby. I'm afraid she'll want to return to Philadelphia to help with her grandbaby."

"Are you happy with the life you've chosen here?" Hudson asked seriously.

"Very happy," Caitlin said, kissing her husband.

Jilly fit into the McFarlane household easily. She rose early and had a delicious breakfast ready when her hosts gathered in the kitchen the following morning.

"Jilly, you are our guest," Hudson scolded.

"I've been working since I was twelve," Jilly exclaimed. "I don't know what to do with myself if I don't have something cooking. Tuck in and enjoy."

Breakfast was enjoyed, but Caitlin insisted that she and the girls would do the clean-up. Hudson rode off toward the farm, and Jesse went outside to complete his chores. When the girls were settled in the office reviewing their schoolwork, Caitlin sat across the kitchen table from Jilly and took her hands in hers.

"Tell me the truth," she insisted. "How are you and your family doing?"

"I've written every week," Jilly said with a smile. "Those doctors were wrong, but it took them several weeks to admit it. A younger doctor took over Lincoln's case, and he said it wasn't his heart at all. It was something he called a gut reflux. We common people know it as heartburn or a sour stomach.

"That young doctor suggested we change Lincoln's diet, and he sent my son home with a long list of foods he can't eat anymore. It took Della and me several weeks, but we figured it out. Once we got Lincoln eating what the doctor advised, he's been improving daily. He's lost weight too, and he needed to lose it.

"Honey, I didn't come out here to spill our woes. The Mason family is doing fine. I talked to that lawyer, Mr. Deveraux, about stopping those monthly bank vouchers, but he said he wasn't authorized to do it! Those orders have to come from you."

"I won't stop them," Caitlin said firmly. "That money is for whatever you want to use it for, and I hope it makes your life easier."

"Well, it did pay off those hospital bills," Jilly admitted. "But, honey, you don't owe me nothing. I was paid by your aunts."

"Not nearly enough to put up with Beaula's meanness for all

those years and for protecting me," Caitlin whispered, and she began to cry.

"Honey, are you happy?" Jilly demanded.

"I am," Caitlin said honestly. "Hudson is very protective. But the sad part is that I occasionally jump back from my husband's touch. I'm expecting him to pinch or grab me hard enough to leave bruises. When he reaches to stroke my hair, it bothers him that I draw back. I'm not afraid of Hudson. He's never given me a reason to be. It's a leftover response from living with Beaula.

"He was angry when I told him about Beaula and how she treated us. He's been a kind and wonderful husband to me and a good father to the girls. We have our little spats, but doesn't every couple?"

"Yes, they do," Jilly said with a smile. "I'm glad you found a man that won't let you get away with misbehaving."

"I don't misbehave," Caitlin protested, laying her face on Jilly's shoulder.

"Oh, honey," Jilly said with a smile and a light smack to Caitlin's bottom. "The tales I could tell about the revenge plots you enacted on Beaula are epic. The only reason I didn't stop you was because she deserved it."

Caitlin winced. "Can we keep that part of my past a secret?"

CHAPTER 13

*H*udson was late coming home from Magnolia Farm. The better part of the day had been wasted talking the farm foreman out of quitting. He had pulled all the workers together and tried to settle the differences between the men in charge and the permanent workers. He put two men on probation and fired the man who seemed to be the leader of the trouble.

Three steps from the back door, Jesse stepped out of the little storage room attached to the back porch with a cocked revolver.

"Sorry," the boy mumbled, lowering the weapon and disappearing behind the closed door.

Moving around the kitchen quietly, Hudson found a covered cast iron pot half full of something that smelled good.

The door to the housekeeper's room opened, and a large woman wrapped in a flannel wrapper joined him.

"Since Jesse didn't shoot you, I'm assuming that you are Caitlin's husband?" the woman said.

"You assume right," Hudson said. "Can I assume that you are Jilly Mason?"

"I am," Jilly said, joining him at the stove and stirring the stew. "This is barely warm."

"I've eaten worse, and there's no need to fire up the stove to reheat it. I'm hungry enough to eat the pot," Hudson said, watching the woman fill a large bowl and set a half-dozen saucer-sized biscuits on the table.

"Coffee or milk?" Jilly asked.

"Milk will do if there's enough left for the girl's breakfast," Hudson said, digging into his supper. "Why are you sleeping in the housekeeper's room? You're our guest."

"I'm too old and stiff to climb those stairs," Jilly said. "I've spent the last three decades working as a cook. Caitlin tried to get that boy to take a room upstairs, but he said he couldn't guard the house from there. We'll get him sorted out tomorrow."

"Jesse is doing his job," Hudson said with a grin. "How was your trip? I wanted to meet you in Tyler, but something came up."

"Caitlin explained," Jilly said. "And you were doing your job."

"Well?" Hudson asked.

"Well, what?" Jilly asked, buttering a biscuit.

"Are you satisfied that my wife is happy? Do I cut the mustard?"

"You'll do," Jilly agreed. "My girl is happy, and knowing that makes the trip worth it. She deserves happiness, but she also needs a firm hand sometimes."

"I agree," Hudson said with a chuckle.

"How is she getting along with her father?"

"She is holding her own," Hudson said. "I know everyone excuses Florence as a weakling, but one letter or telegram would have made a lot of difference in Florence's life and Caitlin's. Angus would not have abandoned either. I know that for a fact. Angus met Florence after his marriage had turned

167

into a disaster. The woman he thought was his wife turned out to be a hustler. Even so, he paid her to disappear and raised her daughters as his own."

"I haven't met the man," Jilly admitted. "I'll judge him when I meet him. I started working at the Ridgeway Estate when Caitlin was just a youngster. I saw right away that something was awful wrong in that house."

"You would have quit working in that hellhole if you hadn't decided to stay and protect me," Caitlin said, entering the kitchen. She kissed Jilly on the cheek and was pulled into her husband's lap for a kiss.

"What have I told you about swearing?" Hudson growled.

"The girls are sound asleep and can't hear me," Caitlin said. "Anytime I speak of Beaula, it should be with nasty swear words. Did you get everything settled at the farm?"

"Right now, it's more of a stalemate. I'll check in again in a couple days. If they resort to fisticuffs again, we'll hire some new workers," Hudson reported. "Did you like your surprise?"

"It couldn't have been better," Caitlin admitted, beaming at her husband.

"We can talk tomorrow," Jilly suggested. "It's been a long day for me."

Even though it had been a long, hard day, Hudson wasn't about to ignore his husbandly pleasures. A single man for years, he enjoyed making love to his wife. Physical pleasure could be slow and delightful, or it could be fast and hard. Caitlin usually let him guide her, but tonight, she set the pace, and he thought it was because she'd been delighted by Jilly's appearance. He had nothing to do with her friend's return except receiving the telegram and suggesting it would be a good day to go to town.

In the darkness of their bedroom, he enjoyed her arousing him until he needed her desperately. Then Caitlin relinquished control to him and wanted him to use her body as his personal playground.

Hudson took his wife at her word when she whispered what she wanted. He roamed over every inch of her beautiful body. Kissing her with a hunger that needed to be quenched, he entered her body with a slow, deep plunge.

Caitlin gasped at her first orgasm and moaned during her second.

Hudson's mission was to satisfy his wife. When she was in a frenzy of passion, he turned her over and entered her with a deep thrust. Gentleness was cast aside as they wanted their desires to be sated. They came together, a union of needs to be satisfied. His body was rigid, seeking release, as Caitlin was compliant with however he wanted to use her. Pleased as lovers and partners, they fell asleep in each other's arms.

Sequestered in the Ridgeway Mansion and treated as a servant, Caitlin hadn't made female friends. The ladies in Beaula's circle occasionally brought their daughters to the house, and Caitlin was expected to serve the guests.

Listening in the background, Caitlin was appalled that most of those unmarried girls were allowing their parents to choose their future spouses. They were marrying for social standing and wealth. Love was rarely cited as a reason to marry.

When the social gatherings were over, Caitlin and Jilly would talk about the overheard conversations. Jilly claimed that a man wasn't worth his weight if he married for money, and neither was a woman.

Caitlin tried to shake off her unsettling thoughts. She loved Jilly, but her appearance had resurrected bad memories. The past was the past, and it was over and gone. Nor, she realized, would she have wanted to change the past if it meant missing out on what she'd gained since moving to Texas.

She added Angus to her mental list of family and new friends in her groggy sleep, although they were still tip-toeing around each other. Turning over, she felt Hudson tuck her closer to him, and she smiled. Her life changed when Florence finally admitted her motherhood with the strokes of her signature on her last will. The Ridgeway fortune had freed Caitlin. It had also made Jilly's life easier in her time of need and Bert's, although the stubborn old goat wouldn't admit it. She doubted that Bert lacked money, but he was missing love and friendship. Now, he was saturated with love and respect with the McFarlanes in his life.

Caitlin awakened when Hudson left their bed. "It's barely dawn," she complained.

"I have a full day ahead, and I'm meeting with Angus first thing this morning," Hudson said, kissing her.

"What about breakfast?"

"Mrs. Brimmer always knows when to expect me and the other foremen," Hudson said. "Behave and stay out of trouble."

"You say that every day," Caitlin teased. "When have I ever caused you trouble?"

Hudson leaned over, kissed her, and gave her bottom a rub and a light smack. "You've been trouble from the first day I met you. You vamped me, and I've been *in love* ever since. I still want you to behave and be careful."

Breakfast was loud, with the girls trying to talk over each other and Jilly scolding them for their lack of manners. When the dishes were done, and the girls were settled in the office for their lessons, Caitlin asked Jilly if she would watch the children while she rode her horse to a patch of her property where a half-dozen peach trees had been planted.

"Didn't I read in your letter that Bert sold this property to you because he didn't want it turned into a peach orchard?" Jilly asked.

"That's true, and part of the feud between Bert and Angus is that Angus planted trees on Bert's property without his permission. It was a test to see if the trees would grow. The trees have flourished over the years, and so has their feud. Bert's not one to waste, though. He's already brought me several bushels of peaches. I canned them like you taught me. I want to pick the last of them before the season ends."

"Take Jesse with you," Jilly said.

"No, Jesse has chores, and I'd rather he stay around here. The peach trees are only a short distance from Bert's cabin. That was one of the reasons he was so angry about the trees being planted. Augus tried to steamroll over Bert, but he didn't get away with it. I made Bert promise not to cut them down when I bought the property because I thought I could use or sell the fruit. Bert should be home today, and I'll be fine."

"I don't like this," Jilly said. "Shouldn't that boy be escorting you? I heard in town that there have been several hold-ups recently."

"Jesse has chores, and I won't be gone for long. We've lived here for months now, and we've never had any problems," Caitlin assured her friend. "I'll be back in a couple of hours."

"Two hours," Jilly said firmly, pointing her finger. "If you're not back in two hours, I'm sending that boy to look for you."

Caitlin agreed, although she still thought Jilly's worrying was unnecessary.

It was a quick trip to the peach trees. Caitlin could see the roof of Bert's cabin in the distance. She quickly realized she should have driven the small horse-drawn cart as she had done before. She had stood on the wagon bed for height.

This time, she'd come by horseback and climbed into the small trees to reach the fruit. The job required constantly climbing up and down in the trees because the fruit had to be handled gently.

Placing three peaches into her sack carefully, Caitlin looked around, wondering if there was an easier way to complete the job.

She mounted her horse, Bucky, and guided him under the

tree limbs, where she found picking the fruit was easier. She had half a sack full when Bucky jolted, knocking Caitlin off balance. She screamed as she tumbled out of the saddle and landed flat on her back. Before she could recover her breath, there was a feral hissing growl, and her horse bolted.

Gasping for breath, Caitlin sat up but stopped breathing again as she saw a bobcat not six feet from her. The wild cat moved closer, and Caitlin grabbed a peach and threw it at the animal. She didn't hit the cat, and it didn't attack. It streaked away in a fraction of a second and disappeared in the tall weeds.

Regaining her breath, Caitlin tried to stand, only to fall back onto the ground.

"Ohhh... ouch!" She moved her foot and wiped her tears at the pain. Scooting over to a tree trunk, she used it to help her stand but couldn't put any weight on her foot. Looking around the small stand of trees, she didn't see her horse anywhere. He'd been spooked by the sounds of the bobcat, not that she blamed him.

She glanced toward Bert's cabin, but her foot and ankle hurt too much to walk that far. Next, she screamed a few times, but either the cabin was too far away for him to hear, or Bert wasn't home.

Glancing at the tall weeds every few seconds, she picked up a broken branch to fend off the bobcat if it came back.

There was nothing she could do except wait for Jesse to come find her.

* * *

When the clock hands marked two hours, Jilly hollered for Jesse and told him to go looking for Caitlin.

Jesse saddled a horse and headed to Bert's cabin. He wasn't overly concerned about Caitlin until he spotted her horse heading toward Rose Hill, saddled but without a rider. Then he kicked in his heels and rode like the devil himself was after him to catch Bucky.

Hudson stepped in through the kitchen's back door and then took two steps back to get out of the way as Jilly carried a blackened, smoking skillet outside. He hadn't returned home to a burnt meal offering in a while. It hadn't taken his wife very long to learn the skills of providing a decent meal.

"Where's Caitlin?" he asked, following Jilly back inside.

"She went to pick peaches, and she was supposed to be back by now," Jilly said. "I sent Jesse to look for her."

"What time did she leave?"

Jilly looked over her shoulder at the clock hung on the kitchen wall. "She was supposed to be back an hour ago."

Hudson nodded but went through the house to a room he'd turned into a small office. One glance told him that the rifle his wife was supposed to carry when she left the house by herself was still on the gun rack over the fireplace. Angry now, he unlocked a wooden box, strapped on a hip holster, loaded the revolver, and stuck a small box of bullets in his shirt pocket.

Hudson knew the exact location of the test trees since he and Caitlin had previously discussed her picking the fruit. They were on Rose Hill property, but she was supposed to be with Bert or Jesse if she wanted to ride a distance from the house. He'd spoken twice with the Sheriff recently. His men had found evidence that drifters had been camping on Magnolia property.

Caitlin must have been in one of her moods again. They'd talked several times about the safety of a single woman being miles away from help. She didn't seem to understand that some men weren't the kind and helpful sort. Sheriff Bensen did his best to encourage the jobless and vagrants to move along, but his job was primarily to protect the town of Tyler. Bert had been her protector when she'd first bought the property. Now that she was married, the old man spent less time at Rose Hill.

Hudson caught up with Jesse, who was leading Caitlin's horse. "Where did you find her horse?" he demanded.

"Over by Bert's gate," Jesse said. "He's been spooked bad and was hard to catch."

"Have you been to the trees yet?"

"No," the boy answered.

"Let's go," Hudson said.

They rode toward the trees, and even at a distance, Hudson saw his wife sitting on the ground in the shade of a peach tree. He dismounted, handing the reins to the boy.

Hudson walked over to his wife. "What the hell were you doing out here by yourself?"

"Waiting for someone to come and help me," Caitlin said honestly. "I lost my seat when Bucky was scared by a bobcat. At least, I think it was a bobcat. It wasn't much bigger than a house cat, but it scared Bucky. Me, too, but it ran away and hasn't returned."

Hudson nodded toward the sacks. "Are those full?" he asked.

She nodded, and he picked up the two sacks, carried them over to Jesse, and slung them over the back of his saddle. "Take these back to the house and her horse," Hudson ordered. "Tell Jilly to make sure the water reservoir is full. I'm bringing Caitlin back, and she will need a bath and some first aid."

"Yes, sir," Jesse said. "Boss, Mrs. McFarlane didn't tell me she was leaving."

"She will from now on," Hudson promised.

"Yes, sir," the boy mumbled as he turned to leave.

Hudson returned to Caitlin.

Standing with his hands on his hips and barking out orders, Caitlin knew her husband was angry. "I think I sprained or broke my ankle," she explained.

Hudson squatted beside her as she pulled the left side of her riding skirt up. "I can't get the boot off."

Hudson tried to pull off her boot, but she was gritting her teeth in pain. He went back to his horse and brought back a canteen of water. Pouring it inside the boot, he tried to ease her foot out, but she was still in pain, and tears were running down her cheeks.

"Just pull it off!" Caitlin said.

"It's going to hurt," he warned. "I can cut the boot off."

"I've only had these boots a few months. I don't want to ruin them."

"You can afford to replace them," Hudson growled.

It hurt, even as Hudson tried to cut through the leather. Caitlin sucked in her breath and thought for a few seconds she was going to faint, but the boot finally gave way. Her ankle, now freed, was swollen and throbbing.

"Damn it," Hudson swore when he saw the swollen and bruised ankle. "What the hell have you done to yourself?"

"I'm the one that's hurt," Caitlin snapped. "Why are you angry?"

"I'm pissed, there's a difference," Hudson said, gingerly feeling her ankle. She jerked away from his probing touch.

"I hope it's just sprained," she said.

"I'm pretty sure it's broken," Hudson corrected her. "That means you'll have an uncomfortable ride back to the house, and then I have to take you into town to see Dr. Martin. We'll discuss your not following orders later."

"I'm not one of your hired workers," Caitlin snapped.

"No, you're my wife, and I won't allow you to ignore what I think is best for you," Hudson said.

"This was an accident," Caitlin exclaimed. "I didn't want the peaches to go bad."

"I don't care about the damn peaches," Hudson growled.

"I'm more concerned about you not sending Jesse to pick the fruit and you not carrying a rifle."

"I said I was sorry, and I did take a gun. I took the revolver."

"Sorry is a lousy excuse," Hudson warned. "And, so far, you haven't managed to hit one bulls-eye with a revolver."

Caitlin shut up because she knew the words he spoke were valid. She'd also left without telling Jesse where she was going. Although she had told Jilly. Even she had to admit Hudson's anger was justified.

The trip back to Rose Hill was slow and jarring to her ankle and silent. Hudson turned the horses over to Jesse, and he carried his wife inside, where she was immediately pampered by Jilly.

"Get her cleaned up and dressed, and I'll wrap the ankle," Hudson said. "I'm going to take her to Tyler to see Dr. Martin. He will have to decide whether her ankle is sprained or broken. Pack a bag for us because we might have to spend the night."

"You've done it this time," Jilly said in a hushed voice when Hudson left the kitchen.

"He's angry," Caitlin agreed.

"He has the right to be," Jilly scolded.

* * *

THE TRIP to Tyler seemed twice as long. Unrestricted from the leather boot, Caitlin's ankle had swollen more and was throbbing. Hudson took her straight to the doctor's office. He went back outside and lit a cigar, something he rarely did. When the door finally opened, Caitlin stepped out on crutches.

"The ankle is probably broken, but I can't cast it until the swelling goes down," Doctor Martin said. "Soak the foot in cold water tonight and bring her back in the morning. Sprain or broken, she'll be on crutches for about six weeks. He gave

Hudson an envelope with powders wrapped in paper and suggested she use them if the pain worsened.

Hudson swept his wife into his arms and carried her outside to the wagon. "We'll be back in the morning. We'll spend the night at the hotel."

Dr. Martin followed them outside and tucked a set of crutches into the back seat of the buggy. "Keep that foot in cold water. Once the swelling goes down, I'll know if it's a sprain or a broken bone." He shrugged his shoulders, "Sprains versus small broken bones are hard to diagnose. I can't see through the skin and muscles."

"I'll keep an eye on it," Hudson promised. He drove the buggy to the hotel and carried Caitlin to their room. "I'll be back in a few minutes. I have to take the buggy to the livery, and then I'll go to the Rusty Pot for dinner. Eleanor can fix us something."

Hudson did what he promised, but Caitlin was becoming uncomfortable. Her husband was barely speaking to her. He was talking to her, but it sounded like he was barking orders. Hudson had never been this angry with her since they had married.

"I'm sorry," Caitlin whispered.

"Are you?" Hudson asked. "I don't ask much of you, Caitlin. I do expect you to respect me enough not to defy my wishes. I am the head of our home. It's my job to support and protect our family.

"I do respect you!" Caitlin exclaimed.

"Do you? I took our vows seriously. Our vows weren't just words spoken before a Justice of the Peace to make our marriage legal."

"I meant them too," she whispered.

"Good, because when we get home, I'm giving you a spanking that you won't forget for a while. If you had listened, you wouldn't have been hurt and wouldn't be in trouble!"

CHAPTER 14

*H*udson woke in the darkness of night and realized the sounds he was hearing were Caitlin crying. He sat up, lit the lantern, and turned his wife to face him.

"What's wrong?" he demanded.

"It hurts," Caitlin whispered.

Hudson pulled back the covers. He couldn't see under the bandage, but he could see that the binding was loose, and her ankle was purple and black from bruising. Bolting from the bed, he poured a glass of water and opened one of the powders Dr. Martin had given him.

"Sit up and take this," he instructed, offering the pain medicine. "Wet your mouth first, then pour them on the back of your tongue. Follow that quickly with water and swallow."

"Ack!" Caitlin choked but cleared her throat with the water.

Hudson looked at the clock on the mantel. "It's three a.m. I'd hate to wake Dr. Martin, but I will if that powder doesn't help. I've had it before, and it should make you sleep." He grabbed an extra pillow and lifted Caitlin's foot carefully onto it. Then he pushed his bed pillow against the headboard, sat up against it, and pulled her into his arms. He kissed the top of her head. "I'll get you to the doctor's office when daylight breaks."

"I'm sorry," Caitlin whispered. "Jilly is going to skin me for being so careless."

Hudson tightened his arms around her. "She'll have to get in line. I don't know how long Jilly expected to stay, but you will need help. By the way, what is Jilly's real name?"

"I don't know," Caitlin said, sounding sleepy. "All I know is that she hates her name and refuses to tell anyone what it is. I asked her son Lincoln once, but he said he didn't dare tell me."

Hudson made himself comfortable as Caitlin drifted into sleep. He didn't know what was in those powders, but they'd had the same effect on him when he'd needed them a few times over the years.

In the morning, Dr. Martin changed his mind. He was now sure that Caitlin's ankle was broken. He wrapped her foot in strips of muslin and plaster, warned her to stay off her foot as much as possible, and told her to continue to use the crutches.

When they arrived at Rose Hill, he carried Caitlin into the house and parlor, followed by Jilly and the children, who were all asking questions.

"Calm down, everyone," Hudson said firmly. "Caitlin will not be on her foot for a couple of weeks. She will need help during that time, and we'll all be here to supply her with that help."

"Does it hurt?" Charlotte asked.

"Yes," Hudson said before Caitlin could answer. "I expect all of you to help Momma as much as possible. Is that understood?"

Heads nodded all around.

"Maisey, would you please run upstairs and bring down a couple of pillows and a blanket. Momma will spend a couple of days here on the couch, and I'm sure you girls will be helpful and not let her get up or try to walk. If she does try to get up, I want you to run and tell Jilly," Hudson said, to more head nods and a smug look from Jilly.

"Charlotte, Naomi," Jilly said, getting the girls' attention. "Go into the office and get your schoolwork. You can do it in here today while watching over Momma."

"Dr. Martin gave me these medicine packets," Hudson said, handing over the powder packets to Jilly. "She can have one every six hours or so. Most likely, she'll sleep after taking them. I've had broken bones before, so I know what to expect. Caitlin should be able to get around on the crutches in a couple of days. She couldn't keep breakfast down because of the pain this morning, but she needs to eat."

"I'll see to her," Jilly promised. "You'd best be getting to work. I'll take care of everything here and bring a tea tray immediately. Tea always settles her stomach."

"Thanks," Hudson said as Jilly left the parlor. He kissed Caitlin gently on the forehead. "You should be feeling better in a little while. I've got to talk to Angus about what was decided yesterday at the farm. Behave and get some rest while I'm gone."

"Are you still mad at me?" Caitlin whispered.

"The mad has settled down to concern," Hudson said. "I should be back by supper time."

Caitlin had never had a broken bone before, and she found it painful and annoying. The powders she took helped, but they also made her sleep. She hated being dependent on everyone, and keeping the girls focused on their schoolwork was challenging. Jilly could read and do primary sums, but her handwriting was almost indecipherable. The only history she knew was of her family, who had been fugitives of the War of the Rebellion. They had been part of the Great Migration north to avoid the repercussions of the poverty conditions of the southern states.

Angus surprised Caitlin on the third day, visiting her at

Rose Hill. He arrived at the front door, demanding to see his daughter. Bert disappeared out the back door to return to his cabin.

Angus stayed several hours, scolding Caitlin for being careless, and promised to do his best to ensure Hudson was home on time every evening while she was laid up. Introduced to Jilly, he thanked her for being there in his daughter's time of need and for being her support when she lived with the Ridgeway aunts.

When Angus left, Bert reappeared with a plucked chicken, and Jilly invited him to a fried chicken supper, which was his intention.

Caitlin was restricted to the first floor during the day until Hudson came home. He carried her down the stairs in the morning and upstairs in the evenings to bed. After the first week of being on crutches, most of the pain subsided, and she was hobbling around and resumed some of her duties as wife and mother. She was teaching the girls and helping Jilly in the kitchen with the jobs that allowed her to sit while doing them. Peeling potatoes and prepping vegetables wasn't her favorite chore, but she could do it sitting at the table.

Bert was coming around more often and helping Jesse with his chores. He spent a lot of time in the kitchen with Jilly and seemed to be finding excuses to be at Rose Hill. Bert and Jesse had returned to the small peach orchard and picked what remained of the ripe peaches. Bert's wife had done a lot of canning, and there were shelves of empty glass jars in the pantry. Jilly canned the peaches.

Caitlin was fed up by the third week of hobbling around on the crutches. When Hudson rode off for work, she dropped the crutches, wrapped her cast in an old pillowcase so it wouldn't get dirty, and went to the closet where her painting supplies were stored. She carried her easel outside to the rose garden, followed by the girls carrying her supplies.

When Hudson arrived home early, he was met by a furious Jilly. She was upset that Caitlin wouldn't listen to her. Well, that wasn't news to Hudson. He went to the office/schoolroom and was surprised that his wife wasn't there. When he asked where she was, Charlotte pointed to the window. When he walked over to look outside, he saw his wife standing without the support of the crutches in front of an easel.

"How long has she been out there?" he asked.

Maisey looked at the clock on the fireplace mantle. She didn't want to tattle. "She's been out there for a while."

"How long?" Hudson asked again.

Maisey raised guilty eyes. "Over three hours."

"How are the lessons going?" Hudson asked as a general statement.

"Spelling is hard," Naomi complained. "I got five words wrong!"

"That's not too bad," Hudson said.

"There were only twelve words in the test," Maisey said. "Momma said Naomi has to keep writing the words she missed over and over until she can spell all of them correctly.

Hudson nodded. "I think Momma is right. You ladies, keep studying. I need to have a few words with Momma."

Caitlin heard the footsteps behind her and turned to face Hudson.

"It's a beautiful painting," he acknowledged. "Where are your crutches?"

"I left them on the porch."

"The bone hasn't had time to mend," Hudson scolded.

"My ankle isn't hurting anymore, and I can get around without them."

"I don't doubt it, but Dr. Martin has been doing his job for thirty-some years. I think he knows more about broken bones than you do. You're also not setting a good example for the girls."

"I get enough of that from Jilly," Caitlin complained. "I love her, but she and Bert are driving me crazy!"

Hudson walked over to the sitting area and returned with two wooden chairs to where she'd set up her easel.

"Sit!" he ordered. "We all want what is best for you, and I know it's not setting well with you, but it's for your own good. If you fall, it could set your recovery back to the beginning or damage your foot permanently. You have an appointment next Monday, but I have to go to Tyler tomorrow, so if Dr. Martin has the time, he can look at it."

"Why do you have to go to town?"

"Mr. Thomas at the train station sent a courier to Magnolia with a telegram. Abigail, Angus' younger daughter, is arriving tomorrow for a visit. I'm not sure what her relationship with Angus is at this point," Hudson said.

"Why isn't Angus going to pick her up?"

"Because he's at one of our outlying camps, that's a four-day ride. I've sent a rider with the news, but it will take him four days to get there and the same back.

"Abigail knows she's not kin to Angus, doesn't she?"

"Since they left to live with their mother until they married, I would think so," Hudson said.

"I don't think Angus' daughter is going to think highly of me," Caitlin said. "She'll probably think I'm after his money."

"Who knows what kind of trouble she's up to. Angus has already told them that they aren't going to inherit Magnolia," Hudson said. "I don't know what was said, but Angus returned disgusted with them.

"Most likely, she and Emma have decided to fight Angus for Magnolia, although they don't have any right to it. Both times his daughters have visited in the last twenty years, they wanted money. The only time I met them, they were hoity-toity and thought they were better than everyone. Snooty as hell!"

"You don't like them," Caitlin said with a laugh.

"I only met them once, and no, I didn't. Emma and Abigail were snobby, obnoxious, and greedy like their mother. I met Louise several times at a distance. She kept coming back, wanting money. The problem with trying to help someone who doesn't deserve it is that if you fall for their 'pity me' excuses once, they'll keep coming back for more. Louise came around several times, but Angus finally sent her packing. She didn't come back, but that was because she died.

"Angus didn't marry for love. He married because his father wanted male offspring to pass on the ranch. That didn't happen, and Angus didn't know love until he met your mother."

"Why do you want me to meet this Abigail. You don't like her, and she doesn't sound like someone I would like!"

"I don't particularly. It's a coincidence that you need to see Dr. Martin, and I have to pick up Abigail at the train station. Still, you meeting them is unavoidable, and I would prefer to be present when that happens," Hudson said.

Caitlin smiled and leaned over to kiss him. "You're trying to protect me."

"That's my job," he admitted. "We'll worry about that tomorrow. Right now, I'm taking you inside, and if you argue, sitting on a wooden buggy seat tomorrow will be uncomfortable."

"My ankle isn't hurting," Caitlin protested.

"It's not your ankle you need to worry about right now," Hudson grumbled.

* * *

Leaving early the following day, Caitlin was Dr. Martin's first patient. The doctor didn't remove the cast, repeating his warnings to Caitlin about using the crutches. He warned her that walking on the cast could damage the fracture. Rather than listen to another scolding, she promised Hudson she'd keep using the crutches. While they were in town, they visited with Nell and the baby and then went by Ben's office and invited them to lunch at the Rusty Pot.

The next stop was at the bookstore, and James was glad to see Caitlin. He'd heard the gossip about her accident and was relieved to know she was recovering. The bookstore was making enough profit for him to repay Hudson's loan and leave him enough to live reasonably well. He even admitted that he was courting Eleanor Foster.

Dinner at the Rusty Pot continued with everyone informing each other what they'd been up to for the past few weeks. Hudson was watching the clock. When it was time for the train to arrive with Abigail, they said their goodbyes and headed for the train station. He settled Caitlin on a bench and went inside the station that also served as the post office, picking up the Magnolia mail.

Returning, he joined Caitlin with the news. "The train is running twenty to thirty minutes late," he said.

"Are the trains ever on time?" Caitlin asked.

"Not often," Hudson said with a smile. "It gives me time to scold you again."

"I'd rather sit here and enjoy the sunshine in peace," Caitlin said.

The eastbound train was forty minutes late. When it finally pulled into the station, two women, not one, disembarked. The porter unloaded several trunks and satchels.

Hudson didn't recognize the women, but they were the only passengers to leave the train. He approached them. "Would you be Emma and Abigail Ballard?"

"Emma Stratton, and this is my sister Abigail Norris," one of the women nodded. "Have I met you before?"

"Yes, you have, but that was nearly fifteen years ago. I'm Hudson McFarlane."

"Are you the boy that worked with my father the last time we visited?" Abigail demanded.

"I am," Hudson said. "I'm afraid Angus won't be back for a few days, but I can take you to Magnolia Ranch, and you can settle in there. It may take a few days for him to return."

"We sent him a telegram announcing our arrival," Emma exclaimed.

"Unfortunately, it arrived after he'd left," Hudson said, turning to the porters. "Jack, Hank, would you put their trunks in the back of the buggy?"

"Sure thing, Hudson," the porters said with smiles.

The women weren't traveling light, and Hudson was afraid that meant they were planning on staying a while. When the luggage was stored in the buggy, he steered them toward the platform bench.

"Emma Stratton, Abigail Norris, I'd like you to meet my wife, Caitlin McFarlane," Hudson said.

"You are the woman who claims to be our father's illegitimate child?" Emma exclaimed.

"Yes, I am," Caitlin said calmly. "And, you are the offspring of Louise Gibbons and your mother's real husband, Buck Lambert. My understanding is that you are not related to Angus. It's a tricky situation, isn't it?"

Emma Stratton, the oldest of the two women, looked furious at Caitlin's words. She raised her hand, but Hudson stepped between the women. "There will be none of that," he said, making Emma back off a few steps.

Abigail's chin and nose rose in an arrogant gesture. "Take us to the hotel. We'll stay there until our father returns. When Angus returns, inform him we are here."

"Not a problem," Hudson said amiably. He turned his back to the two women and spoke quietly to Caitlin. "Why don't you visit with Mr. Thomas while I take these two to the hotel." He turned back to the two women. "Wait here until I help my wife inside. As you can see, she is on crutches."

Caitlin smiled at Hudson and whispered, "Now I know why Angus doesn't speak of them as his daughters anymore. They have the manners of black widow spiders. Now I feel sympathy for him."

"Keep that to yourself and behave," Hudson warned.

Hudson left the sisters in the buggy while he went inside the hotel. "Where have you been, friend?" Daniel Foster exclaimed with a smile. "We need to get together for a hunting or fishing weekend."

"That sounds good," Hudson agreed. "I have the Ballard sisters outside. They want rooms until Angus comes to fetch them."

"Do I have to house them?" Daniel asked. "The last time they were here, they insulted my cleaning ladies, and they quit. I don't want that to happen again!"

"I can't force you to house them," Hudson said. "That's your choice, and this is your business. Give it to them straight. You'll toss them out in the street if they don't follow your rules. I wouldn't mind witnessing that myself."

"I don't want Angus mad at me," Daniel said.

"It's your business," Hudson repeated. "You don't have to accept their insolence or their attitudes. You make the rules."

Daniel stood up straighter and puffed out his chest. "You're right, and I will set them straight this time."

Hudson went back outside to help the sisters from the buggy and caught the attention of a man he knew on the sidewalk. His friend lent a hand in carrying the stack of satchels and trunks into the lobby. Hudson left the sisters there with a wink and a tip to his hat at Daniel.

"What do you mean we have to share a room!" He heard Emma exclaim at the desk. He stuck his foot out so the door wouldn't close and he could listen to the exchange of words.

"Just what I said," Daniel said. "This is my hotel, and I make the rules. Take it or leave it. I don't care. And, this time, you'll pay up-front and carry your bath water and luggage upstairs."

"How dare you," Abigail exclaimed.

"Take it or leave it," Daniel said. "I own the only hotel in Tyler! You're welcome to go to Harriet Wilder's boarding house. She always has empty rooms, but complaints will get you thrown out. They'll get you kicked out of my hotel too!"

Hudson smiled. He wasn't fond of Angus' daughters, and they had mistreated him. He could have dealt with it, but they had also been snotty to Nell, and she'd only been twelve.

Emma was the worst of the two. She had made fun of them for being orphans. He hadn't told Angus about their mistreatment for several years, and when Angus heard of it, he apologized for their behavior.

The daughters had only stayed two weeks at Magnolia Ranch and had not made any friends on the ranch or in the town of Tyler. Everyone had been relieved when they'd left town. Fifteen years later, the sisters wouldn't receive a parade for their return. Most of the town and ranch residents wouldn't welcome them. Personally, he hadn't forgotten how they had treated him as a youth, refusing to address him by his name and calling him 'you boy' when they addressed him.

Hudson returned to the train station and found Caitlin eating a large square of chocolate.

"Try this," she exclaimed. "We have to stop by the mercantile and get some of this. It's delicious! Are the sisters settled?"

"I left them in Daniel's care, and they are not my problem," Hudson said. "They have decided to stay at the hotel until Angus returns."

The rest of the week was quiet. Caitlin gave up her battle with the crutches and accepted there was no way around using them without being scolded or spanked. Yes, Hudson had spanked her, and it wasn't a playful or sexual spanking. It hadn't been hard, but it had stung enough that she didn't want to risk another.

The Ballard daughters showed up at Magnolia Ranch several days later. Daniel had evicted the sisters from his hotel after only two days. They were also banned from the Rusty Pot, belonging to Daniel's sister, Eleanor. The only other place to eat in town was the saloon.

"They moved their belongings to Harriet Wilder's boarding house but hadn't learned a lesson. After two days of constant complaints, Harriet tossed them out of her boarding house with their luggage. With nowhere else to go, the sisters hired a buggy and a driver from the livery and were taken to Magnolia Ranch.

Hudson had his hands full in Angus' absence. He'd sent word to Angus, and it shouldn't have taken the rider more than a couple of days to reach him. When one of the hands sought him and told him he was needed at the main house, he trotted to the main house, assuming Angus had ridden long hours to return home.

He was wrong. Mrs. Brimmer was sitting on the porch with two suitcases. "What's wrong?"

"I want you to take me to Tyler," Mrs. Brimmer exclaimed. "I will not stay here and be at the mercy of those two horrible women!"

"What did they do?" Hudson asked.

"I'll not repeat what they said, and I will not cook and clean for them!" Mrs. Brimmer declared. "If you don't take me to Tyler, I'll walk!"

"Are you quitting?"

"That will depend on Angus," Mrs. Brimmer said. "I've worked here for twenty-two years, and I've never been treated so disrespectfully. Those two women are the spawn of the devil, and I will not tolerate their impertinence!"

"I'll take you wherever you want to go, Mrs. Brimmer, but

please don't quit," Hudson agreed. "Rufus is in barn one or two. Would you walk over there and tell him to hitch a buggy and load your suitcases. I'll be with you as soon as possible. I want to lock Angus' office."

Mrs. Brimmer nodded her head in agreement. "That's a good idea, and I'm sorry I didn't think of it first."

Hudson entered Angus' office, but Emma and Abigail had beat him to it. They had already opened the drawers to Angus' desk.

"Ladies, I suggest you remove yourselves from this office," Hudson said.

"You can't tell us what to do," Emma snapped.

"I can, and I will," Hudson said.

"You can't..."

"Shut up and do as you're told," Hudson ordered. "Leave this room, or I'll have you on the afternoon train heading west."

There was a stare-off, and the threat worked. Abigail was the first to stomp out of the office.

"We'll see about this when Angus returns," Emma exclaimed, with her nose tilted so high that she would have drowned if she'd been rained on.

"Yes, we will," Hudson said. "I'm putting an armed guard in the house. You are allowed in the parlor, the kitchen, and your bedrooms. You are not allowed in any other rooms until Angus returns. You are not allowed to move or break anything. If you do, you will pay for it. If you don't follow my orders, I will put you on the next train out of town, and I won't be particular about where it goes."

"You can't..." Emma spat.

"I can do anything I damn well please," Hudson snarled. "You have been given your restrictions and been warned. Follow them or pay the penalty. If you make any messes or destroy anything, I'll put you in the cellar where the hogs used to be kept!"

Hudson slammed the office door closed. He walked over to Angus' desk and opened the bottom drawer. Pulling out a metal box, he set it on the desk and produced a key from his pocket. Then, he opened the safe and deposited the cashbox and a few ledgers inside. Looking at the paperwork the women had scattered over the top of the desk, he removed a few envelopes, adding them to the safe. He put the papers back in desk drawers and locked the desk drawers. Angus would have to straighten out the mess when he returned. He locked the desk and deposited the key back in his pocket. Hudson spun the safe lock and tested it several times to ensure it had locked correctly. Crossing the room, he left the office, locking the outside entrance.

Walking around to the front of the house, he saw Mrs. Brimmer sitting rigidly on the buggy's seat. He stopped to talk to Rufus, his second in command.

"I want an armed guard on Angus' office, and I do mean armed," Hudson repeated. "Those women are restricted to the parlor, the kitchen, and the bedrooms they use. They are not allowed in any other rooms. The guard is to follow them from room to room and not let them separate. They are to retire at no later than nine o'clock at night, and I want a guard stationed in the hallway outside their old rooms. They are not allowed to leave their rooms for any reason until morning, and if one leaves, the other has to do the same. Do not let them separate. Even if they go to the outhouse, it is to be together. If they cause any trouble, lock them in the cellar."

Rufus' eyes widened at the orders. "Yes, sir!"

Hudson climbed into the buggy seat and tipped his hat to Rufus. Mrs. Brimmer was silent, although she looked over her shoulder several times. When they reached the road to Tyler, he stopped the buggy.

"Do you have any particular place you want to go?" Hudson asked.

The housekeeper shook her head and wiped her eyes.

"I have an idea," Hudson said. "Why don't I take you to Rose Hill? We have plenty of room, and Caitlin will welcome you with open arms."

Mrs. Brimmer shook her head. "I heard you have company."

"Our guest is family, and so are you," Hudson said. "You filled the role of mother to me and Nell for almost two decades. Caitlin and I will welcome you into our home as a family member."

Mrs. Brimmer wiped her tears again and patted Hudson on the knee. "Thank you. It would be rude for me to decline your offer."

Hudson covered her hand with a squeeze and smiled. "You helped to raise us. I remember all those scoldings and those swats when no one was looking. I can also use your help to keep Caitlin off her broken ankle!"

CHAPTER 15

*H*udson pulled the buggy to a stop at the front door of Rose Hill. He turned to Mrs. Brimmer. "Mrs. Brimmer, give me a minute to tell Caitlin you are here. She hates being slowed down by the crutches."

Mrs. Brimmer nodded. "I think it's about time you called me Gladys."

Hudson smiled and kissed her on the cheek. "That may take some practice." He burst into the house calling for Caitlin and Jilly. The women came from two different directions, at different speeds, as his wife had heeded his warnings and was using her crutches.

"What's wrong?" Caitlin exclaimed.

"I have Mrs. Brimmer outside in the buggy. She's left Magnolia Ranch and needs a place to stay until Angus can straighten out his daughters and teach them manners," Hudson said in a lowered voice.

Caitlin turned to go outside, pushing open the screen door and stumping across the front porch on crutches. "Mrs. Brimmer, please come in!"

The housekeeper hurried to the porch. "My goodness, what have you done?"

"I fell off my horse," Caitlin admitted. "Come in, please. Mrs. Brimmer, this is my friend and foster mother, Jilly Mason. Come in, and we'll get you settled."

To her surprise, Mrs. Brimmer was welcomed into Rose Hill without explanation. She was taken to the parlor, where Charlotte came running, hugged her, and introduced her sisters again. Jilly said she would bring a tray of coffee and tea.

"Where should I put the luggage?" Hudson asked from the doorway.

"We have several unused rooms upstairs. Take whichever one suits you," Caitlin told the woman.

"Any room is fine," Mrs. Brimmer said to Hudson. "I'm grateful I won't have to stay at the boarding house."

"I've heard that Harriet Wilder is strict, but I haven't met her yet," Caitlin agreed with a laugh. "You're welcome to stay as long as you wish, Mrs. Brimmer."

"Please call me Gladys. I have known Harriet for years," the housekeeper said. "She is persnickety about who stays in her house and won't put up with disrespect. I may be here for a while. Why Angus puts up with those two horrible women is beyond understanding."

"Angus doesn't strike me as a man who would put up with a lot of nonsense," Caitlin said.

Mrs. Brimmer shook her head. "What you don't know..."

Hudson poked his head into the parlor. "Mrs. Brimmer, uh... Gladys. Your bags are upstairs in the blue room, third door on the right. I've got to get back to Magnolia."

"Thank you," the housekeeper said, standing up and hugging Hudson. "You've always been a good boy."

"Yes, ma'am," Hudson said, knowing he was blushing at her words. No one had referred to him as a boy for a very long time.

"I'll do my share of the housework and cooking while I'm here Mrs. McFarlane," Mrs. Brimmer assured her hosts.

"Nonsense," Caitlin said. "I'm Caitlin, and I see no reason for formality. I am a little useless now, and your help would be appreciated."

"Come into the kitchen, and I'll send you out with a jar of coffee," Jilly said, and Hudson followed her.

Hudson spoke quietly, "Jilly, Mrs. Brimmer has been the housekeeper and cook for Angus for twenty-two years. I didn't get a complete explanation of what Emma and Abigail said to set her off, but I did catch them red-handed going through Angus' office. If you can get her to tell you what those women said to her without prying too much, I would like to know. Please allow her to help with the cooking and cleaning as much as she wants. She is not the kind of woman to sit around and be waited on. I have known her for years, and she's one of the best. Right now, she needs a little bit of pampering."

"Don't worry," Jilly agreed. "I'll care for her and keep Caitlin off her feet!"

"Thanks, but don't run yourself ragged," Hudson said, accepting the quart jar of coffee she handed him. "I'll be back around seven."

Hudson drove the buggy back to Magnolia Ranch, spoke to Rufus, and headed to the house. Leon Wilson, a cattleman, wasn't happy about his assignment. The Ballard women had already threatened his job and had even claimed they would have him arrested. Hudson assured the man that his job was not in jeopardy.

The Ballard sisters were arrogant and rude, but Hudson had no problem putting them in their place. His next stop was to talk to Rufus and devise a rotating schedule for guard duty day and night. He didn't trust the sisters to not violate Angus' privacy again. Hudson was good at judging people and didn't trust the sisters. They were up to no good, but he wasn't responsible for figuring out what. Repeating his warnings to the women, he returned to work supervising the men who made and kept Magnolia one of the finest ranches in Texas.

Going home that evening after a long day, Hudson was presented with a delicious supper. The three women seemed to be getting along, and there were no complaints, not even from the children. The only chip in his amiable evening was that Bert was at their table, although he was getting used to it. If the old guy was going to supply fresh fish, chicken, and wild turkey to their table, he couldn't complain.

Mrs. Brimmer settled into the household, and between her and Jilly, the women kept Caitlin off her ankle as much as possible. His wife didn't stand a chance against the two older women. The women at Rose Hill were getting along, and Hudson's only problem was remembering to call Mrs. Brimmer by her first name. It was hard to break a sixteen-year habit.

When he checked with the guards the following morning, the women under house arrest attacked him verbally with enough profane language that would have earned his wife and daughters a trip to the woodshed. Hudson told Emma and Abigail bluntly that they had choices. They could accept the restrictions, return to Tyler, or go home.

Emma was the most outspoken. When she asked Hudson, *'Who do you think you are?'* He answered her truthfully. "I'm the man in charge. I am responsible for Magnolia when Angus is busy or out on the range. If you have a problem with that, take it up with him."

"Oh, we will," Abigail threatened. "And you'll be the one who will be thrown out and arrested!"

"Ladies, and I say this facetiously, you have outstayed your welcome," Hudson snorted. He tipped his hat and walked away.

"Can she have you arrested?" Caitlin demanded that evening when she heard about the latest threats.

"I guess they could try, but I don't see Sheriff Bensen getting involved in what he calls a Domestic Dispute. I'm doing my job. I doubt I will be kicked out."

* * *

HUDSON WAS UNSADDLING his horse when Angus stormed into the barn one morning.

"What the hell is going on?" he demanded.

"What took you so long to get here?" Hudson demanded.

"I had business to finish," Angus growled. "I bought the Fergman ranch. What the hell has been going on with Emma and Abigail. They said you've had them under an armed guard since they arrived."

"I have," Hudson admitted. Then he explained the sisters being kicked out of the hotel and the boarding house and Mrs. Brimmer quitting.

"What? Why did Mrs. Brimmer leave?" Angus demanded.

"Because they are rude, ill-mannered, and demanding. Gladys refused to jump to their every whim. She's at my house now, helping to keep Caitlin off her broken ankle. I caught Emma and Abigail in your office, going through your desk and your paperwork. I kicked them out, locked your safe, desk, and office, and put your daughters and your office under guard. You may think Emma and Abigail are ladies, but the way they have been behaving, they take after their mother. They've been acting trashy, and both need a trip to the woodshed.

"They are here for a bigger slice of Magnolia, Angus, and don't pretend you don't know it. They tried to intimidate Caitlin, but she was having none of it. They called her illegitimate, and she fired back that Louise wasn't legally married to you, and they aren't your daughters at all.

"Handle this as you want, but it's about time you stopped pretending and faced the facts. Emma and Abigail are just like their mother. Louise was never shy about telling the truth, no matter who it hurt or who was destroyed by it. Emma and Abigail haven't treated you decently for the last two decades, maybe longer, but I wasn't around then. Now, they are trying to swoop in, claiming they have a right to Magnolia. That's pure greed.

"I know you kept them as smaller children rather than them being raised by a whore, and a card shark, but it didn't work. They're trying to blackmail you into giving them something that doesn't belong to them. You tried, Angus. You know what has to be done. Don't let them use you or try to destroy what you've spent your entire life building."

"I loved those girls, even after discovering they were Lambert's and not mine," Angus said. "Louise poisoned them against me. I can see Buck Lambert in them now as they age."

"They probably see it too," Hudson said. "You shouldn't have told them you plan to leave Magnolia to me. I kinda wish you hadn't told me."

"Well, that's not going to change," Angus said. He looked over to the ranch house and rubbed his chest. "But, there will be some changes made to the will. Emma and Abigail left Magnolia before I met you. They have never shown any interest in the ranch or the farm except to write asking for money. Now, it's none of their business." He squared his shoulders. "Go home, Hudson. Tell Mrs. Brimmer I'd appreciate it if she would come home once Emma and Abigail are gone. Magnolia is where she belongs."

"I'll tell her," Hudson said. "By the way, what happened to the breeding stock you went to purchase?"

"They are on their way. If they don't arrive by Saturday, you'll need to be here Sunday," Angus said. "They are big, but slow."

"Keep the guards until you're rid of them," Hudson advised.

"I can handle them," Angus said. "It's about time I put them in their place. When Emma and Abigail left, they broke the ties that held them to Magnolia. They are Louise's daughters, and she admitted the truth in writing when I paid her off. I tried to be generous, but they are just like their mother. Greedy and always wanting more. I've had enough, and now they've embarrassed me in front of the whole town! They aren't my daughters, and they need to return to their fancy husbands. They don't belong here."

Hudson nodded his head in agreement. Angus was working up a temper. It didn't happen often, but you didn't want to be in his line of fire when he exploded. Emma and Abigail would get an earful, and he hoped he'd be there when it happened.

* * *

"So, are they going to leave?" Caitlin asked. Hudson was explaining his conversation with Angus. The girls had been sent to bed except Maisey. She was in the office reading because she was allowed to stay up an extra hour.

Hudson detailed his conversation with Angus with the women.

"I can't see them going without a fuss," Caitlin said.

"You've never seen Angus mad," Hudson said. "When he goes off, it's duck and pray time. He wants you to return, Mrs. Brimmer, although he's accepted that you won't return until Emma and Abigail are gone. Now is a good time to wrangle a raise from him."

Gladys smiled. "I've never complained about my salary, but then I didn't have to deal with those obnoxious creatures. I'd only met them once before, but I was too new to complain. And shame on you. It wouldn't be Christian to take advantage of Angus' problems."

It took two days of arguments and accusations before Angus sent for Judge Albertson, the county law, and the man who had drawn up his previous wills. The armed guards in the house were still intact.

Emma and Abigail received a dose of hard reality. Regardless of what their husbands had told them, the two women were not blood relatives of Angus, and he had proof. He did not 'owe' them anything. Louise Gibbons had signed an affidavit stating not only was she still married when she married Angus, but both of her daughters were fathered by Buck Lambert.

Angus' so-called daughters would now be written out of his will altogether. Angus sent a rider to bring Judge Albertson to Magnolia to compose a new will. He didn't inform the women of the changes except to tell them they had been written out! The Judge wrote the new will and validated it with his signature and the signatures of a half-dozen Magnolia men as witnesses.

Greed, the *Lambert* sisters learned the hard way, would get them nothing, and Judge Albertson assured the women the will was unbreakable, except by Angus.

During the ruckus, Hudson stayed away from the main house. He always had plenty of work to do, although he was surprised that Angus hadn't called off the guards after the judge had arrived.

The morning after the judge left, Angus ordered a buggy to be hitched, and he loaded what he now called the *Lambert* women and their luggage and took them to Tyler. The *Lambert* women sent telegrams to their husbands and had to wait several hours before their train arrived. Word spread, as it always did in small towns, and the women spent several uncomfortable hours sitting on the outdoor station bench receiving nosy looks as the town folk passed by, looking in their direction.

The McFarlane family was sitting down for supper when

there was a knock on the front door. Mrs. Brimmer opened the door to Angus with his hat in his hand.

"Mrs. Brimmer, I came to apologize for Emma and Abigail. I don't know if you've been told that although I raised them, they are not my true daughters. I did my best raising them, but they turned out just like their slut of a mother. I have disowned them for their recent behavior, and I apologize for how they treated you. I'm pleading with you to return to your job at Magnolia."

"Of course I will," Mrs. Brimmer said. "Have you had supper?"

"Not yet," Angus said. "I've about starved, as neither of those women can cook worth spit."

"Neither can you," the housekeeper reminded him.

"Yes, ma'am, I know that," Angus agreed. "I'm looking forward to your fix-ins and Magnolia settling down now that they're gone."

"If you're through apologizing, join us for supper," Hudson said behind Mrs. Brimmer. "The food is getting cold!"

"I surely will do that," Angus agreed, hanging his hat on the coat tree.

* * *

CAITLIN WAS WAITING ANXIOUSLY the next day for Hudson to come home. When he arrived, she tried to corner him, but that didn't work because the first few hours were spent with the girls and Jesse.

Mrs. Brimmer had gone back to Magnolia with Angus. When the children were sent to bed, and Jesse and Jilly retired for the day, it was finally private time for the couple.

"Tell me what happened between those women and Angus!" Caitlin demanded.

"What makes you think I know," Hudson teased.

"Because Angus tells you everything," she pounced. "Will they come back? Or try to sue him?"

"I wouldn't think so, but you never know what chiselers will do for money," Hudson said derisively. "What I'm telling you is only repeating what I've been told because this happened before my time.

"Emma and Abigail were babies when Angus discovered that his wife Louise already had a husband and was still sleeping with him in addition to Angus.

"When Angus discovered what was going on, he kicked Louise out. She could have been arrested for bigamy, but he didn't file charges. Angus wanted Louise out of his life, but he didn't want to lose the girls. He decided to raise them as his own. Even though Louise told him they weren't his children, he didn't want to abandon them. Slicing Angus' heart into pieces wasn't enough for Louise. She kept in contact with her daughters and secretly turned them against him."

"How could he prove that he wasn't the father?" Caitlin asked.

"Buck Lambert has a birth defect in his left hand. His ring and little finger were grown together from the knuckle to the first joint. The two fingers had to be cut apart to have use of the little finger. Emma and Abigail had the same defect. Dr. Martin said that fault wasn't common and would run in families. Those women were not Angus' offspring.

"The trip to California was his last attempt to make them believe he still cared for them. He had a will drawn up before he left, and it was generous considering that neither Emma nor Abigail ever made any attempts to stay in contact with him after they left except when they wanted money. When he showed up in California, they initially treated him well. But then they started questioning and demanding to know who would get Magnolia. They thought the property should go to them, even though they hadn't had anything to do with the ranch in over twenty years."

"They were greedy, just like Beaula," Caitlin whispered.

"Yes, and for reasons beyond my understanding, they thought they were entitled to the property," Hudson said. "It was my misfortune that Angus had decided to leave me in charge while he was making a deal for breeding stock. Those women didn't count on me protecting Angus' business and home."

"Three sentences out of their mouths, and I knew they were like Beaula," Caitlin agreed. "Has Angus got everything settled now?"

"This isn't for public knowledge," Hudson said sternly.

"I know how to keep a secret."

"I'm counting on it," Hudson said. "Angus has decided that since I am his heir to Magnolia, he won't keep secrets from me. He has written a new will with the help of his old friend, Judge Albertson.

"Emma and Abigail will get one hundred dollars each, and it's stated in the will that they are not his daughters and have never acted as a family toward him since they left Magnolia. One hundred dollars is a drop in the bucket compared to what he'd previously left them. Their greed and bad behavior have cost them a fortune.

"If they try to contest the will, they will get nothing. It was spelled out in the will why he has changed his mind. Judge Albertson claims the will is written, so it can't be challenged. Angus promised Magnolia will be mine someday, but I'm not concerned about it. I want Angus to live as long as possible. He's the closest to a father that I've had for a long time."

"Me, too," Caitlin agreed.

Hudson frowned. "He is your father by blood."

"That doesn't matter to me," Caitlin said softly. "Family is more than blood. It's accepting love from someone and returning it. I just hope Angus wasn't hurt by those scheming bitches. They ignored him for decades but thought they were entitled to what his family had built over generations. I don't understand how people can think like that!"

Hudson frowned and gave his wife a stinging smack across her bottom. "What have I told you about swearing?

"Ouch," Caitlin howled. "They are, and you swear."

"Don't push me. You won't like the results," Hudson growled. "I still owe you a paddling."

Caitlin ignored his threat on purpose. "As soon as I get out of this cast, we need to start visiting Angus more at the ranch and having him to supper here more often. He's a very accepting man. He took you and Nell in, and he's taken me and the girls in. Angus pretends he doesn't need anyone, but he's wrong. He needs a family to surround him with love."

Hudson wrapped his arms around his wife and smiled. "We'll provide the family for Angus, just as you have for Bert. Now, if we could get those two hardheads to play nice together, it would be a major accomplishment."

* * *

THE FOLLOWING DAY, Bert loaded what he called his womenfolk into a buggy and told Jesse to drive them to Magnolia to help Gladys get the house back in order. Bert told Jesse to visit with his folks and that he would do the chores and keep an eye on Rose Hill in their absence. Bert had heard the entire saga from Jilly. Gladys had been warned by Angus that the house looked like it had been hit by a tornado, a very dirty one.

With all hands given jobs, it didn't take long for the house to be scrubbed clean. The younger girls did the dusting and rug sweeping while Jilly and Gladys handled the bigger jobs. Caitlin was given jobs that didn't have her standing. For the most part, she was ironing and folding linens. Even the office was cleaned, although the paperwork that Hudson had tossed back into locked desk drawers would have to be gone through by the man himself.

Gladys accepted the help and was relieved that 'her' house was again spotless. She enjoyed the company and the assistance. Most of the time, she worked alone.

Angus came in from what he was doing and called it a day, spending the rest of the day talking to Caitlin and playing games with the girls. After a feast of a supper made by Gladys and Jilly, Hudson left with his family, giving himself enough time to get them home before dark. Before he left, he reminded Angus that he was taking Caitlin to Tyler to have the cast removed from her foot the next day.

Caitlin assumed she would regain mobility immediately after removing the cast, but that wasn't the case. There was pain when she put weight on her ankle. Dr. Martin told her it wasn't uncommon because her muscles and joints had been weakened and were stiff. He suggested she continue to use one or both crutches as support until her foot regained its full strength.

"It won't be much longer," Hudson promised. "I've been in a cast before. You'll just have to be patient for a little while longer."

Patience was not a virtue Caitlin was well acquainted with. She wasn't happy, but at least the cast was gone. While in Tyler, she and Hudson visited Nell and little Ben, now a chubby little fellow. Then they made their way around town to see all their friends. Visiting Daniel at the hotel, they heard about the screaming arguments that had taken place in the hotel before he'd thrown Angus' daughters out. He also told them about the scene caused by the women at the railway platform. The women had made a scene, shouting at him and calling him names in public. Angus had told the women he was done with them before driving away.

Emma and Abigail had walked to the hotel and demanded a room, but Daniel had refused them. "I sent them on their way," Daniel said proudly. "And they knew better than to try going anywhere else. Those foul women wore out their welcome in Tyler, and we sent them on their way!" The troublesome sisters had returned to the station and had left on the next westward bound train.

The next stop was visiting with Ben, Nell's husband, before visiting James Bennett at the bookstore next door. The young man was looking fit and proud. He claimed the bookstore was doing well. He proudly told Hudson that his loan would be paid off in six months, not the year they thought necessary.

"James is doing well for a town this size," Hudson said when they left the shop, and he shifted a sack of books they had purchased to his left side so he could use the other to make sure Caitlin didn't trip on the rough, uneven sidewalk. "He made a deal with Mr. Thomas over at the train station. He has a display of books and ten-cent novels that anyone waiting for the next train can purchase. He also made a deal with Daniel at the hotel and has a display in the parlor that can be purchased."

"He can't be making much money on ten-cent novels," Caitlin said.

"Maybe not, but every penny counts. I read in a newspaper a couple of years ago that the publishers of those books make millions. Church-based people were trying to get the government to shut them down. They were claiming that the books were immoral. They must have lost their case because the books are still being sold."

The mercantile was the next stop for supplies, and they stood around talking with the Ellisons between customers. Rob Ellison brought out a chair so Caitlin could sit while she talked with Alma. Caitlin invited them to supper on Sunday, and the couple promised to be there. When they left the mercantile, they met with Nell and Benjamin for lunch at the Rusty Pot.

They were invited to Sunday supper but already had plans. After lunch, Hudson went to the mercantile for their ordered supplies, leaving Caitlin behind to spend a few minutes with Eleanor.

Eleanor gave Caitlin a few more details about how badly the Ballard women had behaved in town before they hired the buggy to take them to Magnolia Ranch. Caitlin invited her friend to Sunday supper.

"May I bring a friend?"

"Female or male?" Caitlin asked with a tease.

"Male," Eleanor reported with a smile.

"Anyone I know?" Caitlin teased.

"The new man in town, James Bennett," Eleanor said with a smile. "Have you met him?"

"Yes, I have," Caitlin said with a smile. "And he's already been invited."

CHAPTER 16

*a*n unexpected cold front settled over eastern Texas in late September. In its wake, the red foliage of the sassafras trees and golden, rust, and orange-colored leaves of the sycamores and hickories made for a beautiful landscape of colors. The rose bushes wouldn't produce again until late spring.

Coats were needed, and Jesse drove Caitlin into town with the girls to get them outfitted for winter. Coats were purchased larger than required to be used for several years. Caitlin had been told that Tyler would get cold during the winter, but not like the East Coast. Snow was rare, maybe an inch in one of the snow months, and it would only last a few hours, as most winter days, temperatures would rise to the low fifties during the day.

Jilly began to drop hints that it was time for her to return to Philadelphia. Her grandbaby was due in late October.

The problem was Jilly didn't want to return to city living. She had never lived in the country before and loved the solitude and the quiet. Even with three little girls and a strapping boy, it was quiet most of the time. She enjoyed being involved with Caitlin, her new family, and their new friends.

Jilly got along with her son and daughter-in-law but not well enough to want to live with them. Getting another live-in position at her age was an idea she didn't like to contemplate.

She knew Caitlin would support her for the rest of her life, but that didn't sit well with her. She'd taken the support when her son was in the hospital and had appreciated every cent, but he was well now and had a better job. Jilly had been self-supporting since her husband had died more than thirty years ago and had left her to support herself and her son Lincoln. As much as Lincoln was her son, Caitlin was her daughter, and Jilly knew Caitlin reciprocated the feelings.

Jilly worried about the situation, and she finally made a decision. Caitlin was doing well and didn't need her protection anymore. She had reconnected with her father and married a good, decent man. She was the mother of three young children who adored her and had the Ridgeway inheritance to fall back on.

When Caitlin stopped limping, a leftover from breaking her ankle, Jilly decided she would return to Philadelphia, and she brought up the subject after supper one evening.

Charlotte was the first to react. "You can't leave us! You're our Grandma!"

"Grandma's don't leave," Naomi cried, jumping from her chair and running around the table to hug Jilly.

"Oh, honey," Jilly exclaimed, pulling Naomi into her lap. "I can't be your grandma. Can't you see I'm different? I'm brown."

"We see," Maisey said, wrapping her arms around Jilly's neck. "We see, but we don't care. You are our grandma."

"Papa, tell Jilly she can't go away," Charlotte cried.

"Honey, I can't tell Jilly what to do," Hudson said. "I don't want her to leave either.

"Neither do I," Caitlin said, wiping tears from her face. "Can we talk about this?" she pleaded.

Jilly nodded, surrounded by tears.

When the girls were settled that night and sent to bed, Jilly faced Caitlin and Hudson.

"I thought you were going back to visit, not to stay," Hudson said.

"I understand you want to see your grandchild, but I thought you were coming back? " Caitlin said. "You don't get along with Della. She only tolerated you when Lincoln was sick because you were helping pay the bills. You said so yourself. That's not your fault, but one of the reasons you came with me to Texas was to let them live their own lives without what Della called interference."

"I can't stay with you forever," Jilly said.

"Yes, you can!" Caitlin exclaimed. "Look around, Jilly. Our children love you. I love you. It was us against Beaula. And why did you bring up your color? It has never mattered before. Never."

"I may have made a mistake in my thinking," Jilly admitted. "I do love all of you."

"We may not be the textbook definition of a family," Hudson said. "But we are a family, and that includes you." He pointed his finger at Caitlin. "Besides, I depend on you to keep my wife corralled and out of trouble!"

"Oh!" Caitlin exclaimed, and she threw a pillow at him. She turned to Jilly. "I need you to help me keep Mr. Know-It-All in check!"

"All right, all right! No fussing," Jilly exclaimed, laughing. "I'll give some more thought to what I said at supper. I still need to visit my son and see my grandchild."

"Of course you do," Caitlin exclaimed, and she hugged and kissed her friend on the cheek. "You can go every year if you want to, but don't forget that we love and need you. And you have to be back before Christmas. Maisey and Naomi haven't had a decent Christmas since they lost their parents. Naomi doesn't remember ever having a Christmas tree, and they were never given gifts."

"Yes, I want to be home for that," Jilly agreed.

"Home," Caitlin repeated. "See? You do think of Rose Hill as your home. We are part of your family."

At breakfast, Jilly explained to the girls that she planned on staying at Rose Hill. But she did have to travel to Philadelphia to visit her son, daughter-in-law, and grandbaby. She would leave in early October and come home at the end of November.

"When do we get a baby?" Naomi asked.

Jilly smiled. "I think that's a question you should ask your Momma and Papa."

* * *

WHILE THE WEATHER around them was changing, so were their routines. At least once a week, Jesse would drive them to Magnolia Ranch, and Angus would make time to spend with Caitlin and his granddaughters. Caitlin mostly listened as Angus reminisced about his courting days with Florence. He remembered Florence as a beautiful young woman.

If Angus was busy, Caitlin and the girls would spend more time with Mrs. Brimmer. So far, Angus hadn't received any mail from the Lambert women, and Mrs. Brimmer would have known if he had.

In return, Angus came to Rose Hill to join the family for Sunday suppers. He still resented Caitlin's friendship with Bert. But the two rivals buried their animosity and behaved at the supper table. Sometimes, if one or the other was particularly antagonized, Jilly would eat with Bert in the kitchen. Even so, there would be no arguing at Rose Hill.

Caitlin was trying to prepare herself to live without Jilly

around to help. She'd never been pampered and was well acquainted with keeping a house clean, but the cooking was another matter. She and the girls could live off her meager efforts, but cooking for men meant dealing with meat, chicken, beef, lamb, and fish. Caitlin could eat meat if it was served already cooked. But preparing the raw meat sent her outside to be sick. No matter how hard she tried, she couldn't stop her reaction to raw meat.

"I'll teach Maisey," Jilly said after sending Caitlin to her bed one afternoon.

"No," Caitlin said firmly. "She's had enough responsibilities piled onto her young shoulders. I want her to enjoy what is left of her childhood. Chores around the house are acceptable but not major responsibilities."

"Then we have two choices. I can cancel my trip, or you'll have to hire help," Jilly said. "I know you don't want to admit to this problem to Hudson, but you can't live off vegetables."

Caitlin raised her head off the pillow, but Jilly stopped her. "I know you and the girls can, but men want meat! Talk to Hudson! I'm supposed to leave next week and won't return until early December."

Caitlin kept putting off talking to Hudson because he was dead tired when he came home from work. Winter was coming, and he spent most of his time at Magnolia Farm as the crops had to be harvested before the first frost. It wasn't uncommon for him to stop at Rose Hill on his way to the farm.

During one of those stops, Jesse talked to Hudson about hiring his sister. He'd overheard Jilly chastising Caitlin and sending her upstairs to her bedroom because she was sick. Hudson didn't understand what Jesse was talking about until he mentioned Caitlin being sick.

Concerned, he went straight to the source, Jilly.

Jilly admitted that Caitlin had a problem but also admonished Hudson. "Now, don't you go flying off the handle. My girl is trying, but sometimes, in life, there are things we can't control. Men as well as women. I don't know why she hasn't admitted this problem to you, but I'd bet you my traveling money that it has something to do with that nasty Beaula Ridgeway."

"Where is she?" Hudson asked.

"Upstairs lying down. It takes about a half-hour or so to settle her sick stomach."

Hudson was halfway across the kitchen when he stopped and turned to face Jilly. "Is this why she's been losing weight?"

"Most likely. My girl is stubborn and doesn't give up easy," Jilly admitted.

Hudson opened the bedroom door quietly and saw that Caitlin was stretched out with a towel covering her face.

"Caitlin."

She sat up and tossed the wet towel aside. "You're home early!"

"Someone told me you are having a problem dealing with raw meat. Why didn't you tell me?"

"Jilly told you!"

"It wasn't Jilly, but she did confirm that you get sick when you're dealing with raw meat. Cutting it up and dealing with cooking it. I'm glad someone told me. What's going on?"

"I know it's stupid, and I'm trying to get over it, but nothing seems to help. If anything, it's getting worse," Caitlin admitted.

"Why didn't you tell me?" Hudson demanded again.

"It's stupid," Caitlin said. "I can't expect you to understand."

"I can't understand if you're hiding things from me," Hudson said sternly. "All you had to say was: *We need to hire a cook while Jilly is away*. Why is that so difficult? Instead, you're forcing yourself to be sick several times a day? You can't keep this up. I've asked you several times why you're losing weight, and you've made excuses. You claimed you weren't when I know you are! How long have you had this problem?"

Caitlin shrugged. "It started before Jilly was hired. Aunt Beaula was on a rant, firing all the servants. She fired the cook and told me it was my job to cook for us. Only, I didn't know how. No one had taught me. I tried, but I was a child, Maisey's age. One day, she brought some meat to the kitchen and told me to cook it. I didn't know how. When she cut into it on her plate, it was raw. She was so angry, I thought she was going to kill me. Beaula tried to force me to eat it. She slapped me when I choked and tried to force the bloody meat down my throat. I was crying and sick, but she wouldn't stop.

"Finally, I bit down on her fingers, and I didn't let go until she was screaming and bleeding. I had a mouthful of her blood, and I spat it out and vomited all over her. She shoved me to the floor and kicked me.

"I couldn't eat for a week without thinking about that blood. I couldn't even keep bread down. Then, Jilly was hired, and I was never forced to try to cook again. Jilly became a barrier between me and Beaula."

Hudson wrapped his arms around his wife and hugged her to him. "Are you still supporting that evil woman?"

Caitlin nodded. "Mr. Deveraux, the attorney, warned me that if I didn't give Beaula something to live on, she could try to take me to court. She is on a tight budget. The small brownstone where she lives belongs to me, and she is fully aware that I can make her homeless with a single telegram."

"And you never told me about this problem," Hudson said.

"Hudson, I hate Beaula, and I won't allow her in my new life," Caitlin whispered. "I will be glad when she is dead and gone. If that makes me a bad person, I can live with it."

"It's understandable, and she can't hurt you anymore," Hudson said. "What isn't acceptable is that you kept this from me. I'm your husband, and you should feel safe confiding in me. I won't hold your past against you. I'm here for you, and I love you. But I'm not going to allow you to keep secrets from me, and I'm not going to allow you to make yourself sick over stubbornness."

"I'm sorry," Caitlin whispered.

"Saying sorry doesn't mean much," Hudson said sternly. "We are supposed to be a team, and you can't keep secrets. We have talked about your past several times. I don't hold it against you, and I try to understand. I'm your partner, and everything that is going on in our lives is my business," Hudson said. "This lesson will teach you that you are not alone." He pulled Caitlin facedown across his lap and smacked her across the bottom.

"No!"

"Oh, yes!" Hudson answered, tossing her skirts over her back, pulling down her bloomers, and exposing her bottom. She was trying to wiggle and squirm away, but he tightened his hold and spanked her bottom with hard, stinging swats.

"Hudson!" Caitlin cried as she struggled to get loose. This was not a playful swat he gave her occasionally. This was a full-out spanking!

Caitlin kicked and cried, but he spanked her harder with stinging smacks.

"Stop!" Caitlin sobbed.

"No!" He continued spanking and lecturing her about keeping secrets from her husband!

Caitlin was crying and having a difficult time listening. Hudson had strong, hard, calloused hands. Her bottom was stinging and burning. Every whack caused her to gasp and cry.

Caitlin was sobbing by the time Hudson yanked her bloomers back in place, pulled his wife into his chest, and let her cry.

"I am your husband," Hudson warned sternly. "I didn't think I'd ever find love again after my Malinda passed, but I found it with you. It's my duty to protect you, even if it's from yourself. I don't care about you being unable to cook meat. I don't give a damn if you never step foot in the kitchen again. We will manage.

"It's your other skills that make you the woman I love. Your endless ability to take in people and care for them makes you unique, and I love that part of you. I'll talk to Jesse's sister, Brenda, and her folks tomorrow. If she wants a temporary job, and her parents will allow it, we'll hire her. Are we clear on this matter? I don't expect you to ever touch raw meat again. Is that clear?"

Caitlin closed her eyes and took a deep breath. "Yes, we are clear," she cried.

"As soon as you feel better, you should apologize to Jilly," Hudson said, getting to his feet and walking to the door. He turned back to look at his wife, who resembled a chastised child more than a grown woman. "I want to see you eating more, and I want you to gain the weight you've lost. I'll be back in a few hours."

* * *

Maisey was setting the table for the dinner meal when Caitlin came downstairs. Breakfast and dinner were the most significant meals of the day because ranchers and farmers needed more nourishment during the day because they worked so hard.

"Are you feeling sick, Momma?"

"A little bit," Caitlin said honestly. "I'll be in to look over your schoolwork in a few minutes. She wandered into the kitchen but kept her eyes away from the dry sink where Jilly had been trying to teach her how to prepare lamb chops earlier.

"Got your fanny whacked, didn't you?" Jilly cackled.

"Why did you tell him?" Caitlin asked.

"I didn't. Hudson already knew something was wrong when

he came to me. I'm glad he did because he needed to be told," Jilly snapped. "It ain't your fault. Some women ain't made for cooking. He asked, and I told him the truth. Something you should have done a while back."

"Did Hudson say anything on his way out?"

"Not to me, but I'll bet he had plenty to say to you!"

That was the truth. Although Hudson didn't mention the subject when he came home from work. Later that evening, though, was different. When they went to their bedroom, he was still scolding Caitlin for not taking care of herself and not being honest with him.

Caitlin sat on the far edge of the bed with her back to him. Suddenly, Hudson hauled her up against his side, kissed her, and gave her a light smack on her already sore bottom.

"Sweetheart, you can be angry, but I've warned you before. I won't tolerate you taking foolish chances and doing things that can get you hurt. Forcing yourself to do something you despise and makes you sick is not acceptable." He gave her another slightly harder smack on her already tender bottom, wrapped his arms around her, and closed his eyes. "I love you, sweet-heart. I will always protect you, even from yourself."

It took a while for Caitlin to relax into her husband's embrace that evening. She listened as Hudson went to sleep and the slight sound he made, not quite a snore, but more of a hissing sound. Her bottom was sore, but Caitlin knew the spanking could have been worse. Her husband was fit and strong, although he was usually gentle with her and the girls. He could be firm and stern when it was necessary.

Most men believed they had the right to discipline their wives and children. There were even laws that supported a husband and father's rights. Women didn't have those same rights. Still, Hudson was careful with discipline. If the girls misbehaved, a swat or two and standing in the corner was punishment enough. He wouldn't embarrass her by standing her in a corner, but he would take his frustration out on her bottom.

"Go to sleep, woman," Hudson mumbled in her ear. "All will be better in the morning."

He spooned into her, and Caitlin felt his muscled body against her own. She closed her eyes, letting the scent of the soap he used envelope her in his warmth. Despite the spanking, she always felt safe in his presence. One of his hands caressed her in his sleep, and she blinked back tears. Hudson, the girls, and the friends she'd made since coming to Texas were what she'd sought all her life.

Hudson woke up to an armful of his woman, and he smiled. Caitlin had almost crawled on top of him. She was lying face down on his chest with her little bottom up in the air. He rubbed that little fanny with his hand, and her eyes flew open. She started to move, but he pulled her back down. "Now, darling," Hudson said, gently kissing her. "We have to settle on what happened yesterday."

"What do you mean?" Caitlin asked.

"I mean," Hudson said firmly, "we talk about what happened yesterday and then move past it. You put your health and maybe your life in danger, and that's not acceptable. I spanked you. It's done, and it's over, and now we kiss and make up."

His hands gripped her hips, lifting her so she was straddling his lower parts. His manhood was hard and hot, and he nudged it toward her. "Are you ready and willing?"

"Yes," Caitlin whispered.

"Good." Hudson rolled them over so he was on top, and he thrust deep into her, taking what he needed but also fulfilling her needs.

It was past daybreak when Caitlin tried to slip from the bed, but Hudson wasn't ready to let her go yet. Giving her a kiss that made her female parts swoon, she gave herself to him again.

They didn't have time for another long lovemaking session, but neither was willing to separate. The same strong hands Hudson used to spank her were now making Caitlin ache with need. Stroking her most sensitive parts, she was ready when he thrust into her again. A primal need for one another was evident and covetous. She gasped when her body shuddered. Hudson buried his mouth in a pillow to silence his groans of satisfaction.

"Caitlin, I need you so much," whispered Hudson as he held her close, enjoying her body, her softness, and her passion.

Caitlin felt a wave of emotion rise for this man she had chosen as her lifelong companion.

Her husband fondled and played with her body. When he was ready again, he rolled her over on top of him and entered her hard and fast. Because she was on top, he smacked her already tender bottom, just hard enough that she would feel the sting. Her bottom was sore, but Caitlin didn't mind. Their mating seemed to go on forever, and she knew she would feel the aftermath for hours.

She lay in his arms for a long time, tired but comfortable.

"I wish I could stay like this for hours," Hudson whispered."

Caitlin leaned over and kissed him but reached for her wrapper. "I wouldn't mind, but that's not likely. The rooster is crowing, and the girls will be awake soon."

Hudson rose up on his elbows. "We didn't have much time together before we married, and I'm still glad you said yes."

Hudson went to work on one of his horses, but returned at midday in a buggy with a young woman beside him. Jesse hugged his sister and carried her sack of clothing into the house. Brenda Cole was introduced to the entire family. She was invited by Jilly to share her room until she left for Philadelphia, and that day was coming closer.

CHAPTER 17

*B*renda Cole was seventeen and planning to marry one of the wranglers on Magnolia Ranch when she turned eighteen. Her parents wouldn't let her marry before her birthday, and they didn't have a place to live. She and her beau, Homer Evans, were waiting for a cabin to be built on Magnolia Ranch. Building several new cabins was on the fourth quarter ranch schedule, but it hadn't been started yet. In the meantime, she would take Jilly's place and earn a wage cooking at Rose Hill. There wasn't much for the wives to do beyond caring for their families on the ranch.

It only took a few days for Jilly to agree that Brenda would keep the family from starving in her absence. Jilly quietly explained Caitlin's aversion to meats but didn't explain the why of the problem. Hudson was still kicking himself for not noticing before.

Caitlin still *'helped'* in the kitchen. She was good at making cakes, pies, and cookies, involving the girls in making and baking the treats. Jilly shooed her out of the kitchen when meat or fish was being prepared. It would be weeks before she began to nibble on meat again.

She also helped with the canning. Bert brought a lot of garden produce for a single man who said he wasn't a farmer. He'd already warned Caitlin that she would have her own garden to tend in the spring.

When it was time for Jilly to leave, she didn't want to upset the children. So she kissed *'her babies'* goodnight and promised to return before Christmas. She dealt with the tears but didn't want to upset the children again. Bert drove her to the train station the following day before they woke.

With the fall foliage, Caitlin spent as much time as she could outside painting. She involved the girls with her hobby, instructing them on their levels of interpreting what they saw onto paper, as she used canvas.

Bert returned from Tyler a week later, delivering a letter from Jilly and a package from Mr. Corman Deveraux, the Ridgeway attorney. Caitlin couldn't help noticing an envelope addressed to Bert in Jilly's jerky handwriting sticking out of his shirt pocket.

When she opened Jilly's letter first, Caitlin discovered her friend was now a grandmother to a baby boy named Ambrose John after his deceased grandfather. She wrote that she was getting along with her daughter-in-law but missed everyone in Rose Hill. Caitlin read the passages where Jilly had written that she missed her girls and looked forward to seeing them when she came home. She was moved by those words. Rose Hill had become home to all of them. Caitlin carried the large envelope from Lawyer Deveraux into the office and left it on the desk. Truthfully, she was a little afraid to read it.

Hudson arrived home with Angus in tow, and they had a good time playing games with the children until supper time. Conversations were always stiff and careful when Angus and Bert were at the same table, but the old-timers wouldn't start a ruckus when they were the guests.

Bert said his goodbyes first and told Brenda he was going fishing in the morning.

Angus hung around talking and reading to the girls from one of their books before they were sent to bed. Then he left, riding back to Magnolia Ranch under a full moon.

Caitlin and Hudson were finally left alone.

"Angus was in a good mood tonight," Caitlin said.

"He's had some good news from Judge Albertson," Hudson said.

"What about?"

"He got a letter from Emma's husband a while back, and it was almost a declaration of war. He claimed that Angus had no right to disown his daughters and change his will and that Emma and Abigail were going to sue him for their rightful inheritance of the Magnolia property."

"That's good news?"

Hudson laughed. "I haven't got to that part yet. The sisters could try, but the law is on Angus' side. A man has a right to change his will any time he wants. He also has the right to distribute his assets as he pleases. Angus forwarded the letter to Judge Albertson and asked him to settle the matter.

"The Judge's response was to warn Emma's husband, John Stratton, that he would ruin Stratton's reputation and political career by making their selfishness publicly known. His response must have scared her husband because Angus received an apology letter from Stratton saying neither Emma nor Abigail would bother him again. I guess their husbands feared for their reputations, as they are political men."

"Why do people have to be so greedy?" Caitlin said, taking a deep breath. "Angus raised Emma and Abigail as his own and gave them everything they wanted. He took them in, knowing their mother and father were worthless, yet they sided with their mother. It was never enough for them, and it's sad."

"It's not our problem," Hudson said. "Let's call it a night."

"There's a package on the desk. I received it this morning. It's from the Ridgeway attorney in Philadelphia, Mr. Deveraux."

Hudson frowned. "What did it say?"

"I'm almost afraid to open it," Caitlin said. "Beaula may be trying to sue me!"

"Isn't he still forwarding money to your Aunt?"

"Yes, the bank is doing that from an account set up for her," Caitlin said.

Hudson rose and went to the desk, and she followed him. Picking up the package and a letter opener, Hudson pulled out several documents clipped together.

"Holy Moses," Hudson exclaimed, sinking into a chair and pulling Caitlin into his lap. "This is a Great Atlantic & Pacific Tea Company bank draft. It's your share of the profits."

"Mr. Bones at the bank will be pleased by it," Caitlin said, looking at the bank draft.

"Before you deposit it with the bank, you need to talk to Angus," Hudson said.

"Why?"

"Because he's the only person I know with that kind of money. You need his advice. Angus doesn't believe in putting all your eggs in one basket. In this case, it means don't put all your money in one bank, and this is one heck of a bank draft!" Hudson said.

"What are those other papers about?"

Hudson laid the bank draft aside and picked up another contract. "This is a purchase contract for a brownstone on Washington Square, Philadelphia." He pawed through several more documents and hugged Caitlin to him. "This is the death certificate and the paperwork for Beaula Ridgeway's funeral."

"She's dead," Caitlin whispered, closing her eyes and dropping her forehead on Hudson's shoulder. "That's why there is a contract on the brownstone. I gave him permission to do so before I left." A single tear streaked down her cheek. "She was the last living relative on my mother's side of the family."

"You have a new family now," Hudson said gently.

"Don't misunderstand these tears for sorrow," Caitlin said, wiping her eyes. "They are tears of freedom. I hated Beaula. If she had a single redeeming quality, I never witnessed it. She was a cruel woman who enjoyed hurting others."

"I'll try my best to shelter you from people like her," Hudson said.

"I'm not a child anymore," Caitlin said, swiping the tear away.

"It's my job as your husband to look out for you," he retorted. "Tomorrow, I'll take you to Magnolia so you can get advice from Angus. If you'd opened this envelope before, he could have advised you tonight and saved a trip."

"I'm not sure I want to share the knowledge of my wealth with Angus. He'll be after me to buy more land, plant peach trees, or buy cattle. We have more than we can deal with now. One good thing from this is that I will write to Mr. Deveraux and tell him to take the money that Beaula was receiving and add it to Jilly's account."

Hudson smiled at her bigheartedness. "But, you still need advice, and you wouldn't get unbiased advice from John Bones. I can sit in and listen when you talk to Angus. I won't let him steer you toward planting a peach orchard, although I still think it would be a good investment."

"I won't break my promise to Bert, even for Angus," Caitlin said. "He stepped into the father position for me before I met Angus, and I won't turn my back on him."

"I'm not asking you to do that," Hudson said seriously. "Just keep giving Angus a fair share of your time. He deserves the chance to be a father to his only daughter."

Angus rode alongside Hudson to Rose Hill that evening, and they had a long discussion about Caitlin's inheritance and the fact that she would continue to receive dividends from the Ridgeway investment of shares in The Great Atlantic & Pacific Tea Company.

Angus suggested that Caitlin open several accounts within a hundred-mile radius of Tyler. Towns that were anchored by the railroad coming through them. He distrusted banks because they could fail miserably under bad management. If a bank closed its doors, all the customers lost their money. That very scenario had happened to his great-grandfather, and he'd nearly lost the ranch. Since then, Magnolia's holdings had been spread out among several banks.

Meanwhile, Brenda and Jesse discussed with Bert how they would be helping Caitlin during Jilly's absence. Hudson had already had a private conversation with Bert explaining Caitlin's *'problem,'* and Bert agreed to bring his offerings of fish or meat ready to be cooked. However, he'd been doing that already with the fish because he'd noticed that Caitlin was squeamish.

One Saturday morning, Bert stopped by, as always, when he was going to Tyler. When he drove away, Caitlin and the girls were with him.

"Can we go to the bookstore?" Charlotte pleaded.

"If we have time," Caitlin agreed. "We need to visit Nell and baby Ben, and then we'll go to the mercantile while Bert picks up the supplies for the animals."

Bert drove them to Nell's house and estimated he would be gone about four hours. He didn't tell her he was going to the saloon for a few hands of Faro with his buddies.

Visiting with Nell was catching up with town gossip and playing with baby Ben. The girls treated him very much like they did their dolls until it was time to change his diaper. When they left, Caitlin made the offer she always repeated. It was an invitation to come for Sunday supper.

The next stop was the bank, where Caitlin withdrew money

from her husband's and her account. Hudson was insistent on supporting his wife and family, regardless of the fact that she was an heiress, and thus far, she hadn't been able to budge him on the subject. Truth be known, he didn't like that they were living in her house, on her property, but as she'd told him firmly, that wouldn't change anytime soon, and he'd agreed.

Living at Rose Hill was also beneficial to him. It was the first time in years that he wasn't the man in charge who was awakened from his sleep if anything went wrong on the ranch. That duty had been switched back to Angus.

The bookstore was the next stop, and they spent a good half-hour there before Caitlin gave the girls five minutes to make their selections. She'd found two books right away and had spent most of her time talking to James.

"I can't thank you enough for helping me and bringing me to Tyler," James said quietly. "I thought I was a failure, and moving here has been a godsend."

"Living in Texas has been eye-opening for me, too," Caitlin admitted. "It's been quite an adjustment moving from Philadelphia, but I love it here."

"Do you miss the city life?" James asked.

"Not at all," Caitlin admitted. "I came here on a mission, not intending to stay, but one thing led to another, and my whole perspective on life and my future changed."

James nodded. "I can understand that. I was just a boy when Chicago burned, and I lost my father in the fire. My mother and I lived in a single room for years while the city was rebuilding. A wealthy politician who didn't live in Chicago donated money to build a library across the street if it would be named after him. People were angry about it, thinking homes and shelters should be built first, but that library became my refuge. It was somewhere warm in the winter. Chicago has fierce winters, and the man who ran the library introduced me to books and literature."

"I was the same when introduced to drawing and painting," Caitlin agreed.

"You paint?" James asked, and a moment of recognition made him smile. "The paintings in the parlor at your home are yours, aren't they? They're beautiful! I was looking at them when Eleanor and I were there for supper. Your maiden name must be Ridgeway."

"It was," Caitlin admitted.

"Do you sell them?" James asked.

Caitlin shook her head. "It's a hobby, and who would buy them in Tyler?"

"I would," James said. "I have an empty wall or two upstairs, and I would be proud to hang a Ridgeway painting. I think others would, too!"

Caitlin blushed. "It's a hobby, but the next time you come for supper, I'll give you a painting of your choice. I can always paint another." Naomi pulled on Caitlin's dress, trying to get her attention. "What, Naomi?"

"Can I have this book?" Naomi asked.

"No, I said two books apiece, and you have already picked your two books," Caitlin scolded. "You'll have to wait until our next trip into town."

"I'll hold it for you," James said, taking the book with a wink at Naomi. "I'll store it behind the counter until I see you again. But don't forget to ask for it because I may forget that I took it off the shelf."

"Thank you," Naomi whispered shyly.

"We have to go," Caitlin said to James. "I'll see Eleanor before we leave town, but the invite for Sunday supper is always open. Are you... Oh, I'm sorry, I'm being nosy."

James laughed. "Eleanor and I are officially courting. I have Daniel's permission."

Caitlin smiled. "That's good news! Please come to supper if you can."

The next stop was the café, although they only had time for a piece of pie for the girls and a few minutes of private whispering with Eleanor because she was busy serving customers.

"I'll check with James later in the week, but I don't see any reason why we shouldn't be able to come," Eleanor said.

Caitlin checked her watch brooch as they walked down the wooden sidewalk toward the mercantile. Suddenly, Maisey stopped, and Caitlin bumped into her. "What?"

"There's that man again," Maisey said, pointing. "The man who asked how old I was at the train station."

Caitlin instinctively gathered her children closer to her.

The man the sheriff had called Chester Brigham stood outside the mercantile, staring at them. Then he pulled his hat down over his forehead and shuffled away.

Caitlin loosened her grip on her girls when he disappeared down an alley. "Let's go to the mercantile. Everyone stay inside, please. You can look but don't touch. I don't want to purchase broken merchandise."

"Can I have a licorice stick?" Charlotte asked.

"I don't like licorice!" Naomi said.

"I don't either," Caitlin said to Charlotte. "I don't like the way it turns your teeth black. I'll give you one penny each for candy if you behave, but not licorice."

"I like licorice," Charlotte pouted.

"One penny's worth, but only if you behave, and it will not be licorice," Caitlin repeated.

"Papa lets me have licorice," Charlotte pouted.

"Papa isn't here," Caitlin said firmly. "And I don't want your teeth looking like they are rotting."

"Can I have a peppermint stick?" Charlotte whined.

"Yes, but whining is not behaving," Caitlin warned.

Bert had already dropped off Caitlin's supply list, and her merchandise was boxed and waiting for her. She went to the small section of the store set up for women's needs. Alma helped her find spools of thread to match fabrics she discovered in the attic. Caitlin was planning to make several dresses for Maisey, who had recently had a growth spurt and had already gained three inches. She also saw a calico fabric in a pattern of sky blue with a pattern of scattered small flowers, and she bought seven yards to make Charlotte and Naomi matching dresses. The now eight-year-olds pretended they were twins, although they didn't look alike.

Hudson would scold her for spoiling the girls, but she didn't care. What was the benefit of having money if you couldn't spend it on the ones you loved?

When Bert appeared with the wagon outside, Rob helped him carry out the boxes of supplies while the girls carried the wrapped packages of books and fabrics.

"Did you win today?" Caitlin asked quietly when the girls were settled in the wagon.

Bert grinned, with a peppermint stick hanging out of his mouth. "I left twenty bucks ahead."

"This week, you won. Next week, you'll lose," Caitlin scolded. "Do you ever break even?"

"It's not about the money," Bert said. "It's about the friendships and keeping in touch with old-timers like myself. Friends are important, especially when you get older and start losing your friends and family. Those left behind become even more important."

"I guess that's true," Caitlin said, leaning her head on his shoulder. "You were a lifesaver when I came to Tyler. You were always there when I needed you. I never had a father or a grandfather, and you filled those empty boots."

"You've got the real thing in Angus," Bert growled.

"Yes, but you took me in first, and I love you dearly," she responded.

"Should I warn Hudson that you have a new boyfriend?" Bert teased.

"He already knows," Caitlin said with a smile, and she kissed him on his cheek. "I have room in my heart for all of you."

Some fall days were still warm, and a person could enjoy the seasonal color outside. But, as the days passed, they were colder, with blustery winds. Fewer hours were warm enough to let the girls play outside. Caitlin used those days to light fires in the fireplaces and spent the time making wool dresses for her daughters. Charlotte and Naomi thought running around indoors in their undergarments was great fun when they had to keep trying on the dresses.

Maisey, who would have her eleventh birthday in a few weeks, was uncomfortable if she wasn't fully dressed. She had to undress and redress many times when Caitlin was fitting her dresses. Maisey was also a budding artist. Her drawings were becoming realistic. There was no need to guess what she rendered in her sketch pad. Her subjects were realistic.

One afternoon, when the younger girls were baking cookies in the kitchen with Brenda, Maisey looked around to make sure the younger girls weren't in the room and spoke very frankly with Caitlin.

"When did you become a woman?" Maisey ask.

Surprised by the question, Caitlin didn't know how to answer. "What do you mean?"

"When did you start bleeding?" Maisey whispered.

Caitlin was shocked, "Who told you about that?"

"At the orphanage. A woman talked to all the girls over nine about growing up and marrying. We were told we were being sent away, and our futures would depend on who wanted us. She also warned us that most girls twelve and older would be claimed as wives because women were scarce in the West. We were told not to argue with those who took us in because it could be the difference between living and starving.

"She said many young girls would be claimed but not

married immediately. Then she explained that most girls around the age of twelve bleed every month for a few days, and we weren't to be frightened when it happened to us. The woman said it was natural and something we had to accept as we approached womanhood. She explained how to keep ourselves clean."

Caitlin put her sewing aside and hugged Maisey. "It's a horrible thing those people are doing to children. I don't know how they can call themselves Christians. It hurts me to think how you and Naomi have been treated."

"Living at the orphanage wasn't all bad," Maisey said. "We didn't go hungry very often and were given a bed to share."

Caitlin hugged Maisey again. "You deserve so much more, and your father and I will make sure you get it. Trust me on this—none of you girls will marry at the age of twelve!"

"Brenda is seventeen, and she's getting married," Maisey said.

"She'll be eighteen before she takes the vows," Caitlin said firmly. "A lot of growing up happens between twelve and eighteen. You have plenty of time to be our precious little girl."

"What about the bleeding?" Maisey asked.

"I'm afraid that's true, but you don't have to worry about that yet. It's part of growing up. When that time gets closer, I'll make sure you are prepared and understand what is happening so you won't be frightened. You only have to worry about schooling, behaving, and having fun. I promise you and your sisters will have the best childhoods we can provide."

CHAPTER 18

*B*renda Cole was as hard a worker as was her younger brother, and they often worked as a team.

Hudson considered the youngsters a Godsend when he came home tired and discovered the chores were done. With Jesse and Bert pitching in, Hudson spent more time with his family.

Fall was the time to prepare for winter. Even though eastern Texas didn't get much snow, winter preparations had to be made. The previous winter had been mild if they didn't figure in the lightning storms and the tornados in the early spring months.

Still, the old-timers claimed this winter would be colder than usual, and Hudson believed their predictions. The old folks said they could feel the weather in their bones, and they tended to be correct. It was October, and the winds were chilling. The trees damaged by the violent storms in the past spring had been tagged, cut down, cut apart, stacked, and left to season during the summer months. In the fall, they were sawed and chopped into fireplace or stove-sized lengths of wood. Jesse and Bert had split the wood at Rose Hill, stacking it alongside the fence, closer to the kitchen back door, and covered it with tarpaulins.

Looking out the bedroom window one morning, Caitlin gave a sigh.

"Something wrong?" Hudson asked behind her, buttoning his shirt.

"Not really," she responded. "I was told when I came here in the spring that all the rain and storms were uncommon. It's barely October, and the terrible weather is back."

"You'll have to take that up with the man upstairs," Hudson said with a smile.

"That's almost blasphemy," she responded.

"This from a young lady who refuses to attend church."

"I don't like Reverend Cormac," was her response. "He acts like he knows everything, and he doesn't!"

"I'm not real fond of the man myself," Hudson agreed.

Caitlin turned in his arms to face him and finished buttoning his shirt. "You'll be soaked before you reach Magnolia."

"I'll be soaked before I leave the yard," Hudson said. "But I have extra clothes at the ranch. "Keep the girls inside. We don't want them getting sick."

Keeping the girls inside wasn't a problem. Jesse took care of most of the outside chores, although Maisey insisted on milking Mary Bell the cow as it was her chore. The cow responded better to her light touch. Maisey milked Mary Bell in the morning and in the evening. There was plenty of milk for the girls to drink, use in cooking and supplying Bert. Some was for himself, but most of it, he took to a widow in town with two small children. Mrs. Thompson, the widow, washed and mended clothes to earn enough money to feed her children and put a roof over their heads. Caitlin joined his efforts, giving him extra eggs and canned goods to deliver. She'd only met Mrs. Thompson once, at the mercantile.

The trips into town were less frequent as the colder weather set in.

"This wasn't what I expected when I decided to settle here," Caitlin complained to Bert. "You told me the weather was mild here."

"It is. The daytime temperatures from October to February are usually in the fifties," Bert said. "If you want heat, you should have gone to the deep south. I heard parts of California don't have snow either, but I ain't been there. I'm a third-generation Texan, and proud of it. You should be proud of your Texas heritage, too!"

"I didn't know about that heritage until recently," Caitlin said.

"Well, now you know," Bert grumbled. "Be proud of it, even if it's linked to that bastard Ballard!"

"I heard you used to be good friends with him."

"That was a long time ago," Bert growled. "There's been a lot of dirty water under that bridge."

"What does that mean?" Caitlin asked.

"That's between him and me, Missy, and none of your business," Bert grunted. "I'm going into town tomorrow if you want to go along."

Understanding that she wouldn't get any more information from Bert, Caitlin nodded. "Same time?"

"Same time," Bert agreed. "If you've got extras, they would be appreciated."

"I can spare some," Caitlin agreed.

Bundled in a thick wool cape, Caitlin joined Bert on his trip to town. He stopped just outside of town and knocked on the door of a small house. Mrs. Thompson opened the door, and Bert introduced the two women.

While Bert was talking to the widow, Caitlin was looking around. The house was tiny and obviously heated by a small stove used for cooking and heating. The two children were toddlers. The little boy looked about three, and the little girl barely walked, taking a few steps and then falling on her bottom and resorting to crawling. Therese Thompson was a young woman, close to Caitlin's age, but the hardship of her life had aged her. Her face had worry lines, and her hands were red and raw from scrubbing clothes on a washboard to feed her children.

Bert handed over a wooden crate of food goods and several milk jugs.

The young woman accepted the gifts with tears in her eyes. She hugged Bert, thanked him, and shook hands with Caitlin, introducing herself.

"I'll be coming back this way in a couple of days," Bert said with a smile. "I'm going hunting tomorrow."

When they left Mrs. Thompson's house, Caitlin looked over her shoulder at the rundown little house. "How is she surviving without her husband?"

"It ain't easy," Bert admitted. "She's had two marriage proposals, but both men would have made sorry excuses as husbands. Therese needs to find a decent fellow, but most men don't want to take on another man's young'uns to raise. I'd marry her if I wasn't so dang old. She'd probably get a belly laugh at the idea."

"Drop me off at the mercantile," Caitlin said. "I can run errands and visit my friends while you're playing faro. Some-day, you need to teach me how to play it."

"Cards and gambling ain't for women," Bert grumbled.

Caitlin stood on the sidewalk, and when Bert turned the wagon into the alley beside the saloon, she ran across the road and entered the bank.

"Mrs. McFarlane, how nice to see you," John Bones exclaimed.

"It's nice to see you too," Caitlin said. "May I speak with you in private?"

"Of course," the banker agreed. "Come in my office. What can I help you with?"

"Are you aware of Mrs. Thompson's situation?"

"Yes, it's tragic. The poor woman has no family to help her," Mr. Bones said.

"Does she own her little house?" Caitlin asked.

"No, ma'am, she doesn't," Mr. Bones said. "It's a rental property owned by the bank."

"How much is it worth?"

"The house and the small plot of land it sits on would sell for around a hundred dollars," Mr. Bones answered.

"How much does it rent for?" Caitlin asked.

The banker opened the large book on his desk. "Aw, here it is. The rent is five dollars a month, and I can assure you, Mrs. McFarlane, that the bank is not overcharging Mrs. Thompson."

"I'm not suggesting that you are," Caitlin said. "Would the bank consider selling the property?"

The banker closed the book. "What is this about Mrs. McFarlane?"

"I'd like to purchase the property, but I'd like to remain a silent owner, and I would like the rent lowered by a half. Mrs. Thompson doesn't have to know why the rent is lowered. Just that it is. I'm sure it would make her life easier."

"That's a generous offer," Mr. Bones said.

"Can you arrange it? And keep it a secret?" Caitlin asked.

"Of course, but I'll need your husband's permission."

"You didn't need Hudson's permission when I opened my account," Caitlin said, surprised by his words. "Or when I purchased Rose Hill."

"That was before you married, ma'am. If Hudson agrees, I will sell you the property. What you do with it is your business," Mr. Bones said. "If you want to hide the ownership, I will assist you in keeping it a secret."

"I don't want Mrs. Thompson to know the property has changed hands," Caitlin repeated.

"I can make that happen, and no one beyond this office will know about it. But only after Hudson agrees."

"Draw up the papers, please," Caitlin said with determination. "We'll be back as soon as he has the free time."

* * *

"Why do you want to buy a property for someone you just met?" Hudson asked. "You have nearly a thousand acres that you're not using!"

"It has nothing to do with this property," Caitlin said. "I want to help Mrs. Thompson but allow her to keep her pride. As hard as living with Beaula was, I never had to worry about putting a roof over my head or going hungry so my children could eat."

"Isn't that the church's responsibility?" Hudson asked.

"She went to the church for help, and that idiot Reverend Cormac stood on the pulpit and told his followers to be generous because one of their flock was suffering. His *flock* responded by dropping off boxes of trash and expecting her to be grateful. Bert has been helping her by dropping off milk, eggs, wild game, and fish. She does his washing for him in return. If I purchase the house and continue renting it to her at a lower cost, it's not a loss to me. The rent would pay for the house in a few years. No one has to know, and Mr. Bones has promised to keep it a secret."

"Are you going to do this kind of thing regularly?" Hudson asked.

"If it's needed, I don't see a problem," Caitlin said, raising her eyes and looking around the well-appointed office. "Except for buying this property from Bert, I've spent very little of my Ridgeway inheritance. I have a great deal of money in Mr.

Bones' bank, and there is a bank voucher over there in the desk drawer that hasn't been deposited yet because we decided to put it in a different bank.

"I will receive those vouchers twice yearly as long as the Great Atlantic and Pacific Tea Company stays in business. Two and a half dollars for rent is less than I spend on the girls for books, drawing supplies, and candy each month. We are privileged, and the difference of those few dollars a month will mean Mrs. Thompson can buy food and necessities for herself and her babies. I would like to become her friend, and Mr. Bones will come up with a reasonable explanation of why the rent was lowered."

Hudson kissed Caitlin on her forehead and hugged her. "I never expected to marry an heiress. Why are you explaining all this to me if you've already decided?"

"Do you disagree with what I want to do?" she asked.

"No, and I think it fits with who you are," he said. "You're a selfless person who wants to help people. I agree with what you want to do. I'm also glad you remembered to involve me in the decision."

"I didn't have a choice," Caitlin admitted. "Mr. Bones said, even though the money is mine, I have to have your permission as my husband to use it."

"Ha!" Hudson laughed, giving Caitlin a light smack on her bottom.

"Texas law is unfair to women," Caitlin complained.

"Not from where I'm standing," Hudson said, pulling her into a hug and kiss.

Hudson rearranged his workload so he could go to Tyler several days later to talk with Mr. Bones and pick up some supplies for Magnolia. Caitlin had gone with him, and they signed the contracts on the little house. Mr. Bones was pleased with the transfer of the house deed, as the property had been a foreclosure and he hadn't been able to sell it for several years.

The banker also agreed to the transaction's secrecy and would speak to Mrs. Thompson about the lowered rent. The banker would also return two and a half dollars to her for each rent collection she'd paid since moving into the house. He would explain that she had been overcharged by mistake and assure her that the landlord would not ask her to move.

Hudson also asked that the property be serviced to see if any repairs were needed. Even from a distance, he could see the roof required patching or replacement, and the picket fence outside needed repairs.

While Hudson ran errands for the ranch, Caitlin went to the mercantile and the bookstore. The next stop was the Rusty Pot, where she and Eleanor talked until the dinner crowd began to fill the tables. Before heading home, they bought a chicken pie and visited Nell, Ben, and the baby for a quick dinner.

"Do you want to stop by Mrs. Thompson's house?" Hudson asked.

"No, that might be too coincidental. I really don't want Therese to know or even guess what we're doing," Caitlin said. "I'll give her a week or more and come in with Bert when he makes one of his trips and drops off his clothing. I know you always lean to the side of Angus, but Bert is a sweetheart."

"I wouldn't call him sweet, but he definitely has a side to him that I never expected," Hudson agreed, giving the reins a hitch.

With winter weather setting in, they woke up one morning to a light covering of snow. It would melt at daybreak, but not before the girls were rousted from their beds and had a chance to play in it.

Allowing the girls to get wet and cold was the wrong decision. Charlotte and Naomi came down with colds and were isolated to their bedroom. Maisey moved over to a room she'd been offered before but had refused because she was afraid of being separated from her sister. She seemed to be enjoying the privacy now.

Jilly wrote that she would return to Rose Hill in the first week of December. Caitlin and the girls received the news joyfully, but Brenda was upset.

"What's wrong?" Caitlin asked of the young woman because she looked worried.

"I knew this was coming," Brenda said in an unsteady voice. She looked like she was going to burst into tears. "I knew Jilly was returning, and this job was temporary." She shrugged.

"It's just that my Ma and Pa won't let me marry until we have a place to live. We were promised a cabin, but it hasn't been built yet. I can't marry Homer until we have a place to live, and I've been working here so we can buy some things we're going to need."

"Don't worry," Caitlin exclaimed, hugging Brenda. "I'll talk to my husband and determine what is delaying the construction. And, if you need furniture, that's no problem either. We'll go upstairs to the attic. Hudson claims there's so much stuff up there that it's a fire trap. I'm sure we can find some furniture pieces you can use, and you can use the money you've saved for other things. We need to go up there anyway. Bert told me there are Christmas decorations somewhere in this house, but I haven't found them yet. They must be stored in the attic with a lot of leftover stuff. I want this Christmas to be extra special for the girls. It will be their first Christmas out of the orphanage."

Hudson left for Magnolia earlier than usual the following day. He kissed her, passed on breakfast, and said he'd eat with Angus at the main house because they had a lot to discuss. When asked 'what?' he smiled and said, "Angus is buying a new breed of cattle called, strangely enough, Angus, and like their namesake, they are a tough breed. He wants to cross-breed them because the calves would be sturdier." Then he tipped his hat and closed the door behind him.

"Darn!" Caitlin exclaimed when she accidentally jammed her toes into the bedframe, and she was hopping on one foot.

The bedroom door reopened. "I heard that!"

"Darn isn't a swearword!" she retorted.

"Close enough!" Hudson warned, and he crossed the room to her. "I might have to get real close to your fanny again! It's been a while."

"I haven't done anything wrong!" Caitlin hissed, knowing he was referring to spanking her.

"You don't have to do anything wrong," Hudson whispered. "You know it, and I know it. You like a spanking when we're together."

"Hudson!" Caitlin blushed. "The girls might hear you!"

"They're still sound asleep. I'll see you later," he said, dropping to one knee to see if she'd hurt her toes. When he stood, he cupped his hands one each on her buttocks and gave them a squeeze. He kissed her, tipped his hat, and was gone.

Caitlin went to the window and saw Jesse join her husband as they walked to the barn. She didn't see Hudson leave because she was dressing, and then she was waking up the girls and getting them dressed.

"Why isn't Maisey sleeping with us?" Naomi asked.

"Because she is older, and she likes having a room of her own," Caitlin explained. "She still loves you, but she's grown enough to want her own room and privacy."

"What's that?" Charlotte whined.

"Privacy means sometimes she wants to be alone," Caitlin said. "Now finish getting dressed. Breakfast is probably ready, and we don't want to disrespect Brenda by letting it get cold."

After the breakfast dishes were done, a chore that belonged to Caitlin and the younger girls, they were settled in the office with the schoolwork. Caitlin led the way to the attic with Brenda and Maisey.

"All this furniture was left behind by Bert?" Brenda exclaimed.

"Yes, it came with the house," Caitlin said. "Bert said he'd taken what he wanted; the rest was my problem. Let's see what we can find that will help you when you marry. You'll be entering a marriage with a dowery of furniture."

"If they ever build a cabin for us," Brenda said unhappily.

"I forgot to ask Hudson about that last night," Caitlin admitted. "He was late and exhausted, but I haven't forgotten, and I will talk to him. We'll set aside what you want, but I'll still ask Bert if it's okay to give it to you. A lot of these pieces hold memories of his wife, Pansy."

"I knew her from church when I was little," Brenda said. "She was a nice lady, and the gossip was that Bert spoiled her."

"Good for him," Caitlin said. "I've heard of men who treated their wives worse than they do their dogs! Don't let your future husband get away with behavior like that."

"Homer isn't like that," Brenda said, shaking her head. "Besides, he knows if he mistreats me, he'll have to face my Pa, my brothers, and my uncles. They all work at Magnolia Ranch. But he's more afraid of my mother!"

"Good for your mother," Caitlin said, laughing while she was uncovering furniture.

They cleared an area near the attic stairs, and she and Brenda uncovered and inspected furniture. They carried small tables, chairs, and the separate parts of a rope bed. There were three trunks that Brenda liked, and when they were opened, she liked what was in them more. One trunk was filled with a complete set of china, while another was filled with cast iron pots and pans for baking. The third was filled with outdated women's magazines.

"Don't you need these?" Brenda asked, pointing at the dishes.

"Is there anything here that isn't in the kitchen?" Caitlin asked. "You and Jilly know more about what's in the kitchen than I do."

"Not that I can see," Brenda said, looking at the pile of stuff she had collected. "I don't know if Homer will accept all these things when we get a cabin. He's a proud man who will want to provide for me. We've been saving what I've earned and most of his salary for a while."

"You're thinking ahead," Caitlin said. "Tag the trunk with the magazines. I like reading the magazines. I'm going to drag Bert up here and show him what we've discovered," Caitlin said. "I'm sure he won't have a problem giving you and your beau these things. When Bert was helping me rearrange the house more to my liking, he got upset one day and said I needed to cart all this furniture off to burn it. But I wouldn't let him. He returned a few days later and said I was right, not to waste the furniture, but to find a home that needed it. I think women value furniture far more than men."

"My Pa is that way," Brenda agreed. "My mother was complaining about needing a new table, and he ignored her until the legs gave out, right in the middle of supper! The Sunday supper hit the floor, and my Ma was fit to be tied. She used a few cuss words, I didn't know she knew!"

"Did she get a new table?" Caitlin asked.

"Yes, Pa built her a new one on his next day off. He also gave Ma a walloping for swearing in front of the kids," Brenda said. "They're still using the table."

Caitlin and Brenda spent several hours in the attic, but she didn't find the Christmas decorations. She'd almost given up the search when she opened a cabinet door and found it full of ornaments for a Christmas tree. The younger girls were already making colored paper chains. Maisey was drawing small pictures on canvas and embroidering red and green stitching around the edges.

As Caitlin had predicted, Bert wouldn't even climb the stairs to look at what Brenda had selected. He claimed it didn't belong to him anymore. He had taken what he wanted. If Caitlin wanted to give the stuff away, it was her business.

Hudson wasn't interested either. He told Caitlin to clear out the rest. Caitlin and Brenda returned to the attic to find additional items that the soon-to-be newlyweds could use. Caitlin was also making a second pile for someone who could use some pretty things.

Brenda sent word to her beau, and he joined the McFarlanes for a Sunday supper. Homer was easier to convince than Brenda, and he accepted the household offerings, giving Hudson a handshake, although his boss had nothing to do with deciding what to give away from the attic.

When Caitlin and Hudson were alone that evening, Caitlin asked her husband if he was still occupying his old cabin at Magnolia.

"Yeah, I am," Hudson said. "Why?"

"There has been a delay in building the cabins for Magnolia's married men," Caitlin said.

"That happens sometimes," Hudson said. "Other work on the ranch is more important."

"Why do you have a cabin that you're not using?" Caitlin asked.

"I use it," Hudson said.

"You haven't missed coming home at the end of the day since we married."

"True, but I still use it," Hudson said. "I keep extra clothing in there and store my guns there."

"You have clothes and guns here," Caitlin reminded him. "If you just need a place to change clothes or to store weapons, what's wrong with using one of the empty rooms in Angus' house. He has four empty bedrooms."

"That feels like overstepping," Hudson said, scratching his head.

"Why? Magnolia will be yours someday," Caitlin said.

"Maybe so, but I don't want Angus thinking I'm trying to push him out," Hudson admitted. "He's been delegating more and more responsibilities to me in the last few years, and I've accepted them. I know my place with your father. I've known it for years. I don't want Angus to think I'm trying to take control. I will try to give the building of the cabins a higher priority."

"Cabins as in multiples?" Caitlin asked.

"Yeah, we need four more cabins at the ranch and three more at the farm. Rebuilding from the spring damage set our goals back. I'll look over our schedules and see if we can start building earlier," Hudson promised.

CHAPTER 19

After a lengthy discussion with Hudson, it was decided that Brenda would keep her job until she married. Brenda would help Jilly with the cooking and cleaning after she returned. How long Brenda would keep her job depended on Magnolia's building schedule.

Several weeks passed before Caitlin rode along when Bert went to town. Her goal was to visit Therese Thompson, and she'd brought a cake as a gift.

"I know I've shown up without warning, and I'll go away if I'm bothering you, but I desperately need to speak to another woman outside my home," Caitlin pleaded.

"Of course, you are welcome," Therese said with a smile. Bert carried a crate into the house, tipped his hat, and left.

"Please have a seat," Therese said, motioning to a table and chair. "My circumstances have changed recently, happily in my favor."

"Does that include a beau?" Caitlin inquired.

Therese shook her head. "I'm not ready for that yet. No, the bank sold this house under the condition that repairs would be made."

"Does that mean you have to move?" Caitlin said, pretending to be worried.

"No," Therese said. "I did have to sign a rental agreement, but the rent is less than before. Mr. Bones apologized and returned half of what I've been paying since I moved here. It's a miracle, and I can afford to buy milk now if you want to sell the extra."

"Oh, no," Caitlin said. "I was raised not to waste, and you taking the milk makes me feel better knowing it won't go sour and be thrown away. I'm a city girl, and when I bought the cow, I had no idea they had to be milked twice daily! We have twice the milk we need!"

Therese laughed. "I've never been to a city before."

"I'm so glad for you, Therese. You look less worried than when I first met you."

"How about you?" Therese asked. "You took on a big load, marrying and taking on children."

"The children and I are fine, but Hudson and I have been butting heads lately," Caitlin said.

"Oh, I'm so sorry..."

"It's not that big a problem," Caitlin said. "It's probably a silly problem, considering what you've been through. Please don't repeat this because I love Bert as a grandparent. He has been wonderful to me and the children."

"Then what is the problem if you want to share it?"

Caitlin took a deep breath and silently said three Hail Mary's before lying. "When Bert agreed to sell me the property, it came with all the furniture. The house was full of furniture, trunks, and boxes filled with everything you could imagine, and so was the attic. There were even beautiful fabrics that had been stored for years. Luckily for me, the moths didn't get into the trunks. I can use most of the fabrics, but the attic is full of leftover furniture. Hudson wants it cleared out. He says the attic is a fire trap."

Lowering her voice, Caitlin spoke softly. "I think Bert's wife must have been what they call a hoarder."

"What's that?" Therese asked.

"It's a person who collects and stores things and never gets rid of anything. So far, I've found five sets of china and enough silverware to feed an army! The attic is full! There is so much furniture up there! I don't know what to do with it. Hudson found guns and ammunition up there, and he was furious because it was a danger to the children. I've asked Bert to help, but he said the property came with the full attic, and he's already taken what he wanted. I love that old goat, but he's not willing to help.

"Anyway, I have to clear the attic because I don't want to get into trouble with my husband again. I've already offered a wagonload to Brenda Cole and her beau. They are planning to get married soon. I know you've had a hard time since you lost your husband, but could you please come over and help me by taking a few things?"

Therese looked conflicted. "I don't like to take charity, and you can't possibly know how much I hate taking what Bert gives me. I did it for my children."

"This isn't about charity," Caitlin exclaimed. "This is about me getting into trouble with my husband! This is about saving my backside! Oh! I shouldn't have said that!"

Therese smiled, and she nodded. "Don't be embarrassed. I was married to a spanker, but I loved him deeply. If it helps you, I'll come over and see what I can use."

"Thank you," Caitlin exclaimed, hugging her new friend. She'd played her part perfectly. "My girls are going to love playing with your little ones!"

* * *

JESSE LEFT in a wagon one morning and returned with Mrs. Thompson and her small children. Maisey was tasked with playing with the little ones and watching over her younger sisters. Therese joined Caitlin and Brenda and trooped up the steps to the attic. Caitlin told Jesse he would be called when needed.

Upon entering the attic, Therese was amazed. Caitlin turned in a circle. "Do you see what I mean? That pile of things belongs to Brenda, but she has nowhere to store it. Hudson promised to start building the cabins, but he hasn't done anything yet. Everything up here, except Brenda's pile, must be moved out. I've tagged anything I wanted to keep, but I haven't had time to go through everything. I'm not sure about how to do this. Wander around and claim what you want. I saw several child-size bed frames somewhere, but I don't remember where. I don't know why they are here. Bert told me he didn't have any children. There seem to be a lot of small tables, and there are rolled carpets in the corner."

"Let's split up," Brenda suggested. "We'll holler if we find something we think you might be interested in seeing." She clapped her hands together. "I'll be looking for a few things for my mother. All the wives at Magnolia are planning a trip down to Rose Hill. Hudson is serious about clearing out this attic."

"Don't I know it," Caitlin said, rubbing her bottom and then laughing with the other women.

Therese was amazed by the generosity. She was called from one end of the attic to the other and helped to carry the items to what the women called 'her pile.' Her benefactor was more interested in opening trunks and boxes to discover what was hidden in them.

"Therese!" Caitlin called when she discovered hidden treasures.

Another set of china with a beautiful blue pattern and another set of silverware were found. So far, five sets had been discovered, and all of them needed to be cleaned and polished. Therese agreed on the smallest setting of six because she doubted she would ever have that many people over for supper. Then they laughed because they were searching for matching chairs to go with a kitchen table.

Brenda found a small kitchen cabinet where the china could be displayed and a missing chair. The cabinet and chair were carried to the 'pile.' She wished she'd found the cabinet first for her mother and was delighted when she found another slightly larger cabinet that would fit in her mother's kitchen. The cabinet was tagged and put in her 'pile.'

Therese had to remind these determined women that her house only had four small rooms.

Jesse was called to carry boxes to the first floor. With the larger pieces, he needed help, and it became a two or three-person lift to get the furniture down the stairs to the porch.

Bert rode in while the women were trying to pack the wagon. He dismounted to help Jesse load the heavier pieces. When no one was looking, he kissed Caitlin on the top of her head and whispered in her ear. "Pumpkin, I knew I could count on you."

When the wagon was full, Therese was in tears. She couldn't believe what was being given to her. She kept asking Caitlin if she was sure, and Caitlin repeatedly thanked her for helping clean out the attic.

Bert offered to drive the borrowed wagon back to Therese's house and help Jesse unload it. He and Jesse tied their horses to the back of the wagon. They would ride home after they unloaded the wagon and returned it to the barn.

There were hugs all around. Caitlin promised to stop in and visit Therese when she returned to Tyler. She also thanked her new friend for *helping* clear the attic, although there was still a lot left up there.

"That was a good deed for the day," Brenda announced as

the women waved off the wagon. "Now I know why you are so generous. It's a wonderful feeling to help a person in need."

"It is, and it takes no effort. I believe in sharing," Caitlin said. "We would have never used that furniture, and how many sets of china does one household need?"

"Did you give away all your furniture when you left Pennsylvania?" Brenda asked and then quickly followed the question with an apology. "I'm sorry, it's none of my business."

"Nonsense," Caitlin said. "I sold some of the furniture to the new owner. I sent the rest to an auction house and gave the proceeds to the Sisters of Charity Orphanage. I was there from birth until I was five years old."

"Really?" Brenda said. "But, aren't you Mr. Ballard's daughter? Oh, I'm sorry again. Ma always gets on me for not minding my own business."

Caitlin shrugged. "I am Angus' daughter, but that's all I'm saying about it." She wagged a stern finger at Brenda. "You are not, and I mean never, to gossip to anyone, including your family, about what goes on here at Rose Hill. Our privacy is important to us, and we won't tolerate anyone breaching it."

"Yes, ma'am," Brenda said, crossing her hand across her chest. "I won't forget. Honest, I won't. My Ma would have my hide if I did. She hates gossip, and I wouldn't anyway. You've been real generous to me and Homer."

"I'm just giving you fair warning," Caitlin said, smiling. "Meanwhile, I'd better see what the girls have gotten into. Maisey doesn't get into mischief too much, but the younger two are a handful."

"And we'd better figure out what we're having for supper," Brenda said.

* * *

JILLY ARRIVED in Tyler on December first. She'd planned her trip back to Texas so she would arrive on a Wednesday because she knew Bert would be playing Faro with his friends. She wouldn't enter the saloon, but Daniel Foster at the hotel was happy to run down the street and tell Bert that she had arrived.

Bert tossed his cards on the table and made a bee-line to the hotel lobby.

Jilly was as pleased to see Bert as he was to see her, and he immediately went to the livery to hire a buggy to take her home.

Caitlin and the girls were thrilled to have Jilly back. She was hugged and passed from one person to the next.

Unloading Jilly's bags, Bert couldn't get near the woman.

Caitlin invited Bert to supper so Jilly could tell everyone about her trip. The reunion was loud, with squeals from the girls and smiles from Brenda and Jesse.

All was right again at the McFarlane household; everyone was where they were supposed to be.

* * *

HUDSON USED his hat to beat the muck and mud from his trousers and scraped the mud and cattle dung from his boots against the office steps. Finally, he gave up, sat on the steps, and pulled them off. Mrs. Brimmer would have his hide for tracking dung into the house. His socks were surprisingly clean, and when he stood up, he faced Angus standing in the doorway.

"Did we get our money's worth?" Angus demanded.

"We won't know until calving season next year," Hudson said. "Those bulls are as big as Brahmans, and I've heard more dangerous. We've tagged the mounted cows, and we'll keep the bulls separate."

Angus didn't say much, but he nodded in agreement. "Take a seat."

"That's not a good idea," Hudson said. "I need a bath first."

"Go on then, but stop in before you head home. I'll ride with you. I've got something I want to talk to you and Caitlin about."

"Good enough," Hudson agreed. He headed over to his cabin. It was only two small rooms, but it had been his home for nearly two decades. When he'd cleaned himself and changed clothing, he stuffed his dirty garments into a bag. He would take them home and return with a clean set in the morning. He scrubbed his boots clean before setting them in front of a window where he knew the sun would dry them.

Two horses were saddled and tied to the porch rail, and Hudson hoisted himself into the saddle. Angus was quiet on the trip to Rose Hill, but that was his nature. He'd talk when he was ready. He wasn't a man to repeat himself.

Charlotte and Naomi came running when Angus entered the house and dragged him into the office, where they dug games out of the trunk where they were stored.

"What? I don't get even a hello," Hudson teased.

"Of course you do," Maisey said, and she hugged him. "Momma will hug you, too."

"I hope so," Hudson said with a smile as the younger girls ran to him for quick hugs but then abandoned him again for their grandfather.

"Where is Momma?"

"Jilly was preparing a beef roast for supper, so Momma went upstairs to change the bed sheets."

"Will you run upstairs and tell Momma we're home and Angus is here?" Hudson asked.

Maisey nodded. "Watch over the girls; if you don't, they'll pull out every game and puzzle we have."

"Will do," Hudson said, entering the office where the girls

were deep into the trunk of games. "Hey now, select two games only, one each. Supper will be ready in a little while."

Charlotte whined, but she obeyed and set up her favorite game.

Angus moved over to a table and began to play a game with Naomi. Hudson did the same with Charlotte. Maisey and Caitlin joined them a few minutes later, but Jilly interrupted.

"Supper's ready!"

"Good, because I'm hungry," Angus announced.

There wasn't much discussion during supper, as everyone concentrated on what they ate.

Hudson was watching his wife. It had been months since she'd admitted her problem with raw meat. Since then, she'd not had to deal with her problem, but she still wasn't eating more than a forkful.

"I'm glad Bert isn't here this evening," Angus said.

"Bert is always welcome at our table," Caitlin said with a slight warning in her voice. "He's our friend."

"I saw Mr. Bert and Jilly kissing," Charlotte announced.

"What?" Jesse exclaimed wide-eyed.

"Hush. That is none of your business," Caitlin said firmly to Charlotte, then she turned toward Jesse and pointed a finger at him. Jesse looked down at his plate and filled his mouth with food.

Jilly's face turned bright red. "The gravy bowl is empty," she said, snatching it and leaving the table.

"Not another word until you've finished your supper," Caitlin admonished the girls, and she got to her feet. "Excuse me."

"Did I say something wrong?" Charlotte whined.

"No," Hudson said quietly. "Eat your supper. The sooner you finish, the more games you can play before bedtime."

Caitlin entered the kitchen, but Jilly wasn't there, so she

knocked on the door of Jilly's room. She didn't hear an answer, but that wouldn't stop her.

Caitlin joined Jilly, sitting on the edge of the bed. "I apologize for Charlotte. She's too young to understand that she embarrassed you."

Jilly stood up and went to stand in front of the window. She took a few deep breaths. "It's true. Bert has kissed me, and I allowed it."

"What's wrong with that?" Caitlin asked gently. "You lost your husband thirty-some years ago. It's not like you are rushing into a romance."

"I'm too old for romance!" Jilly exclaimed. "He just caught me off guard. I didn't know Charlotte saw us."

"Why are you too old?" Caitlin asked gently. "You've spent most of your life taking care of others. You raised Lincoln by yourself, and when he was grown, you protected and raised me. You deserve to be loved, and not just by the children you raised. You're only in your fifties and a wonderful person. A catch for any man!"

"You don't think we're being foolish at our ages?" Jilly whispered.

"No," Caitlin said firmly. "I love you, and I love Bert, and I think you make a great couple. You're made for each other. You're both cranky."

Jilly smiled, chuckled, and put her hands on her ample hips. "That's enough out of you, Missy!"

"I love you," Caitlin said, teasing her friend.

"Get on back into the dining room," Jilly ordered. "I made applesauce cake for dessert and expect you to be at the table!"

"Yes, ma'am," Caitlin agreed, and she kissed Jilly on the cheek. Then she leaned in and whispered, "You stole my first boyfriend!"

"Get on with you," Jilly hissed.

Caitlin turned around and dodged the smack aimed at her.

Supper continued, and no one commented on Charlotte's slip of the tongue.

Hudson and Angus played games with the girls while Caitlin helped clean the kitchen, although there wasn't much to do, as Jilly and Brenda cleaned as they cooked. When it was bedtime for the girls, Brenda and Jesse excused themselves. Caitlin and Hudson sat across from Angus, expecting him to give them some news. He had to have a reason for coming to Rose Hill unexpectedly.

Angus cleared his throat while Hudson and Caitlin waited for him to speak.

"I wanted to talk to you two."

"We sort of figured that out," Hudson said.

Angus made a face and pulled at his collar buttons at his neck. "Yeah, well, well... Mrs. Brimmer, I mean Gladys, has finally agreed to marry me."

"Really? That's wonderful!" Caitlin exclaimed.

"We would have done it years ago if it had been left up to me. I've asked Gladys many times, but she always turned me down. I know now it was because of Emma and Abigail. She always thought they were like their mother, greedy and rotten to the core, and I reckon she was right. I guess I'll keep the rest of her opinions to myself. It's needless to say, she never liked them, and this last visit proved her right."

"When are you getting married?" Caitlin asked.

"I reckon that's going to be up to her," Angus said. "She said she wanted to make sure you didn't have a problem with it."

"Why would we?" Caitlin asked. "We like Gladys and are happy for you."

"All right then, I reckon we'll get back to you," Angus said, looking relieved. He got to his feet.

"You're not going home in the dark," Caitlin protested.

"There's a half moon," Angus said with a smile. "I know my way home."

Caitlin and Hudson waved and closed the door when Angus mounted his horse.

"Did you know my father and Gladys were interested in each other in that way?" Caitlin asked.

"I've known it for years," Hudson said, shrugging. "But then I spend more time with them than most people at Magnolia. I'd guess that very few know they've been involved with each other for a long time. If they did know, they had the sense to keep their mouths shut."

"Really?"

"Really," Hudson said with a grin. "A certain look, a pat on the fanny, their putting space between them quickly, Mrs. Brimmer dusting his desk while he's still sitting in his chair, and Angus behind her buttoning his trousers. There have been a few inappropriate moments when they've been caught, but I've always looked the other way. It wasn't any of my business."

"My father is getting married," Caitlin exclaimed. "I'll have a stepmother!"

"One that you already like," Hudson said, lowering his head and kissing his wife. Everyone is where they are supposed to be, and I could use an early night."

"To sleep or to...?"

"I want the *or to*," Hudson said, sweeping her into his arms and carrying her upstairs.

He put her down at the top of the stairs, and they opened the doors to the bedrooms and peeked inside. The younger girls shared a bed, and Maisey was asleep in the connecting room.

Once behind closed doors, Hudson stripped his wife of clothing quickly. Why women wore so many garments was a mystery to him. When she was naked, he stripped off his own clothing quickly.

Caitlin's eyes widened at Hudson's size, and she knew instantly that this night would be one of lovemaking and very little rest or sleep. His hands roamed over her entire body, gentle yet searching and branding her as his own.

She began to shiver and wanted more. Her husband covered her body with his large one but held his weight up and over so he wouldn't crush her. He placed one of her legs over each of his forearms and lifted her. They watched as he entered her slowly, giving her body time to stretch to the size of his sex. He moved gradually and carefully, changing his position several times to fit his wife more easily.

With her legs wrapped around his strong arms, she took him into her. Hudson was pleasuring her as he pounded into her deeply. He dipped his manhood so his length rubbed against her womanhood and gave her the most amazing feelings. Her husband had taught her about body parts. She had known they were there but hadn't been told they were named. An orgasm, something else she'd never been schooled about, was building inside her as he rode her hard and deep. When Caitlin's body responded, Hudson followed seconds later.

It was a night of pure pleasure. They woke at dawn as they did most mornings, but neither was anxious to leave their bed.

Hudson knew he didn't have much time, but he wouldn't forgo pleasuring himself and his wife once again.

Hudson's lovemaking was very much as he'd performed before, but Caitlin was in for a surprise. After her first orgasm, Hudson positioned his wife on her knees, stretched her arms out, and wrapped her hands around the brass headboard.

Caitlin had been in this position before. She thought she knew what to expect. She wasn't expecting a stinging spank across her bottom.

"What?" she gasped.

"Shush, you don't want to wake the girls, and you'll learn to like this," Hudson said quietly.

With a stinging bottom, Caitlin sucked in her breath. Her husband rubbed out the sting with one hand while the fingers on the other hand played over and into the folds of her sex. He spanked her bottom again and again while fondling her between spanks.

Caitlin wasn't sure she would like this kind of sex, but then her body began to throb with the need to have him inside her. She tried to shift, but he smacked her bottom harder.

She stiffened for a moment, but he was stroking her, making her need for him palpable. She was squirming and gasping for breath. The spanking continued with a few more stinging swats, and then she felt him. His sex was entering her, and with every thrust, she was closer to that amazing feeling of joining her husband and being a part of each other. Then it happened, and they held onto one another until it passed.

Hudson rolled off Caitlin and kissed her. "How was that?"

Caitlin took a deep breath. "I'm not sure," she said honestly.

"Think about it today," Hudson whispered in her ear. "Have you ever felt so satisfied?"

"It's a little hard to know with my bottom still stinging," she whispered.

"You've got all day to think about it, to feel it," Hudson said. "Try to isolate those few minutes when your body was yearning for mine as much as I wanted to be inside of you. Those are the truest moments between a man and a woman."

CHAPTER 20

*C*aitlin looked out the window and watched Hudson riding north toward Magnolia. He took the same route daily and made the trip so often that he'd worn a path through the brush. She shivered as she looked at the white-covered world outside. It reminded her of Philadelphia snow, but it wasn't the same. As soon as the sun rose, the pale ice would disappear, leaving the ground wet, and even that would disappear in the first hour of dawn.

Climbing back in bed, she gently stroked parts of her body. Living in Ridgeway, in a house of women, she hadn't any idea what happened between a man and a woman when she married. Hudson had been her teacher, and he was still teaching her. The previous night had been amazing and unexpected. Rubbing her bottom, it was a bit tender, but she knew the tenderness would disappear in a few hours.

Cupping her hands on her flat belly, she closed her eyes and prayed for a baby. She loved her children; everyone in her acquaintance loved them, but she wanted to experience motherhood from the beginning. Thinking of a little human growing inside her was scary, but she could almost feel her body preparing for that miracle.

Caitlin opened her eyes a second time that morning because the girls were jumping on her bed and calling her a sleepyhead to wake her.

"All right, all right!" she exclaimed, tucking the covers around her tightly as she was still naked under the quilts. "What is so exciting?"

"Jilly is making pancakes!" Naomi exclaimed. "And it's not Sunday or a special day!"

"I think it was because Bert came over this morning. He was kissing Jilly in the kitchen again," Charlotte said.

Caitlin sat up carefully. "Today is special because our Jilly is home where she belongs. Now, listen, you two. I don't want you teasing Jilly and Bert. They are our friends and family, and it's not nice to laugh and giggle at them."

"They're too old to be boyfriend and girlfriend," Charlotte said.

"Who said so?" Caitlin asked.

"Jilly," Charlotte said.

"All right, that's enough. Bert and Jilly like each other and want to spend time together. That is their business, not yours," Caitlin scolded.

"Jilly and Bert are old people," Charlotte said."

"Yes, they are," Caitlin scolded. "But, no matter how old a person is, everyone needs love."

"Kissing is love?" Naomi asked.

Caitlin smiled and kissed the girls. "Yes, kissing is part of love, but you must be a grown-up to understand. You two are a long way from being grown. Now, I want you to go to the kitchen and see if Jilly needs help. And, girls, there will be no teasing. I'll be down in a few minutes."

Smiling, Caitlin dressed and joined her family, minus her husband, for breakfast. Because he left early, Hudson usually ate breakfast at Magnolia. Halfway through breakfast, Caitlin looked around and asked. "Where is Maisey?"

"The last I saw of her, she was going in the barn to milk the cow," Jesse said.

"Maybe she went to gather the eggs," Brenda suggested. "I'll get her. Everything is going to get cold if she doesn't come in."

"Finish your breakfast. I'll get her," Bert said, rising from his seat.

A few minutes later, they heard Bert shouting for Maisey.

Caitlin snatched a shawl from the hooks on the back of the door and ran outside. "Where is Maisey?"

"She's not in the barn, but the full milk bucket is, and she hasn't gathered the eggs," Bert said.

"Where could she have gone?" Caitlin demanded.

"I don't know, but I'll look in the barn again. Check the privy."

Caitlin ran to the outhouse, but Maisey wasn't there either. She ran inside and asked Brenda to run upstairs to see if Maisey was there. She ran through the house, searching every room, but she wasn't anywhere.

Jilly met Caitlin and Brenda in the dining room. "What's wrong?"

Before Caitlin could speak, Bert joined them. "She's not outside anywhere. I checked all the buildings. But someone has been here," Bert said. "There are fresh boot prints in the corral behind the barn. The hoof prints were made by workhorses."

"Someone has taken her!" Caitlin cried.

"Now, we don't know that yet," Bert said. "She could be off chasing a rabbit or something."

"She wouldn't, where can she be?" Caitlin cried.

"Calm down, I'm going to keep looking," Bert said. "Jesse, you come with me. We'll follow the tracks and see where they're going. Brenda, get the rifle and load it. If she shows up, fire off three rounds."

Bert saddled two horses and tried to calm Caitlin down as she followed them into the barn.

"I'm going with you," Caitlin exclaimed.

"No, ma'am, you are not," Bert said firmly. "Try to stay calm."

As the men mounted their horses, Caitlin turned to Brenda. "Do you know how to ride a horse?"

"Yes, I'm a good rider," Brenda said.

"Take Bucky and ride to Magnolia as fast as you can. Tell Hudson Maisey is missing!"

"I'll be as fast as I can," Brenda promised. She quickly saddled the horse and sped off at a full-out gallop."

Jilly led Caitlin back into the house, trying to calm her down. She only got through to her by telling her she was scaring the younger girls.

"We need to stay calm," Jilly scolded. "Take the girls to the office. They can work on their school work."

Bert and Jesse came back first. "We lost the trail," Bert admitted to the women. He turned to Jesse. "Run over to my place and saddle my horse. These mounts need rest. Then ride into town and tell Sheriff Bensen we've got a missing girl."

Jesse ran across the fields toward Bert's cabin.

"What can we do?" Caitlin cried.

"Nothing until we can get some help," Bert said. "I've done all I could think to do. We lost the trail when the horses were steered onto the road. We couldn't follow the track because there are too many prints and no way of telling which way they went."

"There must be something we can do!" Caitlin cried.

"Pray," Jilly said, wrapping her arms around Caitlin.

The town of Tyler was six miles away, but Jesse rode at a break-neck speed. He jumped down from the horse and burst into the Sheriff's office.

"What's wrong?" Sheriff Benson demanded.

"Maisey McFarlane has gone missing," Jesse said.

"How long?"

Since about six o'clock this morning, it might have been earlier," Jesse said.

"Is she one of those orphans Mrs. McFarlane adopted?"

"Yes, sir, the oldest."

"Have any young fellows been hanging around?" Sheriff Benson asked.

"She's too young for that, Sir. She just a little girl," Jesse exclaimed. "She's a good girl and spends most of her time doing school work and playing with her sisters."

Sheriff Benson stood up and strapped on his gun. Then he opened his desk drawer, pulled out a tablet, wrote a note, and hung it on the jailhouse door. He locked the door as they left the jail. "We'll swap your horse for a fresh one at the livery."

When Brenda rode into Magnolia, she pounded on the front door, demanding to know where Hudson and Mr. Ballard were. When Mrs. Brimmer said she didn't know, Brenda ran back to her horse, mounted, and rode quickly over to the barns screaming.

"What's wrong," Hudson demanded, coming out of a barn.

"Maisey's missing," Brenda explained. "We've looked everywhere, but we can't find her."

"George..." Hudson barked out orders, but the worker was already moving. "I'll get your horse saddled, Boss!"

"Find Angus," Hudson ordered, and three men ran in different directions."

Angus came running in less time than it took Hudson to remove his barn boots and pull on his regular boots. "What's going on?"

"Maisey has gone missing," Hudson said, mounting, and Angus was only seconds behind him. "George, you're in charge. Brenda! Stay here until someone can escort you back to Rose Hill," Hudson ordered as he kicked in his heels.

Angus wasn't far behind, and both men rode as fast as they could push their horses.

It was one of the longest rides of Hudson's life, as he feared for Maisey's life. There were hundreds of ways that she could have been hurt or lost.

When Hudson pulled his mount to a stop, he was surrounded by Caitlin and the girls. "What happened?" he demanded, although Caitlin wasn't able to answer him because she was sobbing in fear.

"We don't know," Jilly answered. "She went out to milk the cow and didn't return. Bert is still looking for her. He lost the trail of a horse past the fishing creek, but he's still trying to pick up a trail again. He said one of the horses had a dent in the horseshoe, and he'd try to pick up the trail from that."

Jesse arrived with Sheriff Benson and three other other men. The trail had already been followed, and the hoof prints led them nowhere. The men split up, searching the landscape for any trace, a footprint, or a hair ribbon, but they found nothing. They checked the creeks, the ponds, and even rock formations, believing the girl might have climbed them and fallen.

Many hours later, without a trace, the Sheriff called a halt to the search. He sent his men back to town.

"I'm sorry, Hudson, but we can't keep looking in the dark," Sheriff Bensen said. "She could be a runaway. Three orphan boys on that last orphan train have run away from their new homes."

"They were probably mistreated," Caitlin cried. "Maisey wouldn't have run away. She wouldn't have left Naomi behind."

"I'm truly sorry, ma'am, but there's nothing I can do until daylight," the Sheriff said.

Caitlin sank into Hudson's arms.

"We'll keep looking in the morning," Hudson promised as the Sheriff left.

"I'll bring the boys back with me," Angus promised, hugging Caitlin. "We'll search every inch between here and Sulfur Springs. We'll find her!"

Angus mounted his horse to ride back to Magnolia, carrying a torch, and he disappeared in the darkness, breaking his rule of never riding in the dark.

Hudson took Caitlin inside and tried to get her to lie down, but she refused.

Jilly fixed a supper, but no one was hungry. Eventually, everyone sat in the parlor in silence. No one was interested in doing anything, and the silence was unsettling.

When the clock chimed eight o'clock, Jilly stirred. "I think it's bedtime for the girls."

"What's that?" Jesse asked, sitting up with a jerk.

"It's a horse," Hudson said, jumping up and rushing to the front door and running to the end of the porch. "It's Maisey!" he shouted, jumping over the banisters to meet the incoming horse and rider.

Maisey was riding double behind a young man. He held her hand and lowered her to the ground.

"You're the man in the orphan train crowd," Caitlin said.

"If you have hurt her..." Hudson didn't finish his threat.

"No!" Maisey exclaimed, standing in front of the thin young man. "He saved me! Ralph saved me!"

"I-I-I would n-n-not hurt her," the young man stuttered.

"Why don't we calm down and go inside?" Jilly suggested.

Hudson unclenched his fists. "That's a good idea."

Maisey took the young man's hand, and he followed her inside, looking disturbed as he passed Hudson.

"May we have something to eat?" Maisey asked. "We haven't eaten since morning!"

"Of course," Jilly and Caitlin said together, backing out of the way.

Maisey sat beside her new friend at the kitchen table and

introduced everyone. "This is Ralph Higgins. Ralph, this is my mother and father, Hudson and Caitlin McFarlane." She pointed out and named the rest of the people in the kitchen."

"Ni-ni-nice to-to-to meet you," Ralph stuttered, although he wouldn't raise his eyes to anyone except for Maisey.

"What happened to you today?" Hudson demanded.

"Please don't shout," Maisey said gently. "It upsets Ralph because he thinks you're making fun of him. He has difficulty speaking, but his hearing is fine."

"I apologize. What happened?" Hudson asked again.

"I went outside like I do every morning to milk the cow. A man grabbed me, tied a cloth over my mouth, and tied my hands and feet together. He carried me out of the barn, threw me over his shoulder, and carried me almost to Bert's cabin. Another man was waiting there with a wagon. They put me in the back of a wagon and covered me with sacks and a smelly quilt. I couldn't get loose, but I could hear them talking. They wanted a woman to cook and clean for them. One of the men was arguing with the other, telling him it was no way to get a woman. The other man said if they kept me long enough, I'd go along with what they wanted. The one named Chester said it was Momma's fault they had to steal me because he was going to take me from the orphan train, but she got in the way."

"Did they hurt you?" Hudson demanded.

"No," Maisey said, shaking her head. "That's because Ralph saved me. He was fishing at the creek, where the man with the wagon was waiting. When they put me in the wagon, he knew what they were doing was wrong, but he wasn't carrying a gun to stop them.

Ralph hid in the bushes. Those men have picked on him before because he stutters. He knew they were doing something wrong, and when they moved on, he followed them. Ralph followed them all day. When they stopped to set up a camp for the night, he snuck into their camp, stole a shovel from their wagon, and knocked them out. He tied them up and untied me." Maisey smiled at Ralph and faced her family. "Ralph didn't want me hurt. People make fun of him because he stutters, and that's wrong. He's my friend now, and I like him."

"I'm so sorry," Caitlin exclaimed, addressing the young man. "Please forgive us for not offering you friendship."

"Yesss, yesss, maaam," Ralph said.

"What did you do with the men?" Jesse asked.

"I-I-I-"

Maisey squeezed his hand. "May I speak for you?"

Ralph nodded.

"After he knocked them out, he tied them up and put them back in the wagon. He covered them with the sacks of grain just like they did to me. We hid the wagon in the brush, and he brought me home. Ralph is my hero."

"Yes, he is," Hudson agreed. "Thank you, Ralph." He held his hand out to shake. "We can't thank you enough for saving our Maisey." He looked around the room. "We can't find or fetch them in the dark, and you're welcome to stay the night. We'll have to wake up the Sheriff at daybreak."

Ralph unbuttoned his shirt pocket, unfolded a piece of paper, and pulled out a pencil stub. He wrote some words on it and handed it to Hudson.

Hudson read the note and looked around the kitchen with a smile. "Ralph says he'll sleep in the barn and take us to the men in the morning."

"I forgot to tell you," Maisey said, beaming at the young man. "He's very good at writing and spelling. He's smart and shouldn't have to talk if he doesn't want to."

"We agree," Caitlin exclaimed. "But, we'll bed you comfortably in the house, not the barn. We can't thank you enough!"

Later that evening, when everyone was tucked into their beds, including Ralph, who was sharing a bed with Jesse, Hudson, and Caitlin, privately gave thanks that Maisey had been returned to them unharmed. Unbeknownst to them, nearly everyone who knew she was safe was doing the same.

Neither Caitlin nor Hudson got much sleep. They were simply waiting for daylight.

Angus arrived with twelve men on horseback and was relieved to discover they weren't needed. The men were sent back to Magnolia, and he shook hands with Ralph Higgins. Angus had run across the young homesteader before and had been told he was deaf and dumb. Angus couldn't remember who had told him that, but he would spread the word that Ralph was indeed an intelligent young man and a hero. He might have a problem with speech, but he was not deaf or dumb and had saved his granddaughter from a horrible fate.

Hudson hugged Maisey extra tight before letting her go the following day before the men left for town.

Caitlin hugged Ralph and gave him a small packet of paper she'd sewn together, the size of his shirt pocket. While Hudson had slept fitfully the night before, she had made Ralph a small pad of paper. "I'll make more of these for your use," she promised. "You don't have to speak to be a brave and decent man. If you need anything, anything at all, just contact us. We owe you a life debt for saving our daughter."

Ralph shook his head.

Angus squeezed the young man's shoulder. "Yes, we do! Now, let's go give those idiots what they deserve!"

As the men rode away, Caitlin turned to Jilly. "Normally, I'm against violence, but those men deserve anything they get!"

With a stop at the Sheriff's office, they gained manpower. Ralph led them to where he had hidden the wagon, and the Sheriff recognized the two men as Chester and Burl Brigham, brothers from Winona. Leeroy had arrested them once before for cattle rustling, but the charges had been dropped.

The brothers claimed innocence, with Chester complaining

that they hadn't done anything wrong. They were just taking what should have been theirs.

"Turn your head," Angus snarled at the Sheriff. Leeroy blinked, but he turned his back and winced, hearing Angus and Hudson trying to beat the stupidity out of the Brigham brothers to think they could kidnap a child bride.

When the beating was over, the Sheriff formally arrested them for abduction and warned them that they would be serving time for their actions.

Life at Rose Hill and Magnolia settled down as they waited for a court day. The only difference in their daily routine was that Jesse milked the cow and gathered the eggs every morning. When he was told those chores were women's work, he just grinned and said the extra chores were fine as long as he got a good breakfast.

A week later, a jury of six men sentenced the Brigham brothers to eight-year sentences in the Huntsville prison. Prisoners, especially lifers, had their own code of behavior. One of them was that children weren't to be harmed, especially innocent little girls. The Brigham brothers were beaten several times in jail. After six months of incarceration, they were found in their cells dead... strangled, and not a single prisoner or guard knew who killed them.

The town of Tyler, as a whole, began to treat Ralph better. He rarely tried to speak, but he was quick enough to get his needs understood by writing it down on his shirt pocket paper. James became a good friend of the young man, secretly loaning him books that were treasured and always treated with the utmost care. They came from the newly released bookshelf in the bookstore, and after Ralph read the new books, they were sold at full price to customers. Ralph was also invited to the McFarlane supper table several times a month, and the friends would often go together, along with Eleanor.

It took months before Caitlin would let the girls out of her sight. Jesse and Bert were more diligent about watching the women and girls when they were outside. The abduction had scared everyone.

Sheriff Bensen cracked down on male visitors to the town. If the travelers didn't have relatives in town, they were encouraged to get a job quickly. He was especially tough on unmarried men. The sheriff had his own vendetta against men like Chester and Burl Brigham.

Angus suggested that the new family cabins needed for Magnolia Ranch and the Farm be built closer to Rose Hill. The more populated an area was, the less chance of no-good drifters causing problems.

Caitlin liked the idea of having more women and wives living close by.

Bert thought the idea was Angus trying to encroach on his land again, but Hudson reminded the octogenarian that the property belonged to Caitlin. As long as his wife didn't plant peach trees, she wasn't breaking their agreement.

Preacher Cormac tried to involve the town in another orphan train, but the Ballards, the McFarlanes, and several other families were dead-set against it. Caitlin claimed the children were being used and abused, and the practice was a form of slavery. The turnout at the train station was sparse, and the lack of interest had the promoters moving on down the line.

CHAPTER 21

 ecember was a busy month. The fright over the kidnapping was gently side-lined, although there was never a second when the girls were left unsupervised.

The marriage of Gladys and Angus wasn't celebrated. The couple went to the Justice of the Peace, said the words, signed the contract, and returned to Magnolia. The only difference Hudson noticed was that the couple were sharing a bedroom, and they seemed to be friendlier with each other. The rooms in the Ballard house were also being changed little by little. More mounted heads and rugs were being delegated to Angus' office until he ran out of space.

Jilly and Bert were more formal about getting married. With the help of Caitlin, Brenda, and the girls, Jilly wanted a simple, quick ceremony and then a big supper at Rose Hill. Bert was okay with it as long as a bar was set up for his card-playing buddies. James brought Eleanor and Ralph Higgins to the ceremony.

The only person in the crowd who had a problem with a white man marrying a brown woman was the Reverend Cormac. He was quickly removed from the house and told to spout his opinions and hatred elsewhere. He hadn't been invited!

When the door finally closed to all their guests, Caitlin was exhausted.

"Tired?" Hudson asked when his wife leaned against a wall.

"Exhausted," she admitted. "And look at the girls! They are still running around. Oh! Girls! No playing hide and seek in the house! Besides, it's past your bedtime. Off you go!"

After pleading and groaning, Naomi and Charlotte raced to see who could run up the stairs the fastest.

"I'll see to putting them to bed," Maisey promised, taking the stairs at a walk.

"Have you noticed a difference in her?" Caitlin asked.

"Yes, she's quieter and has matured suddenly. She has a crush on Ralph, and we'll have to keep an eye on that," Hudson said.

"It's sweet," Caitlin said. "And I hope those damn bastards rot in jail!"

"Hey! We've had a great day, and I'd hate to ruin it by paddling your bottom!"

"I've been trying to compensate for all the bad times the girls suffered in that orphanage, and then she was kidnapped!"

"You can't undo what happened," Hudson said solemnly. "What happened was, and will probably always be with Maisey. We just have to love her a little harder to vanquish her fears. I know I have a lot of respect for Ralph now. So what if he can't talk!"

Caitlin stood on her tip-toes and kissed him. "I'm so glad you are a good father. I don't think Angus would have been a great father if he had known about me. I'm not blaming him for being the way he is, but Magnolia has always come first in his life and always will. Even a piece of land as big as Magnolia shouldn't be a man's main motivation. It should be his family."

"He's trying his best," Hudson said. "He's agreed to build

seven new cabins around the curve in the road. It's his property and his way of making Rose Hill safer. It's a shame that Texas has come to this."

"What do you mean?"

"The morality among men has suffered over the last twenty years, probably longer, but I was too young and sheltered living on Magnolia to realize it. A man's word used to be worth something, but not now. I had to fire three new hires yesterday for stealing."

"It's the upbringing," Caitlin agreed. "God knows how I would have turned out if it hadn't been for Jilly. I would probably be in jail for killing Beaula. Jilly had more to do with my upbringing than the Ridgeway sisters. I was a toy doll for Florence to play with and a servant to Beaula."

"What about the nuns?"

"I barely remember them," Caitlin whispered. "They are faceless white robes in my memory."

Hudson hugged her to him and kissed the top of her head. "Let's call it a night."

"I can't leave this mess until the morning."

"Sure you can," Hudson said. "That's why we pay Jilly and Brenda."

"You're only saying that because you don't have to clean up the mess. You'll be riding off as you do every morning."

"That's my job," Hudson agreed, sweeping his wife into his arms. "Dirty dishes can wait; right now, I want to do exactly what the bride and groom are doing."

"Do you really think they are doing that at their age?"

"I hope so because I'm planning on it even when I get their age," Hudson said.

Brenda watched and listened to her bosses through a partially opened door to the kitchen. She wanted that kind of love with her beau, Homer. When she heard the upstairs bedroom door close, she stacked the dirty dishes quietly and carried them into the kitchen. Homer and her family had been invited, but they had left earlier.

* * *

HUDSON AND CAITLIN were nicely surprised the next morning. What Caitlin had called a mess was gone. Everything was in order except for the furniture needing to be moved back to where it belonged. When Jesse came in with the milk and eggs, he and Hudson moved the furniture back to where it belonged.

Brenda handed Hudson several egg sandwiches to eat on the way to work and a quart jar of hot coffee.

Over breakfast, Charlotte cried because Brenda hadn't fixed her scrambled eggs the same way as Jilly did. She pushed her plate away, demanding leftover cake for breakfast, and screamed when she didn't get her way. Her temper tantrum sent her to a corner, and she wouldn't be allowed out until she apologized to Brenda and ate her breakfast, which was still on her plate.

"I can fix her another plate," Brenda offered.

"No," Caitlin said firmly. "This is *spoiled* behavior. She's pulled this before and should have learned by now that it doesn't work."

"I wouldn't like to eat cold scrambled eggs," Brenda whispered.

"Neither would I, but she's brought this onto herself," Caitlin said firmly. "What did you do with all the extra dishes we used from the attic?"

"They are stacked in the butler's pantry," Brenda said.

"We'll box and carry them to the attic again," Caitlin said. "I didn't think we'd ever have that many guests, but I was wrong."

"Do you want the china you gave us back?" Brenda asked.

"Goodness no," Caitlin exclaimed. "Those things belong to you and don't you dare try to give them back. Oh, and I have good news. Angus and Hudson have decided that the new cabins will be built down the road past the property line between Rose Hill and Magnolia. We'll be neighbors by spring. One of those cabins is for you and Homer."

"Oh!" Brenda exclaimed, giving Caitlin a hug and then stepping back. "Oh, I'm sorry, I shouldn't have done that!"

"Fiddlesticks!" Caitlin exclaimed, pulling the young woman to her in another hug. "Just don't tell Hudson I swore. It slips out once in a while!"

Brenda snickered. "I'm not the one you have to worry about, but little ears might have heard and might tell on you."

Caitlin turned to see Charlotte glaring at her with red, swollen eyes from crying. "I can handle her!" Walking over to Charlotte, Caitlin crossed her arms and tapped her foot on the floor. "Are you ready to eat your breakfast?"

Charlotte shook her head stubbornly.

"We do not waste food in this house," Caitlin said. "Do you know how many corners there are in this house?"

Charlotte shook her head.

Caitlin frowned and looked around because she didn't know the answer to her question. She would fake it. She was not going to be out-maneuvered by an eight-year-old child. "There are a lot of corners in every room, and you are going to stand in every one of them until you are ready to eat your breakfast and stop acting like a spoiled brat."

"I hate eggs!"

"You've been eating scrambled eggs for months with no complaints, often asking for seconds, and have never been refused. You will stay in a corner until you decide to eat, and after you apologize to Brenda. She works very hard, and I won't have you disrespecting her or what she does for us."

"I'm going to tell Papa on you!" Charlotte cried.

"Go ahead," Caitlin said. "He is going to be very disappointed in your behavior."

Two hours went by, and Charlotte cried, screamed, and exhibited a temper she'd never shown before, trying to kick and hit when Caitlin tried to speak to her.

"I don't know what to do with her," Caitlin exclaimed to Brenda.

"I know what my Ma would do," Brenda said.

"What's going on?"

Both women turned around, surprised to face Hudson.

"What's wrong with Charlotte?"

"She has been acting like this all morning," Caitlin explained. "She refused to eat breakfast and demanded leftover cake from last night. I put her in the corner, and her behavior has worsened. She'd gone from screaming and crying to hitting, kicking, and biting."

Hudson tipped his hat back. "Excuse me, ladies, but I have a temper tantrum to attend to!"

The screaming stopped as soon as Hudson walked into the dining room. Crying and snuffling, Charlotte cried, "Papa, they're being mean to me!"

"Upstairs, young lady, into your room," Hudson said with a firm point of his finger.

His daughter didn't stop crying, but she ran up the stairs.

Hudson stopped after several steps, and Caitlin bumped into him. "You stay down here. I'll handle this."

Fifteen minutes later, still crying, Charlotte came into the kitchen and apologized to Caitlin and Brenda.

"Now back in the corner," Hudson ordered. "You're staying there until Momma says you can leave it, and you will eat your cold breakfast."

"We're supposed to trim the Christmas tree today," Charlotte whined.

"Then I suspect you'll miss out on the fun," Hudson said firmly. "That's your fault for misbehaving. Do you understand?"

"Yes, Papa," Charlotte sniffed and returned to the corner. She took each step slowly as if her heart was broken.

"When she grows up, she's going to be the next Lillian Russell," Hudson whispered, shaking his head.

"What did you do?' Caitlin asked.

"I gave her a few swats and laid down the law," Hudson said. "Don't you dare feel sorry for her! She earned it. Charlotte will spend the rest of the morning with her nose stuck in that corner. If she doesn't eat the eggs, send her back into the corner in the parlor facing the room, and let her watch but not participate in whatever you do with the Christmas Tree. Sending her to her room, with all those toys, is not a punishment. You need to be firmer with her. If she gets away with it this time, the next time will be worse."

"I tried," Caitlin said. "Why are you here?"

"I'm on my way into town. I need to arrange for the blacksmith to come to the ranch and then the farm. I stopped to see if you needed anything."

"I'm glad you did," Caitlin said. "I've never seen a child have such a temper tantrum."

"If our daughter knows what is good for her, she won't pull this again," Hudson said. "Oh, and she doesn't get dessert for a whole week. None!"

"That's cruel," Caitlin whispered.

"No, it's not. Charlotte has earned her punishment," Hudson said, kissing her forehead. "Save some of that leftover cake for me. Do you have a list of what you need from town?"

"I always have a list. It's in the kitchen," Caitlin said. "I sent Jesse to find a pine tree. I'm going to postpone the tree decorating."

"Don't deny Maisey and Naomi something you promised because of Charlotte's bad behavior. That's not fair to them," Hudson said. "Do you need help with anything else while I'm here?"

"No, we'll manage," Caitlin said. "We're having party left-overs for dinner and supper. It was good the first time, so it will probably be better the second and third time around."

"Sounds good to me!" Hudson said with a smile, and he was on his way.

Charlotte stopped crying and sat in the corner with a few sniffles. The tantrum was over, but her punishment wasn't.

Jesse came home dragging what he called a shortleaf pine and went to work, standing it in a corner in an old tub filled with rocks and water.

"I thought trees were nailed into boards to hold them in place," Caitlin said, watching.

"Maybe that's what they do in the big cities," Jesse said. "But, my folks never saw the need to kill a tree. They come from the Illious plains, where trees were scarce. After Christmas, we'll plant it in the yard."

"Thank you," Caitlin said, touching the tree. She turned to the girls who were watching. "Let's go up to the attic and bring down the boxes of Christmas ornaments we found."

Maisey glanced over to Charlotte, sulking in the corner. "Momma, can we make more paper chains today? I don't think we have enough. We can put the ornaments on the tree tomorrow when Papa is home. Maybe Jilly and Bert and Grandpa can be here too."

Caitlin hugged Maisey and kissed her on the forehead. "You're a beautiful person, Maisey McFarlane."

"Can we call Mrs. Brimmer Grandma now?" Naomi asked.

"You can ask her," Caitlin said.

"Bert and Jilly, too," Maisey said. "They are part of our family, too!"

"Yes, they are," Caitlin agreed, hugging the sisters, and then she looked over at Charlotte. "You can come out of the corner for a hug."

Charlotte ran to join them.

Taller than all three girls, Caitlin raised her eyes to the ceiling and whispered, "Thank you!"

Gathering all the *'family'* together delayed the tree trimming by two days. The elders became grandparents, with smiles and hugs. Then, everyone joined in decorating the tree and eating the last of the leftovers from the wedding.

Hudson walked down the stairs after ensuring the girls were all tucked in. He looked in the office expecting to find his wife as that was their usual place to relax in the evenings. Instead, he found Caitlin staring at the Christmas tree in lamplight.

"It looks good," he said. "I doubt Bert has bothered with a tree since his wife died."

"It's beautiful, and it's a memory I'll cherish. My first Christmas Tree."

"Your first?" Hudson questioned.

Caitlin nodded. She tilted her head, looking up to her husband. "You really don't believe Beaula would have celebrated, do you?"

Hudson shook his head and wrapped his arms around her. "That woman should have been jailed for how she treated you!"

"It was what it was," Caitlin whispered. "But, I'll make sure our children don't have bad memories of Christmas. I want their memories to be joyful."

"They will be, and so will yours," Hudson promised.

The first Christmas in Rose Hill would always be memorable, and Hudson decided that a budget would be discussed in the following years. Not only had Caitlin been extravagant, but so had he, and the new grandparents.

Bert had given Caitlin a voucher for rose bushes, and so had Hudson. The choice of what kind would be hers, and she would order them in the pre-spring months. Hudson had ordered more paints and canvas and spent nearly an hour in the bookstore, taking James' advice on what books to purchase.

Angus had given Caitlin another riding horse, and Hudson had given in and given the girls the ponies but was firm with them about learning how to ride correctly.

The parlor was knee-deep in tissue paper and love. Grudges and misunderstandings were ignored for the day. Only laughter and smiles were allowed.

When the excitement had finally faded, the guests had left, and the girls were sent to bed, Hudson found his wife in the parlor, still looking at the tree.

"Did Santa give you everything you wished for?" Hudson asked.

"Santa made up for all the lost Christmases before today," Caitlin nodded with tears in her eyes. "It was a day to remember forever."

"In three hundred and sixty-five days, there will be another," Hudson teased.

"Thank you," Caitlin cried. "I'll never forget how much effort everyone put into this day, not only for me but for the girls. Angus and Bert were actually talking and not snarling at each other. That was a blessing."

"I told them both to behave," Hudson admitted. "I can't believe I have to act as a parent to two grown men."

Caitlin laughed. "They did behave very nicely."

"They're a little old to be spanked," Hudson growled.

"I'm not," Caitlin whispered. "I'm all yours tonight, whatever you want."

"I accept," Hudson said and grinned. "I have a few tricks that I haven't shown you yet. It will be a…"

"A night and a lifetime of good memories," Caitlin said, pulling his head down and kissing the love of her life.

EPILOGUE

 *welve years later... 1895*

CAITLIN WALKED across the front lawn carrying a hot cup of coffee to her husband. The Ballard Orphanage was officially opened after five years of arguments with government officials and constant revisions of the original plans.

The four-story building was built on a piece of land Angus Ballard had purchased and willed to Tyler. His instructions had been simple. Build an orphanage where children would be treated decently. The property was within walking distance of the Tyler school. He also bequeathed money to the town to enlarge the one-room schoolhouse to accommodate the influx of children.

Angus Ballard had died at the age of sixty-seven. As he predicted, he hadn't reached the age of seventy. Seven years after finding her father, Caitlin had lost him.

The Magnolia properties had been willed to Hudson as

promised, and no one doubted he would continue to make a success of the ranch and farm.

Surrounded by orphans in the family, Angus had decided to do something about the lost children, and part of his fortune was set aside to build an orphanage like no other.

The orphanage would house boys and girls under the age of sixteen. The first floor would house the caretakers, with an adult monitor on each floor. The second floor would care for children under six, and the third and fourth floors were for the children from six to sixteen, boys and girls separately. A small house outback had been built for the men hired to maintain the facility.

Caitlin and Hudson had been named the facility's overall managers, but the positions had evolved over the years to include Banker John Bones, Caitlin, Maisey, and Jilly running the show. One of the first rules announced was that no one would be allowed to adopt a child without being investigated for their fitness to be a parent.

Today had been the grand opening after years of fighting with government higher-ups about how the facility would be built and run. While the orphanage building had been delayed for years, the planting of a peach orchard that would support the institution had flourished.

"Is this shindig almost over?" Hudson asked, accepting the coffee. "Reverend Cormac is over there talking to the Vice Governor, pretending he had something to do with building this place."

"He won't get any credit. I talked to the Vice Governor earlier. I also talked to the newspaperman from Houston. He got an earful from Jilly that we would no longer allow the orphan trains to stop in Tyler. This orphanage was built by Angus Ballard and his family and shouldn't have government interference. I also told the newspaperman, Mr. Dobbs, that the town, including Reverend

Cormac, was originally against building the orphanage. He's had no say in the funding or the building, and he will have nothing to do with the operation of the orphanage. Mr. Dobbs took photographs for his newspaper and interviewed most of us who have been in this from the beginning. The people in charge will get the credit they deserve. I'm so proud of Maisey's involvement."

"So am I," Hudson said, running his hand over Caitlin's belly. "Are you feeling okay today?"

"Stop that! We're in public!" Caitlin hissed.

"I love seeing you with child," Hudson said with a grin. "It's nothing to hide; people are used to seeing you with a baby belly." He withdrew his hand with a smile. "Here come our rabble-rousers.

"Can we go home now?" Charlotte asked, standing by her father. "I wanted to have time to ride today."

"I'm all for it. Grab the kids, and let's high-tail it out of here," Hudson agreed.

"Papa, I saw you kissing Momma again," eight-year-old Angus said, named for his grandfather.

Hudson lifted the boy and his twin Jacob into the wagon. "I'm always going to kiss your Momma, so get used to it."

"Kissing in public is bad manners," Naomi scolded, joining her siblings.

"Who told you that?" Hudson said, lifting two more stairway children into the wagon.

"Jilly said so!" five-year-old Sarah announced.

"But she and Grandpa Bert kiss all the time!" six-year-old Martha added.

"Good for them," Hudson said as he counted. "One, two, three, four. All accounted for! "Every one of you started with a kiss, so be proud that your Papa loves your Momma!

"You didn't count Charlotte, Naomi, or Maisey," Martha complained.

"I always count them," Hudson said. "Who do you think

taught me how to be a good Papa? But I don't have to worry about them getting lost."

"I only got lost once, Papa," Jacob complained. "Maisey snuck out last night to see Ralph. I saw them kissing. Why didn't she get into trouble?"

"That's enough tattling," Caitlin said as she was lifted gently into the buggy seat. "Maisey is going to marry Ralph in a few months, so please keep your noses out of their business."

"Kissing is ekk!" Angus complained.

"Enough of that," Caitlin said firmly.

"How did I go from one child to seven?" Hudson asked in Caitlin's ear.

"I'll remind you later, and it's very close to eight, so you should have figured it out by now!" Caitlin teased.

"Oh, I have," Hudson said, kissing her.

"Ekk!" was heard loudly behind them.

Hudson laughed, but the sound didn't deter him or Caitlin as she kissed him in front of their children and anyone else looking in their direction.

MARIELLA STARR

Hello, this is Mariella.

I've often wondered what makes a writer. I never claimed to be one, because I wrote for myself. Even now, very few people know that I write.

Of the many gifts I received from my parents, the most important one was the encouragement to try things they didn't do themselves. They didn't understand their strange child so different from themselves and her brothers. I had a need to create. My parent's home over the years became a gallery for my artwork. Most of it now resides in the homes of my children and siblings. There hasn't been an empty wall in my home in years.

What fills a child with lifelong inspiration? In my case, it was my parents and two specific teachers. The first, was a grade school teacher who gave me two compliments in one by praising my art on the cover of a written story and the A+ grade was a boost, too. That was in sixth grade.

The second was a seventh-grade teacher who had a reputation for being tough. I was a new student to the school, my family having moved again because of my father's military deployment. I'd heard horror stories from the other kids about this teacher.

I was shocked when the teacher returned my writing assignment with a red copy editing marks all over my pages—something I'd never seen before. I was so embarrassed. I turned it over on my desk so no one else could see it.

My wonderful teacher, though, was walking around the classroom returning the assignments papers to the students, returned to my desk. He turned over my stapled pages. Without a word, he tapped the top of the page with his finger.

I had missed it. Written across the top of the lined notebook page, in red was:

A+++ Best story I've ever read from a student! Ever! Keep writing!

That single incident has never been forgotten. Mr. Gregory taught me so much that year, but most importantly, he gave me encouragement. I kept writing and I have never stopped.

* * *

Don't miss these other exciting titles by Mariella Starr and Blushing Books!

A Long Way to Find Love
Big Jim and the Doctress
Second Try, Different Rules
Trust Me, Precious
A New Found Love
Running Toward Fate
A New Found Love
Taming the Beast
Now and Forever
A Paper Marriage
Jolene, Jolene
My Sweet Rose
Coyote's Calling
What to Do About Kassie
Those Merrick Women
The Breaking Point
A Different Kind of Woman

Miss Trouble and the Law
Coming Home to Promise
A Widow's Secrets
Violet, A Contrary Woman
Emma Takes a Stand
That's Life: The Patrick and Ivy Story
Simmer Down, Red
The Amazing Maven
A Little Bit of Sass
Heller On Wheels
A Path Worth Taking
Keeping Sunny Safe
Maybe, With Conditions
Posey's Assets
Broken Vows
The Promise
In Search of a Noble Man
Lacy's Rules
Desiree, A Woman of Defiance
Full Circle
Caitlin's Conspiracies
The Awakening of Alexandria
Charlotte's Comeuppance
Teaching Miss Maisie Jane

The McKenna Brothers
The Forever Kind: Sully
Holding Tess

The Overton Saga
Isabel's Independence, Book 1
Britannia's Blaggard, Book 2
Sweet Sarah, Book 3

Anthologies
12 Naughty Days of Christmas 2021

Connect with Mariella Starr:
MariStarr@outlook.com

ROMANCE.ink

Reader's favorite romance eBook publisher of sweet, spicy and sizzling hot romance novels. The best deals on steamy romance books: sexy cowboys, protective alpha males, dangerous mafia men, MC motorcycle club romance and more. Your new book boyfriend crush is just page away. For over over 20 years, Romance Ink has published the hottest taboo and edgy romance books around.

https://www.romance.ink/